Wanda's Girls

To Liz,

Thank you for the support

Hope you enjoy!,

Skyler Tori Sampson

Skyler Tori Sampson

authorHOUSE®

AuthorHouse™
1663 Liberty Drive
Bloomington, IN 47403
www.authorhouse.com
Phone: 1-800-839-8640

Published by AuthorHouse   10/17/2012

ISBN: 978-1-4772-8092-8 (sc)
ISBN: 978-1-4772-8091-1 (hc)
ISBN: 978-1-4772-8090-4 (e)

Library of Congress Control Number: 2012919472

Any people depicted in stock imagery provided by Thinkstock are models, and such images are being used for illustrative purposes only. Certain stock imagery © Thinkstock.

This book is printed on acid-free paper.

Because of the dynamic nature of the Internet, any web addresses or links contained in this book may have changed since publication and may no longer be valid. The views expressed in this work are solely those of the author and do not necessarily reflect the views of the publisher, and the publisher hereby disclaims any responsibility for them.

For Z, with all the love my heart can muster.

Chapter One

"I can't believe he's dead."

Brandice Cartel hadn't moved a muscle in over an hour. Tear-drenched mascara ran down her sun-blazed face, colliding with the snot dripping from her nose. She didn't bother using tissues to clean herself, because in a matter of seconds she would look the same again. So instead, she just sat there in a state of disbelief.

"I can't believe Daddy is dead." She spoke to herself because no one else was in the room with her. After the burial of her father, Brandice had ridden back to her parents' home in the black limousine and locked herself in her old bedroom. Family and friends were gathered in the family's living room to pay their respects and to bring food by. People had been knocking on her door for over an hour, but Brandice didn't want to see or speak to anyone but her father. Unfortunately, that was never going to happen again because he was dead. It still didn't seem real to her. Just last week they had eaten lunch at a restaurant on Newbury Street like they did every Tuesday. They loved this restaurant because of the live jazz band that featured a woman who could give Lena Horne a run for her money. Her father had seemed healthy and in good spirits as always. They had laughed and talked about politics, world news, and when she was going to settle down and give him some grandchildren. All the usual stuff. *He wasn't sick*, she told herself. It had to have been more than a stroke that killed her father, because he was too strong a man to let a stroke take his life. He was her superman, always there to save her from any harm that came her way. He had saved her on the first day of kindergarten when she forgot her lunch at home. He left work to bring it to her and even sat in the cafeteria while she ate the bologna and cheese sandwich her mother had prepared the night before. He had saved her when she first had her period in middle school and didn't have a change of clothes or a sanitary napkin. Her father had picked her up from school and they had gone shopping for everything she needed. Brandice remembered how she had gone numb with embarrassment when he had asked the clerk for a "starter kit" of sanitary napkins. When she was in high school and stressing over the SATs, he had tutored her for months, patiently walking her through quadratic equations and college prep vocabulary words until she felt confident in her knowledge. He had even sent her snack-filled packages every week when she went away to college and felt homesick for the very first time in her life. Her father was always there for her, and now she would never get to tell him how much he meant to her. How much she loved him and wanted to marry someone just like him one day. She wanted to tell him that he meant the world to her and that she missed him already. She wanted to tell him that he was the best father in the world.

Brandice allowed her body to fall back on the firm mattress, the first real movement she'd made in hours. She folded her legs until her feet touched her back and rested her head on her hands. Her eyes darted around the room, not really focusing on much of anything. The light was off, but there wasn't complete darkness due to the curtains being open, letting a ray of light illuminate one side of the room. Her stomach growled piercingly, but she couldn't bring herself to leave her room and face all those people. Everyone would stare at her and ask her how she was holding up. And the only thing she'd be able to say is, "I'm hanging in there." It wasn't the truth, but it was the only thing people would accept. If she told them the truth, that she was a mess inside and hadn't slept in days, they wouldn't know how to respond. People didn't understand death until it hit them directly in the face. Only when it turns your whole life upside down do you truly understand the power of death. *The realization that someone so important to you could be here one second and gone forever in the next puts life in a new perspective*, she thought. The second she heard that her father had passed away, Brandice had known her life would never be the same. Her superman had saved her for the very last time.

A soft knock took Brandice out of her memories. She ignored it the first time, hoping that whoever it was would comprehend that she didn't want to be bothered. But the knock came again, this time accompanied by a familiar voice. "Ice, come on and let me in. I know you're not sleeping." It was her best friend, Junior. It was almost inevitable that they would be stuck to each other like glue since their parents were close friends and Junior was just under a year older than Brandice. But the two had had a special relationship ever since second grade, when she taught him how to jump rope for their school's annual Olympic games. They were paired together for the competition and were inseparable ever since. "Let me in, Ice." He knocked again. "I won't stop until you let me in, sweetheart."

Brandice pulled herself off the bed. She slowly dragged her feet to the door and opened it slightly, leaving just enough room for him to come in but no one else. Junior closed and locked the door behind him. "I brought you a plate." He handed her a paper plate stacked with finger foods. Brandice nibbled on a grape and fell back onto the bed. She felt as though her body weighed a ton rather than the hundred and thirty pounds she actually was.

"I'm here for you, Ice. No matter what you need me to do for you, I'm here." He bit into a cube of pepper jack cheese. "If you want to stay locked in this room for weeks, then I will stay locked in here with you. I just want you to know that you're not alone. I will always be here for you." He bent down and placed a light kiss on her forehead.

Brandice grabbed Junior's hand and pulled his body closer to hers. "Lie with me," she instructed in a soft cry. He was the only person who she wanted to be around right now. Junior took off his black suit jacket and threw it over a chair in the corner of the large room before getting on the bed and lovingly wrapping his arms around her body. They lay together, her back to his chest, in silence for a while. Brandice fell in and out of a light sleep before she said, "I can still hear his voice in my head. It's so clear, like he's still here."

"That's because he will always live in your heart and in your memory."

She turned in his arms to face him. "But I wonder if his voice will always be this clear. I don't want to forget his voice, or his laughter, or the way he smelled."

"You won't," he told her. "Because if you start to forget, then I will remind you. Together we will remember everything about your father. I promise."

Brandice knew that if by some chance she did start to forget her father, Junior would do what he said. He was that type of guy. He always kept his word to her; he had never let her down in their seventeen-year friendship. Junior was the only person closer to her than her parents. He had all the qualities of a good man and was loyal to the end. He reminded Brandice of her father in so many ways.

"Mama said he left me a letter. Something he wrote a while ago but never gave to me. She says it's important that I read it soon, but I don't think I'm ready to open it yet." She sniffled as the tears began to fall again. The thought that her father had had something important to tell her, that he had put it in a letter, was too much to think about right now. She could hardly look at his picture, let alone read his words.

Junior wiped her tears away with his thumb. "You don't have to open it now. There is no rush. There's nothing in that letter that can't wait until tomorrow. For now, I want you to get some sleep."

"Are you leaving?" she asked in disappointment. His presence took away the feeling of darkness that wouldn't seem to go away otherwise.

Junior shook his head. "I'll be here when you fall asleep and when you wake up."

With those words Brandice was content and tranquil enough to allow herself the first real sleep she had experienced in days.

～

Brandice awoke in the middle of the next day fully rested. It didn't even take her being fully alert for her brain to identify the heartache she felt. She immediately thought of her father and wondered if she would ever be able to escape this powerful internal pain. If sometime her first thoughts wouldn't be of his death. She lay with her eyes closed, listening to the voices in her parents' house. She pulled the comforter more tightly around her body and yawned. Forcing her eyes open, she rubbed the sleep from them and lifted her body out of bed, falling back on the first effort but succeeding on the second. She grabbed her satin robe off the back of her door before walking out of it. She walked down the staircase, tying her robe around her waist.

"Good morning, Mom," she said, entering the kitchen where her mother sat at the table with Junior. "How are you doing?"

Her mother was a rather tall woman with long blond hair and oval-shaped blue eyes. She was a second-generation German immigrant whose family fled to America after World War II. Brandice knew very little about her grandparents, who had virtually disowned her mother when she married Daniel Cartel, a black man.

She had only one distinct memory of her grandmother. Brandice couldn't have been more than five years old when she came to visit one summer. It was the first time Brandice had seen the woman who looked so much like her mother. She remembered her grandmother telling her daughter that Brandice would've been just as beautiful as the two of them if it weren't for the "nigger" features she had inherited from her father. A few more words were exchanged between the two women before Brandice's mother finally asked her to leave. That was the first and last time she saw her grandmother.

Brandice's mother was the polar opposite. She was the kindest, most caring woman. She never raised her voice or lifted a hand to anyone. Even through the sudden death of her husband, she still remained composed. In Brandice's eyes, she was beautiful on the inside and out.

"Fine, sweetheart. And how are you?" Her mother went to the coffee maker, poured her daughter a cup, and handed it to her. "I'm glad you finally got some sleep." She kissed Brandice's forehead.

"Me too." Brandice leaned against the countertop sipping her java. "What were you two discussing before I came down?"

"Why don't you have a seat, Brandice. We really need to discuss an important matter." He mother pulled out the chair between where she and Junior were sitting.

"Is there something wrong?" Brandice's heartbeat quickened, and she felt a flash of sharp pain shoot though her chest. She sat down. "I can't take any more bad news, so if it's going to be too much for me to handle, then please just don't tell me." She looked exhausted by just the thought.

Junior took her hand in his and rubbed it slowly and lovingly. "Ice, what your mother has to tell you is important because it was your father's wish for you to know."

"Know what?" she asked her mother. "What did Daddy want me to know?"

Her mother moved the plate in front of her to the side and folded her hands, resting them on the table. "I don't know why it was so important to Daniel to tell you this, but for some reason it was."

"Tell me what, Mom?" The patience she had previously was quickly disappearing. "What is going on?"

"You father wanted you to know that he was married once before," her mother blurted out.

Brandice couldn't pinpoint her mother's tone. She never heard her mother speak of her father which so much annoyance. She could tell that for some reason her mother wasn't pleased. "He was what? To whom?"

"I don't know the woman's name. All I know is that he was married and divorced by the time we met. For some reason or other, things didn't work out with him and his first wife. After they divorced, he never spoke to her again." She said the words with no emotion, as if they were rehearsed.

Brandice was lost. She didn't understand why her father would keep this secret from her for so long. The pieces weren't all there, she told herself. "So what? He was married. I don't see why that's a big deal."

Her mother turned away, gathered herself, and looked back at her daughter. Brandice knew that whatever was coming next was the clincher, the real reason behind the secret. "While married to his first wife, Daniel fathered three children. Two girls for sure, but he wasn't around for the birth of the third child, so I don't know if it was a boy or a girl."

"What?" Brandice said in disbelief. She blinked her eyes hastily as if that would change the words she had just heard. It was unnatural for her not to comprehend something that was so clearly stated to her, but this was just too unbelievable to accept. "No. Daddy wouldn't have had three children for all these years and never talked about them. He never once mentioned their names or anything. This must be a mistake."

"Sweetheart, he didn't have a relationship with them. Their mother whisked them off and made it impossible for him to contact them. I never wanted to tell you this because I didn't want to see the look on your face that's there right now. Your facial expression is that of someone who has been bamboozled or cheated out of something. I didn't want to be the one to make that face appear."

"Mom, it's not your fault. You're just the messenger." Brandice stood and began to walk back to her room. "But I was cheated out of something. My whole life I've wanted a sister. I begged you and Daddy to have another baby, and now I find out that I have two sisters, possibly three. And now, more so than before, I wish I could talk to Daddy. I wish I could ask him all the questions you can't answer, but I can't."

"Brandice, sweetheart, I don't know if this will be much help. But Daniel left you a letter that he wrote years ago. He asked me not to read it, so I can't tell you what it contains." Her mother went to the drawer next to the stove and retrieved an envelope, tightly sealed. She handed it to Brandice. "I know that this is difficult to take in all at once, but I think you should read the letter soon. It was important to your father, so I know it will be important for you."

Great. Just what she needed, more surprises. Brandice started to regret ever waking up. Yesterday she was grieving, but by the grace of God she had finally gotten to sleep, and now this. Now she finds out that her dead father had a secret life and for some reason he thought it okay to hide it from her and only bring it to her attention after he was buried six feet under.

She stood in the entryway of the kitchen holding the envelope close to her eyes. She knew the content was filled with explanatory information, but she wasn't sure if she was ready to read it.

"Ice? Do you need me?" Junior took steps in her direction.

"Always."

"Are you going to open it?"

After discussing the possibilities of what the letter might say for over two hours, Brandice and Junior sat on her bed Indian-style with the envelope between them. They both rested their chins on their fists. After going back and forth, Brandice decided that she would indeed open the letter. But every time she reached for it, a force beyond her control pulled her hand back.

"Come on, Ice. You can do it," Junior encouraged her. "How about I open it and you read it?"

"Yeah, I like that plan." She cracked the knuckles on all ten of her fingers as Junior tore open the envelope, straightened out the folded pieces of paper, and handed them to her.

"Okay, I can do this." She spoke to herself, taking the letter and pulling it to her eyes.

"Don't bother reading it aloud. I'll just wait for you to finish, and we can talk about whatever you need to," Junior offered.

Dear Brandice,

First off I want you to know how much I love you. I couldn't have asked for a more perfect child. You have been the light in my life since the day you were born. Not a day goes by when I don't thank God for you. I hope you know all of this to be true in your heart.

I am writing you this letter to explain a few things about my past. I know you would have appreciated if I would have told you this in person, but I just couldn't bring myself to disappoint you.

Over thirty years ago, I married a woman named Wanda. She was such a beautiful woman, and she had a zest for life that was contagious. It didn't take long for me to fall in love with her. Within the first year of our marriage, she gave birth to Raven, my eldest daughter. Raven was a beautiful baby, the spitting image of her mother. A year later my second daughter was born. Leila was a daddy's girl, and I adored her to death.

For very difficult and complicated reasons, Wanda and I decided to part ways while she was pregnant with our third child. Unfortunately, I was not around to witness that birth and have never laid eyes on that child. I do not know where my children are or what type of life they've lived. All I know is that they were denied their father.

My wish is that you locate them and build the relationship with your siblings that I never had. I would like for you to know them and for them to know what a wonderful person you are.

Brandice, I know that this is a lot to ask of you, but I am confident that you can make this happen. If you choose to grant my wish, please let your siblings know that I am extremely sorry. I loved my girls, and I never stopped thinking about them and wondering how they were doing.

I know you will have more questions that haven't been answered, but once you meet your sisters, everything will make sense to you.

I only ask that you always remember the husband I am to your mother and the father I am to you. Never forget that.

Love always,
Daddy

Brandice read the letter three times for clarification and to make sure she didn't overlook important information. Her father wanted her to seek out his children, but he hadn't given her much to go on. His ex-wife's name was Wanda, and Raven and Leila were the names of her sisters. Her father wrote that his eldest daughter was born almost thirty years ago, which would make her five years older than Brandice. Leila would have to be around twenty-eight. And then there was the mystery child's identity. It was going to be a complex task, but Brandice was up to the challenge. Not that she was excited about uncovering her father's secret past, but she loved her father. If this was important to him, it was important to her.

"Raven and Leila." She spoke aloud, dropping the letter in her lap. She looked up at Junior in a daze. "My sister's names are Raven and Leila."

She let their names slip off her tongue and immediately wondered how it would feel to say their names and have them respond. She imagined how they looked. Were they biracial, too? Did they have a clue that she existed? Suddenly she wanted to know everything about the two women who shared half her DNA. She knew nothing about them beyond their names, but a strange feeling came over her. Brandice felt a connection to her sisters that she couldn't explain. They were family by blood, and nothing or nobody could change that. "My father wants me to find them, tell them how sorry he was for not being there to raise them, and eventually bond with them as my sisters."

"Wow," Junior exclaimed. "That's a lot to ask of you. Don't you think, Ice?"

She didn't hesitate in saying, "No. My father would have walked through fire for me, and I was never able to tell him how much he meant to me. Here's my chance to do just that. All I have to do is locate them and tell them that Daddy was a wonderful man and that he sent me to apologize to them."

"Brandice." Junior only used her full name when he needed her undivided attention. "I don't want you to get your hopes up. This could turn out to be a lot tougher than you're expecting."

"Junior," she cut him off. "I have to do this for my father. Will you help me?"

Junior did hesitate. His eyes said that he had apprehensions about what she was asking of him. "I'll do whatever it is you need me to do."

Chapter Two

How can you expect someone to love and respect you
if you don't love and respect yourself? –Wanda

Raven Thompson sat behind her desk completely disgusted at the image before her. Two beautiful teenage girls sat in the chairs across from her. One was holding a plastic bag half full of melting ice over her swollen left eye. The other sat with a similar ice filled bag on her busted bottom lip. The two had ended up in the principal's office after a fight broke out in the cafeteria. From what Raven had heard from a student who was brave enough to come forward and explain, the two girls had been dating the same guy and didn't know it. Instead of focusing on the guy, they did what most girls do: get mad at the other girl and start a confrontation.

How sad, Raven thought. *Two of my top senior girls are sitting in my office, facing possible suspension over a knuckleheaded boy who didn't have an ounce of respect for either of them.* Raven tapped the ballpoint pen she was holding on the desk before she spoke.

"I would recite a speech to the both of you about how your future is bright. It would include all the possibilities that life has to offer you and how you are smarter that what you two are displaying right now. But I don't feel like wasting my time." Raven sucked in a deep breath. She hated to see her students act in such a manner, especially her female students. All 312 were important to her, but Raven always gravitated to the girls. She thought it a great blessing to be a female principal, especially a fairly young one at the age of twenty-nine. She had always known that she wanted to be able to help young girls, and after graduating from Harvard, she decided that heading a school was the perfect way. She'd paid her dues as a teacher for three years but was determined to reach her goal before she turned thirty. And last year she did so by becoming the youngest principal in a Boston public school. "You two obviously don't care about your future, so why should I?" Reverse psychology 101.

"It's not even like that, Mrs. Thompson." The girl with the busted lip spoke. "We do care about our future." She looked at the girl sitting next to her and rolled her eyes heavily. "At least I care about my future."

According to Raven, that was the painful issue with most black women. They were always thinking about their lives, their immediate family: mother, father, brothers, and sisters. Black women were always hustling for more, for a better life, which Raven thought was wonderful. But in the midst of pushing for themselves, somewhere down the line black women lost the desire to help one another out. It used to be about watching each other's backs. Even if you didn't know a sister, you would watch out for her children, tell her when you saw a job opening down the street or making sure keep an eye on her husband when she was away. That was the strategy that had worked for older generations thus far in this Anglo world. That's how this generation's mothers and grandmothers were able to continually progress. But modern black women let all that go. Now it was each woman for herself. *And look how well that's been working out*, Raven thought.

"Then why did you do it?" Raven stood and moved to sit on the front of her desk, bringing her closer to the students she knew very well and admired. "Give me one reason, and make it good."

"Forget it, Mrs. Thompson. You wouldn't understand. Can you just give us our punishment so we can get back to class? I have a test this period."

"What will I not understand, Ms. Jackson? I was seventeen once. I know how it goes when you call yourself really liking a guy. I know the games that these boys like to play on girls. Believe me, I've been in your shoes before, and I know how it ends. Girl meets boy. Girl gives up the goodies. Boy meets new girl. Boy leaves old girl for new girl." Raven released the pen form her grip and let it fall on a stack of papers.

"So if you know the story, why you asking us why we did what we did?"

Raven let out a sarcastic laugh. *The little girl must've gotten hit a little too hard if she thought she would come in my office talking to me in that tone,* Raven thought. Her first instincts were to hand the girl her suspension papers and send her on her merry way, but her heart knew better. The girl was obviously in need of some attention, and that's what she was going to get. But if she didn't check herself soon, she might get slapped as well.

"I'm asking you because I want to know if it makes sense to you. I want to know if throwing your future away over a skinny little boy with no job, who still lives at home with his mama and who is probably out there slopping up another girl right now, makes sense to you?" When they didn't answer right away, she repeated her question. "Does it make sense?"

"No," they both said.

"But what we supposed to do? It ain't cool to not have a man, Mrs. Thompson," Ms. Jackson continued. "Not that you would know about this or anything, but some of us have to fight for ours."

Raven bypassed the comment about herself and focused on the important stuff. "I'm all for fighting for what you want, ladies." She moved back to her seat. "So what is it that you want?"

Both girls opened their mouths as if they had been waiting to be asked that question for years. Raven waved her pointer finger in the air to stop them. "Tell me what you want out of life. Your ultimate goal. Not what you want today or tomorrow. Something that's actually worth fighting for."

Both girls looked at each other then took a minute or two to really ponder their answers.

"I want that." Ms. Jackson pointed to the framed photo on Raven's desk.

"Me too," Ms. Mitchell chimed in.

Raven took the photo in her hand and glanced at it. She held it close to her face and couldn't help but smile back at her two handsome sons, who were in the arms of her loving husband. The three of them were her heart and joy. They were definitely worth fighting for, and Raven was sure of it because she'd done just that. The day she gave birth to her first son, Raven was overjoyed. She had a healthy, beautiful baby boy who even at a few minutes old resembled the man holding him, his father. The day she left the hospital with her newly formed family brought on whole new feelings of agony and defeat. Unlike his peaceful demeanor at the hospital, her son wouldn't stop crying the day he arrived home. She cradled him, burped him, fed him, but nothing worked.

His wailing left her sleepless and aggravated, wondering if she was cut out for this motherhood thing. What kind of mother doesn't know how to soothe her own child? That's when her husband proved himself as not only the breadwinner but also truly her partner. For weeks he dedicated his time to caring for their newborn, doing everything from changing his diapers to bathing him at night, giving Raven the much-need sleep her body yearned for. Smiling, Raven placed the frame back down.

"You want kids?" she asked knowingly.

Ms. Mitchell lowered the bag of ice from her eye and sat up straight in her chair. "I want the whole thing. I want the family, with the husband included." She emphasized "husband."

"Real talk, Mrs. Thompson. I want that too. I know I have good grades, and I've already gotten into several colleges. I know I want to be a doctor, and I'm confident that I can do all of that," she said with a smile in her voice. "But what I really want is to have a man for myself and a father for my kids. I never had a daddy, and I'm not trippin' or anything, but it would be nice if I could change that for my children." She spoke like a person who knew she was on the losing side of the statistics. Single black mothers headed 30.5 percent of American households, and a pitiful 40.4 percent of black women have ever been married. It was a hard pill to swallow, growing up knowing that the odds were stacked high against you. Raven thought about the children in her school and their parents. Most were single mothers. It was rare to see a father come to a parent-teacher meeting, a basketball game, or any other school event.

Raven's heart swelled in her chest. When she had asked the question, she had never imagined getting a response like that. Something so simple yet, it seemed, so out of reach for these girls. It saddened her that all the hard work it would take to become a doctor seemed so attainable but the notion of marriage was too rare to be a reality. But then Raven asked herself, why? Why didn't she expect that answer? For she herself would sit around the table and dream the same dream with her sisters when they were in high school. She would watch the Brady Bunch and replace the blond characters with brown faces, picturing herself as the strikingly beautiful mother whose husband was the ultimate provider and adored her as much as she did him.

"I'll tell you what. Write down everything you want in a man. All the qualities you admire in a person and would like in a future partner. Make that list and bring it to me tomorrow during your free period." Raven walked to the door and opened it.

"That's it?" Ms. Mitchell said, shouldering her book bag and walking towards the door, Ms. Jackson at her heel.

"For now." Raven smoothed out the wrinkles in her teal shirt. "I don't think I have to tell you both that I will not tolerate another performance like the one you put on today, do I?"

"No, ma'am," they said on their way out of her office.

Raven retired back to her desk, her mind running wild. Here she was with the opportunity to help these girls. They wanted to find a man, but Raven wanted to help them find themselves. She wanted to show them how bettering themselves would put them both in the position to have options in life and in love.

"First you have to work on yourself," her mother would tell her and her sisters. "The rest will come to you." Raven took another look at the photo of her family, and her energy and happiness were restored. She would help her students get what they deserved, just as someone had helped her.

Raven drove her black hybrid into her driveway. She retrieved her aluminum travel mug, briefcase, and keys out the ignition before slamming the car door. Her heels made a clacking noise as she walked up the cement path leading to her brownstone. As always, she focused her eyes on her living room window, where her sons were always looking out, waiting for their mother to arrive home. She smiled when she saw her youngest son, Tristan, waving at her. She quickened her steps. She walked into her house and was bombarded with four small hands shoving colorful, childlike drawings in her face.

"We drew these for you, Mummy. To put in your office," her eldest son said, handing her his drawing of their family. Josiah was only four, but he was already showing natural talent in drawing. Raven held the picture of the four of them and kissed the top of Josiah's head.

"This is absolutely beautiful. I love it."

"Mine, mine." Tristan jumped up and down, giving her his drawing. Raven couldn't really make out what the two-year-old had actually drawn, but he had made it for her, and that was all that counted.

"Wow!" She pulled Tristan up to her hip. "This is perfect. Thank you guys so much for these."

"You're welcome," Josiah said, and he ran up the stairs and disappeared into his room. Raven put Tristan and the drawings down in the living room. She slid out of her stilettos and walked to the kitchen, where she found her after-daycare babysitter sitting at the dinner table, her head buried in a book.

"How was your day?" Raven asked, taking a seat at the table.

"It was productive. I got a few pages written, so I can't complain." She lifted her head from the book and closed it. "I seasoned the chicken and made a pecan pie for dessert. All you have to do is fry the chicken and fix the sides." She snapped the top back on her yellow highlighter.

"You're too good to me." Raven took off her coat and laid it over the chair. She washed her hands and prepared to start what was left of dinner. "I don't know what I'm going to do when you become a *New York Times* bestselling author and leave us behind."

"Me neither." The babysitter stuffed her books into her oversized Louis Vuitton satchel. "I think I'm already starting to forget about you guys. What's your name again?" She joked. "I'm out this piece. Tell your husband he still owes me money on that Celtics game. I know he's from

LA, but it's about time he recognizes that the Celtics are killing the game right now."

Raven turned the stove on and filled a deep skillet with vegetable oil. "You don't want to stay for dinner?"

"Nope. I have some research to do, and I don't want to take a break from writing when I'm on a roll." She headed for the door.

"Little sis," Raven called out after her. "Are you good on the money front? Do you need anything?" She knew her sister was a grown woman, but Raven couldn't help but feel protective. As the older sister, she felt it was her job to make sure that her little sister was taken care of.

"I'm fine. I have enough money saved up to last me through the year. You know I wouldn't have quit the magazine if I couldn't afford to."

"I know, I know. I was just checking."

"Oh yeah, and how about we lay off the little sis thing and call me Brooklyn like the rest of the world, Raven? I'm a grown-ass woman."

Raven waved her sister off. "Bye, Brook."

"Bye, Raye."

Raven had just finished setting the table when her husband came through the front door. And just as they did for her, her sons met him there. The sat down for dinner, blessed the food, and ate as a family. Raven and her husband allowed the boys to explain all about their day at daycare and how Auntie Brooklyn had taken them to the museum to see the dinosaur exhibit. After dinner, Raven gave the boys a bath and put them to bed while her husband did the dishes and cleaned the kitchen.

"There is nothing sexier than a man washing dishes. Suds and all." Raven walked into the kitchen and wrapped her arms around her husband's waist. This was definitely the best part of her day: being with the man she loved.

He turned to face her. "When I was mowing the lawn last weekend, you said the same thing, Raye." He turned and kissed her full lips.

"I guess you do a lot of sexy things, then," she said, putting the dishes away in the cabinet. "I just try to point them all out." She smirked.

"Do you know what you do that's sexy?" he asked, throwing the drying rag over his shoulder.

"What?"

He waited a moment, looked away as if he didn't want anyone else to hear what he had to say, and then turned back to her. "Everything."

Raye couldn't help but laugh, and she knew he wanted her to. "Look who's trying to gain all the Kool-Aid points he can tonight." One of the things that attracted her to her husband was his sense of humor. Where she was naturally reserved, he was not. They were like ying and yang on the personality front.

"Is it working?" He massaged her shoulders and kissed her neck.

"Is what working? Your attempt to seduce me?" This time she turned to face him and met his nod. "You just keep doing what you do and all you have to do is ask for it." She laced her fingers around his neck and looked into the dark, round eyes of her husband. He stood at six foot two inches, considerably taller than her five foot six. His skin was the exact shade of brown in a Crayola box. His goatee was trimmed to perfection, as was his Caesar-cut black hair. Everything about him was on point, but Raye absolutely loved his jaw. It was strong and defined, just the way a man's should be.

"After last night, I didn't know if you were too tired. But now I'm asking." He threw the rag down on the countertop and started to unbutton his white dress shirt.

She thought back the love they had made last night. True, she'd felt it this morning when she woke up for work, but it was well worth it. Raye seductively bit on her bottom lip and did her best TI impression. "Baby, you can have whatever you like."

He stopped unbuttoning midshirt and looked at his wife funny. "Now, you know you need to stop that right there." He moved his hand in circles in front of her. "You're watching too much BET."

"Boy, you know I can sing." Raven couldn't even get the sentence out without laughing. She, as well as everyone who knew her, was aware that singing was not one of her talents. Raye knew she'd been blessed with brains and beauty. She could cook and had an eye for good bargains, but Whitney Houston she was not.

Raye slipped her hands into the back pockets of her husband's black dress pants. "How was your day?"

"Good. We picked up a new client. She's married to one of the Sox players and is interested in branding herself. She wants to start a clothing line eventually, but first we have to get her name and face out there." He spoke about his job as a publicist with passion.

"You said this woman is married, right?" Raven's brows lifted in genuine concern for confirmation. Her husband worked nine hours on a regular day and sometimes more. Most of the time directly with his clients. *If I could make it so he only worked with men, I would. And if he had to work with women, I would damn sure make sure they were ugly as hell*, Raven thought.

"Yes, she's married to a Sox player, remember?" he reminded his wife of five years.

Raven knew it had to get on her husband's nerves the way she always wanted to know about his female clients, but she couldn't help it. Some things a woman needed to be assured of, and one of those things was who her man was spending his time with. Her husband was a good man; actually, he was great. Sometimes Raven had a hard time believing that she was not only married but married to a loving man who made her feel content and safe in their marriage. That was hard to come by. She had learned that through various conversations over the years with women who were married or had been at one point. Most of them had similar experiences of anxiety building up when the pressure to keep their marriage as solid as in the beginning became too much to handle without wanting to pull their hair out. The stress of being a black wife, fighting not only for your family but for those who are looking at you to be the example for the younger generations, proving those wrong who had little to no faith that a black family could last, was enough to send a woman into cardiac arrest. But not before she picked the children up from school, prepared a delicious meal for her family, did a few loads of laundry, put it on her husband so good he couldn't even remember the name of the girl who was flirting with him on his way to work, and, oh yeah, cleaned the house just in case company stopped by unannounced. Then, and only then, could she take time out of her day for her heart attack to begin.

Raven thought back to her mother and the rigid life she'd lived, raising three daughters on her own after she decided she'd endured enough blows to the face and kicks to the stomach by her husband. Her mother had no family, no education beyond high school, and no job. All she had were her three daughters and the thought that they deserved a better life. She left her husband, moved into a battered women's shelter, found a part-time job, and eventually enrolled in college. Many days they didn't have food to eat or a definite place to lay their heads at night, but their mother never gave up. She never stopped working towards a better life.

Her way of teaching her daughters about life was by telling them about her own. She never shied away from sharing her struggles growing up alone as a foster child, getting molested and raped by the people who took her in. She had tried hard to overcome low self-esteem and find self-worth. There was a lesson about hope, trust, forgiveness, and the power of God in each story she told them. Sometimes Raven would look at her mother and wonder how she could smile after everything she'd been through. Although Raven's childhood wasn't easy in the slightest, she had always found comfort in her sisters. Everything they went through they did so together. There was always someone there who understood their pain. Her mother not having that saddened Raven deeply.

The worst stories her mother shared were about their father. She tried to make him seem like a half-decent guy for their sake, but there was only so much sugarcoating she could do. As the eldest, Raven remembered the ways her father used to abuse her mother, physically and verbally. He was pure evil. He knew his wife was in search of a family she never had and wanted to love and be loved so desperately that she'd pretty much give anyone the opportunity. He took advantage of her and did it with a smile on his face. The thought of him made Raven's body shudder. Anger built within the depths of her soul whenever she thought about how her mother was no longer living but that evil man still had breath in his lungs. Hatred was too light of a word to describe how Raven felt toward the man who had helped create her. The last time she'd seen him, she was four years old and he had kidnapped her from daycare. He didn't do it because he wanted to spend time with her or because he missed his eldest daughter. He did it to make Raven's mother's life more traumatizing than it already was. What kind of person would be so evil? She'd asked herself that question for years but still had no answer.

"Baby?" Raven was pulled out of her thoughts by her husband's voice.

She shook her head as if to empty it of the awful reflections. "Huh?"

"I said, I love you."

Raven kissed him on the chin and took him by the hand, leading him up the stairs to their bedroom. "I love you too, Sean."

Chapter Three

Guard your heart for as long as you can. It's a skill
that will dissipate after time. —Wanda

"I DON'T KNOW WHY I can't leave Doc," the woman said in a confused tone as she lay across the couch. "I know he's lying to me, sleeping with other woman when I'm at work. He's changed; he's turned into a man I don't even recognize. I want to kick his ass out, but I can't give up on him because he's my husband."

Leila Cartel found it hard to listen to her patient's testimony without offering her some womanly advice. She wanted to tell her that leaving her husband would be the best decision she had ever made, because most men are dogs! They can't be trusted, and unless she learned how to play the game, she'd be paying Leila to counsel her for life.

But Leila couldn't say any of that. As a trained marriage counselor, she knew that the patient had to get to the solution on her own. So she just sat there and listened for the hint of courage that she made it a point to search for in all her sessions. This woman was well aware that she was being treated badly by her husband, but she also admitted that she wasn't about to leave him. There wasn't enough schooling in the world to get Leila to understand women who thought like this. Why couldn't they see that they were worth so much more than what they were getting? Why did they convince themselves that what they had was good enough?

This was her fifth session with Denise. She and her husband Clark had come to Leila over six months ago searching for some help to repair their marriage, which is what Leila devoted her life to doing. She had earned a Bachelors and Masters degree in psychology but focused her dissertation on relationship counseling. As a teenager, she had found herself awestruck over the dynamics of intimate relationships. Men and woman, what can make a successful relationship, and all the factors that can kill one. Over the years, Leila learned that relationships are good. Marriage is not. A marriage just doesn't last anymore, because people don't respect the sanction. Marriage leaves people with heartache, debt, and in some cases children to parent alone. Her jaded opinion might have been influenced by her job; nobody ever walked through her cherry wood doors, sat down on her Italian leather couch, and talked about how happy they were or about how much marriage had improve their quality of life. No. People talked about how depressed they were and how sad and unstable their lives had become.

Denise and Clark were a fairly young couple at thirty years old. Their story was cute; high school sweethearts whose relationship lasted through college. Well, at least Denise's college years. While she went to school, Clark worked at a car dealership. After she graduated, they married and became parents in the same year. Denise was now a real estate agent, bringing in the big bucks, and Clark had lost his job at the dealership two months ago. Their son had turned nine last week, which had prompted Denise to start coming to see Leila without her husband. When he lost his job, Clark became depressed and started moping around the house. At first Denise understood, but when the drinking and late nights out began, she started to worry. It wasn't until she found a woman's number in his jeans pocket that she became suspicious. When she approached him about it, he became defensive and told her that she was trying to find a way to leave him because he didn't have a job anymore. That was the day before her son's birthday party, and Clark didn't show up. He'd stormed out the house the night before and didn't come home for another two days.

"Denise," Leila probed, "what do you want to see happen in your marriage?"

Denise sat up. "I want my husband back. I want us to be happy again. Things were starting to get better until he lost his job, and now he treats me like I'm the one who fired him." She ran her hands through her bobbed hair. "I can't magically make a job appear for him. It's a recession out there, and lots of people are unemployed."

"Do you think that Clark's losing his job is the root of your problems?" Leila asked in a monotone voice, careful not to insinuate anything.

"Yes. He's always been upset that I make more money than him, and now that my income is carrying our family, it's really striking a nerve with him."

"Are you willing to take a pay cut or choose another profession so that your husband can feel more comfortable with the balance of income in your marriage?" Leila really had to keep herself in check with this question. She asked it as sincerely and nonjudgmental as she knew how. But it was hard. It just didn't make sense for a woman to be going through some bullshit like this over something as simple as a paycheck. If Clark was so intimidated, then he needed to get his ass up and look for a damn job instead of wasting the little bit of money he did have on alcohol.

"I've thought about it. I know it sounds stupid, but if it will save my marriage then yes, I would do it." Denise spoke in a sketchy tone, but that didn't matter. She meant what she said, and Leila knew it, because it was written all over her stressed face.

Time the hell out! Because this is some straight-up bullshit. Leila placed her yellow notepad down and looked at the woman across from her. "What will that solve, Denise? You'll have less money to raise your son. You won't be doing the job you love. Your whole lifestyle will have to change, and in the end you still don't know if this is the sacrifice that will restore your marriage."

"So, what are you saying, Doc?"

"I'm saying—" Leila blew out hot air. "Think about what all this would do to you. Evaluate what you will be gaining from this and what you'll be losing. I'm saying you need to consider your son. My job is to help you figure out what's best for your family. So that's what I'm saying. Think about your entire family, and that includes you. Too often women put everyone else first and neglect their own well-being, and that's not healthy."

"I hear you, Doc."

"Same time next week, Denise?"

Denise grabbed her purse. "Same time."

Leila pulled up to the drive-thru window at McDonald's and handed the young man exact change in exchange for her dinner. He left out the sweet and sour sauce, so she munched on her salty fries until he returned with her condiment. She ate her chicken nuggets as she drove her Lexus RX 400 down the rocky streets of Boston. *All the money this city has and the streets all look like they're under construction*, she thought. Her Jamaica Plain apartment was only a five-minute drive from her office, and today Leila was happy about that. All she wanted to do was soak in a hot bath and watch some prime-time television while devouring some strawberry cheesecake Ben and Jerry's ice cream.

An hour after she arrived home, she was doing as she planned. The bath had relaxed her, and the ice cream was hitting the spot. When she heard the front door slam, she knew Trevor was home. She didn't have to see him to know exactly what he was doing. His routine was unchanging. First he hung his coat in the hall closet before putting his work shirt in the laundry. Then he moved to the kitchen to put away the food from the restaurant and finally climbed the creaky, uncarpeted stairs to their bedroom.

"Oooo, give me some," he said upon entering the room. He sat on the bed while unlacing his shoes.

Leila smiled but shook her head. "I think not. You know I don't share the Ben or the Jerry."

"I was talking about a kiss." He unclamped the watch on his wrist and let it fall on the bedside dresser.

"Oh, that you can have." She leaned over and kissed him passionately on the lips, giving him a small taste of her ice cream.

"Did you eat already?" Trevor asked.

Leila took a huge scoop of ice cream and stuffed it in her mouth. She nodded.

"I brought some food home for you. Some healthy food. You don't need to be eating all that fast food every night. It's unhealthy," Trevor scolded her in a loving way.

"I had a salad from Whole Foods," she lied with a straight face.

"Don't lie. I saw the McDonald's bag in the kitchen garbage downstairs." Trevor gave her a pitiful look for her sorry attempt to fool him.

Leila silently laughed. Trevor had been trying to get her to eat healthier since they met. He was a culinary genius and the head chef at a popular restaurant on Newbury Street. He'd bring home food for her every night in hopes that she'd eat at least one balanced meal a day. It was a thoughtful gesture, and Leila really did appreciate him for that. "I'm sorry, babe, but I was hungry and I knew you wouldn't be home for hours, so I ate what my taste buds were asking for. But I'll bring your food with me for lunch tomorrow," she leveled with him. "How was your day?"

"Good. We had a busy lunch, so I was able to prepare almost everything on the menu." He took off his undershirt and pants and disappeared into the bathroom. He came back out with a towel wrapped around his waist. "And yours?"

Leila put the empty carton on her nightstand and leaned against the pillows behind her. "Frustrating. I had this one woman in my office today whose husband is a jackass. She knows it, but she still wants to stay with him. She's even willing to dumb herself down just to boost his sorry-ass ego. If I were her I'd be meeting with a divorce lawyer first thing in the morning," she said with complete confidence in her words.

Trevor looked at her with narrow eyes. It wasn't her bluntness that bothered him. It was the way she carelessly talked about ending relationships whenever there was trouble.

"What?" Leila questioned his glare.

"You're a marriage counselor. Aren't you supposed to help save people's relationships, not encourage them to end them?"

He had an edge on his voice. Leila knew where this conversation was headed. She wished that when he asked her about her day she 'd responded "Fine" and nothing more. But now it was too late. She already had one foot in the ring, and the boxing gloves were on. "I do save marriages, Trevor. But I have the right to my opinion, don't I? It's not like I told her to leave her husband or anything like that. I'm telling *you* how I feel because I thought we could discuss things like this without you jumping down my throat."

Now her arms were crossed before her. "Guess I was sadly mistaken."

"I just don't get it. A marriage counselor who doesn't believe in marriage. That makes no sense to me."

"What are you even saying? I do believe in marriage. I believe it's a real thing. I never said it was fake, made-up, or a figment of someone's imagination, now did I?"

"As much as I love your sarcasm, tonight is not the night and this is not the conversation," he said sternly.

"Okay, Trevor." Leila pushed the pause button on the TiVo remote. "I really wish we could go just one night without having this discussion, but I can see that you aren't going to let it go, so let's have it out." She scooted to the edge of the bed and crossed her legs in front of him while he stood leaning against the wall. "My work is my work, and my personal life is separate. I like what I do, but marriage isn't for everyone, including me."

"I want to get married," Trevor stated outwardly, not liking what Leila had said. It annoyed him to his core the way her mind was unchanging on the matter. No matter how hard he pushed or tried to convince her, Leila was as stubborn as an ox.

"I don't."

Trevor exhaled what seemed like pent-up aggravation. "Most women would kill for a man to get down on one knee and ask the woman he loves to be his wife, but not you. I ask you three times, and you reject me like it's nothing."

The pain of her rejection was in his eyes. Leila knew he was hurt that she had denied him marriage, but in all fairness, she had told him about her views on marriage on their third date. She wasn't the type of woman who strung men along, making them fall in love with her before she revealed her true self. That was a tactic she didn't find fitting for her personality or lifestyle. She considered herself an independent woman. She didn't need a man to complete her life, to make her feel worthy.

Keeping men at a distance was not only easier for Leila. It was also her way of protecting herself from the falling into the deep, dark well that was marriage. Giving herself over fully—body, mind, soul, and money—to a man would never sit well with her. She had promised herself when she was a young girl that she wouldn't make the mistake of trusting a man entirely. She wouldn't be the victim of a failed marriage like her mother, her grandmother, and every black woman she grew up with, for that matter.

She had vivid memories of listening to her mother and her friends gossiping every Friday night. She would sit at the top of the staircase with her ear held closely to the banister, eavesdropping on their conversations about nothing and everything. It didn't matter what the topic was because eventually they would all lead to men. The women would tell stories of their latest drama in that department, reveal the trifling acts of their boyfriends, and turn their pain into laughter as they sipped on wine coolers. It was through her eavesdropping that Leila found out just how much her mother had suffered in her marriage to her father. She heard the sorrow in her mother's voice as she spoke about never wanting that life for her daughters, which was the reason she had to leave her husband. It wasn't that she didn't love the man or that she couldn't take the abuse any longer. She did it because she didn't want her dysfunctional relationship or selfish adoration for the only man she had ever loved to dictate how her three daughters grew up expecting to be treated by men. It was all for them. For their safety, their sanity, and their chance to live a healthier lifestyle. As a ten-year-old girl sitting on those steps, Leila told herself she wouldn't let her mother down. She would do everything in her power to ensure that her mother's sacrifice would not go in vain.

It was their first real date.

"I don't want to get married ever," she told Trevor as they left the Hudson Theater after viewing one of August Wilson's plays. The fall night was chilly, and Leila wrapped her arms around her body to keep warm.

"Why not?" Trevor asked.

"It's just not something I see myself doing. I want kids and hopefully a man to share my life with, but no marriage." She jumped over a pothole in the street.

He slowed his pace. "Maybe when you meet the right person you'll change your mind. You're still young."

Leila was used to people questioning her view and was quite comfortable defending it as well. She had to be. For some reason people thought it unnatural for women to not want to run down the aisle with the first man who asked them. That always puzzled Leila. Why was it that women were supposed to be born to marry but men were bred to detest the sanction? It was something she would never understand. "Age has nothing to do with it, Trevor. I'm certain that married life is not for me, and I won't be changing my mind."

They walked to the train station mostly in silence. The loud sounds of cars and Northeastern University students substituted for the lack of conversation. Leila held on to Trevor's arm as they walked down the rubber steps to the underground Green Line station.

"Never want to get married?" Trevor uttered in disbelief as he flashed his train pass to the T worker. He'd obviously been disturbed by what she had to say on the matter. Leila gave him a reassuring smile. "Never."

That night when he walked her to her door, Leila was positive that that was the last she'd be seeing of Trevor. The way he had reacted to her statement let her know that he didn't share the same view. He probably wanted a wife, two and a half children, a dog, and a white picket fence. Everything minus the husband was cool with Leila.

Trevor kissed her good night and promised to call her the next day. Leila didn't believe him, but she said, "I'll be looking forward to your call" anyway.

As expected, Trevor didn't call the next day. Leila didn't trip, though. *Easy come, easy go*, she told herself every time a man left her life. Her own father had left her, and they shared the same DNA. But Trevor surprised her by calling two days later, apologized for not keeping his word, and asked her out for the following weekend. That was two years ago, and Leila couldn't have been happier in her relationship with Trevor.

"I'm not most women, Trevor. I never claimed to be." Leila stood and walked toward him slowly. "You make me happy. I enjoy spending time with you. I'm not looking for anything or anyone else. I only want you." She stood in front of him, resting her hands on his bare chest. "I love you, Trevor." She'd said those three words a million times to him, and she hoped he believed her, because she truly did love him. He was nothing but good to her, and Leila didn't want him to think she took him for granted. He was the best thing that had ever happened to her life. If only he could see things from where she was standing. If he understood her past, he'd know that there was no way she'd ever marry.

"I love you too, Leila." Trevor wrapped his muscular arms around her petite body.

She smiled. "Good. Let's just focus on how much we love each other for now, okay?"

Trevor was hesitant to answer. It took him a few moments, but he said, "Okay." And then they kissed the way lovers should, and Leila knew that their love was strong. She also knew that this was not the last time they would have this conversation. Each time it got harder to coax Trevor. He was just as determined as she was in his stance. One of them would have to give in, and Leila knew it wasn't going to be her. She deepened their kiss, memorizing his taste and wondering if this would be the last one they shared.

Chapter Four

If you don't have anything nice to say,
don't say anything at all. —Wanda

POETRY. WORDS OF THE PSYCHE *that have the power to connect unknown spirits.*
Rhythms that beat in your soul. Their only goal is to take you there.

And right now I need to go there. I need to get away from here and be
taken to another person's world, Brooklyn thought as she swayed to the jazz
music, feeling the vibrations of the saxophone travel through her body.
Her feet tapped the floor on the same beat as the African drum. The room
was dimly lit by only a few strobe lights highlighting the musicians on the
small stage, setting the right mood for the weekly poetry night.

"Coming to the stage we have our sistah Monica," the emcee announced
over the microphone. The band still played softly. A young woman—
probably fresh out of high school, Brooklyn assumed—with golden locks
hanging down her back came to the stage. She wore jeans and a Malcolm
X T-shirt, looking like the stereotypical poet.

"I'm so tired of feeling like I'm dead inside," Monica said into the mic,
her voice shaky. "That's the title."

She closed her eyes and inhaled. When she opened them, she turned to the band and instructed them on what style of music to play before she spoke avidly to the room filled with ready listeners.

I'm so tired of feeling like I'm dead inside

Like my heart won't beat unless I feel yours beat first

For so long you created the smile on my face and were responsible for why I could look past the pain in my life

Now you add to the reasons why my happiness and depression collide

I'm so tired of feeling like I'm dead inside

Like I'm so deserving of this never-ending curse

Late-night connections washed away hateration and replaced it with admiration

Now I desperately try to recall memories of that situation

Love songs won't cure the pain 'cause none of them capture exactly what we shared and how it went wrong

I'm so tired of feeling like I'm dead inside

The way your arms surrounded my body made me feel so secure you taught me how lovers love when my body was so pure and my conscience was very unsure

Your best friend told me that you didn't deserve me, matter of fact everyone said that shit

But they didn't understand it

I didn't deserve you; my man gave me confidence when no one else was willing to

She took a long pause, feeling her own words and wanting the audience to feel them too.

You used to be my boo

Today that statement is oh so untrue

No lie my heart wants to cry

I'm so tired of feeling like I'm dead inside

Your voice is a distant memory

Like Louise but you still on this earth so how could that be?

Questions roam through the cranium like a tumor, no cancer though

Just won't feel alive till I get that answer, yo

I'm so tired of feeling like I'm dead inside

I don't think this pain will ever go away

But if that means that I still love you then dammit the pain can stay!

I know that something's diluted cause since that day I haven't gotten on my knees and prayed

I just lie in bed and harbor thoughts about the good old days

Trying to figure a new man in my life is the hardest equation

They don't know me the way you do, you were my only temptation

Sneaking off after school to find new places in which you could tempt me some more

And more and more

A good girl never freaks and tells

No more verbs just past tense recollections

Really wish we could have had more sex-tions

I'm so tired of feeling like I'm dead inside

I would rather feel like you were alive inside

I ain't gonna lie

My heart wants to cry

I'm so tired of feeling like I'm dead inside!

Thunderous snaps bounced off the black walls as people stood. Brooklyn snapped her fingers along with the rest, thinking that Monica's poem served as therapy for a lot of brokenhearted people. Brooklyn watched as the young lady returned to her seat. A group of ladies embraced her, and Brooklyn could tell that they were comforting her. Her inquisitive nature wanted to know who had hurt the girl so badly that she felt dead inside. Heartache from an intimate love was something Brooklyn had never experienced in her twenty-six years. She'd never allowed herself to get that close to a man, to become so consumed by another person that his actions and moods dictated her own. She knew nothing about the young girl, but she found herself feeling sympathetic toward her.

"Tonight," the emcee said, returning to the stage. "We have a special treat. Brooklyn is in the house!" he bellowed, tipping his black designer personality glasses her way.

The crowd snapped, and as Brooklyn took the stage, people shouted.

"Yeah, girl!"

"I know she's about to put it down."

She smiled, recognizing most of the people. This was one of her regular hangouts.

"What's up, people." Brooklyn spoke softly as she had learned to do from watching *Def Poetry Jam*. "I want to share a piece I just finished yesterday with you. Is that all right?" she asked, knowing that they were just as eager to receive her words as she was to speak them.

"Yeah," "Hell yeah," and hoots and hollers were her responses. She winked at James, the saxophone player, telling him to play something sharp. He started playing some Coltrane; Brooklyn smiled and nodded her head, closing her already tight eyes.

"Check this. WOMAN-OPOLY." Her voice strong and confident, Brooklyn aimed her energy at Monica.

Pass me the dice
I roll a seven every time
Let's see where I land
This board game with a glass ceiling
Causing people to believe that I will always be behind
Just because my priorities are straight and I color within the lines
Rumor has it that I think with a different side of my brain
So some of you feel I can't hold my own in this chauvinistic game.
Wait not "Some of you"
I don't want U to think I'm talking about a new species
Because if I'm a woman speaking for women then I must be talking about
men
Who think they can control me
Put me in my place
My category
Teacher, nurse, secretary
Pregnant with dinner cooked and high heels on
But the truth is I'm more like the wind
Irrepressible, untamable, uncontrollable, unchangeable
God made me 'cause you couldn't handle the world on your own
I am powerful beyond measure

And you couldn't even say "No" to an apple
How's my apple pie?
Dinner's at eight
The tables have turned and now I'm working late
I've climbed the corporate ladder
I'm the CEO
Your boss
I just bought Boardwalk and put Park Place up for rent
You can be my tenant
My plumber, my janitor
Have a few other roles that you can perform
That will limit your skills and stunt your potential
But you won't mind because you're happy with where I place you
I drew a box that you can't climb out of
I'm the breadwinner
There is no need for you to climb
Just stay home and whine
I'll make you feel better with clothes and shoes
A lil' Calvin Klein
My trophy mate
I won't even take the time to dust you
Only call on you for sex
Even though I cheat on you
I still consider you the best
My turn again?
I just rolled doubles
I'm putting hotels on my property
Making monuments in my name
Painting the white house PINK
Joke, I like orange
Changing HIS-STORY
2 HER-Story
2 SHE-STORY
2 MY-STORY

This is a woman's world
And you're not behind bars
You're just visiting
Woman-OPOLY.

She opened her eyes to see everyone on their feet. There were no snaps. Claps and loud roars replaced them. She hoped her words empowered women, especially Monica. Women were built to endure the battles that life tossed their way. *I hope she feels alive inside,* Brooklyn thought. She threw her fingers in the air, forming a peace sign, the gold bangles around her wrist falling to her elbow. She made her way to the back of the room, straight to the bar.

"Can I have a white wine, please?" Brooklyn asked the bartender as she sat. He returned with the glass and placed in on a magenta napkin. She sipped the drink slowly, letting the bitter liquid simmer on her tongue for a few seconds. A tasty glass of good wine was her vice. Holding the neck of the glass, she swirled the contents, took another small sip, and placed the glass back on the napkin.

"Brooklyn, that's an unusual name."

Upon hearing her name, she looked up to face the man approaching her. "What's so unusual about it? Millions of people say it every day." *This man obviously needs to work on his opening lines,* she thought. *It's so annoying when people inquire about my name. It's the name of a city in the most popular state in America. What more do you need to know.*

Apparently overlooking her less-than-polite response, the man took the seat next to her. "What I meant to say was I never met a woman by that name before, and I like it."

Brooklyn had misjudged him. He wasn't cocky but polite. She took the time to study his face. He was a good-looking man. No facial hair, preserving his boyish charm. His almond complexion was alluring. He wore nice black Levi jeans and a black leather jacket over his black V-neck shirt. He was up on the latest trends. Her eyes diverted to his shoes. The Jordan's were clean. She mentally gave him a nod of approval. *As much as people like to pretend that appearance doesn't matter, it does,* Brooklyn told herself. *The way people dress tells a lot about who they are,* so she always took notice without feeling guilty about her judgments. His curly hair sat about a half inch off his head. It was as black as black gets and matched his eyes. Yes, indeed, he was a very good-looking man.

"I guess I'm supposed to say thank you," she said, facing not him but the bartender. "But I didn't give myself this name, so I can't take the credit."

"You wear the name well, and that you can take credit for," he countered, sipping the beer in his hand. "I enjoyed your poem as well. The metaphors were on point."

Brooklyn turned to him gratefully, smiling. The dimples in her cheeks deepened. "Thank you."

"Aw, so she does know how to take a compliment." He smiled, revealing perfectly straight white teeth.

She pursed her lips and sliced her eyes. "And you know how to ruin a moment."

He put his beer down. "Is that what we were having? A moment?"

Brooklyn changed her mind again. He was cocky. Sexy as all hell, but cocky. She placed him the category of men who run game on any woman with a fat ass and a pretty face. She was sure that he was no good for her. And what a shame because he almost had her fooled. "If we were having a moment, you just ruined it." She turned back to the bar, placed a ten-dollar bill next to her empty glass, and stood.

"You leaving?" he asked.

The surprise in his voice perplexed Brooklyn. This guy was a trip. She decided that he was trying to play games with her, and she wasn't about to entertain him. Men were so damn predictable. Why couldn't he drop the macho attitude and talk to her like he was interested in getting to know her? And Brooklyn knew he wanted to get to know her. But he would never get that chance now. Brooklyn wasn't in the business of handing out second chances or giving second looks to any man. She credited that philosophy as the reason she never had men problems.

"Yup."

"Well, it was nice meeting you, Brooklyn."

His courteousness was starting to irritate her. *Players aren't supposed to be this attentive*, she told herself. "You too, sir." She returned his manners and added the "sir" for good measure.

"Sir?" He chuckled. "That's not my name."

Brooklyn adjusted the belt on her jacket as she wrapped it around her waist. "Okay," she said nonchalantly, shrugging her shoulders.

The smile from his chuckle disappeared, leaving his expression blank. "Aren't you going to ask me what my name is?"

Now it was her turn to smile. "I only ask questions when I care about the answer." Feeling like she had the upper hand, she walked out of the club, leaving the nameless man alone with his drink.

Boston is a beautiful city, Brooklyn thought as she walked the Fenway area en route to her home. She enjoyed the historic scenery, the tall buildings, and especially the people. Boston was full of vibrant people who loved their sports. No matter what time of year it was, people were riled up and excited about their home teams. Although as progressive and liberal as Boston was, racial segregation was alive and thriving. Jamaica Plain, Roslindale, the North End, and the South End were known for being majority white. Blacks, Latinos, and immigrants controlled Roxbury, Dorchester, Mattapan, and Chelsea.

Brooklyn was born in Chelsea and grew up in Roxbury, where poverty was the norm. It wasn't until after college, when she landed her first job as a features editor, which she saved enough money to move out. She found a nice one-bedroom apartment in Jamaica Plain. The neighborhood was nice and clean, but she really liked the place because it was down the street from her sister Leila's place, and she wanted to be closer to her.

Brooklyn was the youngest of her mother's three daughters. "Wanda's girls," that's what people used to call them. People could never really tell the girls apart when they were children, so instead of guessing their names they'd simply say, "Wanda's girls."

The memory of her mother brightened Brooklyn's mood. In her mind her mother would always be the world's strongest woman. Growing up she remembered thinking that her mother had superpowers because she never seemed to get too tired. The way she cared for her daughters, like they were precious crystal and meant to be handled with care, was enough to make any child feel special. She was the ultimate mother, and oftentimes Brooklyn didn't even care that her father wasn't around to help raise her. She hadn't even been born yet when their divorce became final, so she didn't have a clue about who he was or even what he looked like. All she knew about him was what her mother and two sisters told her.

"You're lucky you don't have any recollection of Satan's spawn," her sister Raven would tell her whenever she'd ask about him. "You're better off not remembering him."

Brooklyn knew he was a horrific person who abused her mother and never once tried to fight for visiting rights to see his daughters, which is why she felt bad about missing him so intensely. She was different from her sisters in that sense. Where they hated the mention of his name, Brooklyn wanted not only to hear more about him, she wanted to meet him. She wanted to have a relationship with the man and refer to him as "Daddy" instead of "sperm donor" the way Leila did.

As a little girl she used to dream about the day when he would come to their house with both arms full of presents and buy them all the things their mother couldn't afford. He would pay the light bill so her mother didn't have to burn candles every night. He would fill the cabinets with food, and they would only have to eat ramen noodles if they wanted to and not because it was the only food they could afford. In her dreams, her father would realize that they were good, respectful, intelligent girls with bright futures, and he'd want to be a part of their success. Even if he came around only when they were doing good things, like when Raven would win every scholastic award known to man or when Leila would have a dance recital. In her dreams he loved his daughters and was there when they needed him. In Brooklyn's dreams he didn't use his dysfunctional relationship with his ex-wife as an excuse to not be a father to his three daughters.

But Brooklyn had let go of those dreams a long time ago when reality set in that she didn't have a daddy or a father but a sperm donor, just as her sister said. Daniel Cartel was no more a part of her than the elderly man walking past her smoking a cigarette.

Once in her apartment, Brooklyn took a quick shower, wrapped her hair in a satin scarf, and fell into bed. She turned on the television, setting the volume very low, barely audible. She didn't want to watch it, but she needed the television on to keep her company. She hated coming home every night to an empty apartment. It was lonely. Brooklyn told herself she was too old for a roommate, and having a man lay in her bed was completely out of the question.

She thought back to eight years ago. She was seventeen years old and a high school senior. She had been dating this guy for almost a year. He was nice and good looking, and all the girls at school wanted to be his girl, but he chose Brooklyn. They had a lot of fun together because they had a lot in common. They both loved sports, writing, and movies. So it was no surprise when he asked her to be his date to the senior prom. Like a gentleman, he picked her up at home and posed while her mother took a thousand pictures of them.

They danced to almost every song that night, and when the prom was over, he took her back to his house. His parents were out of town, and Brooklyn knew where this night would end. It wasn't like she didn't want to have sex with him. She did. They'd done basically everything else but have intercourse, and the sexual chemistry was definitely present. On most occasions he knew just what to say and where to touch her to make Brooklyn's hormones rage. He knew how to kiss her. How she liked to be touched in her most sensitive parts. Even the way she wanted to be held. They'd seen each other naked more than once, but for some reason every time his erect penis was inches away from entering her heated core, Brooklyn would lose her breath. And not in the good, "I'm so horny I can't wait to feel him inside of me" way. She would literally start to hyperventilate, even have asthma attacks.

"What's wrong with you?" he asked from on top of her. "Are you okay?"

Brooklyn couldn't speak. She was too busy trying to make sure she didn't pass out. So she shook her head. *How embarrassing,* she thought.

What kind of woman hyperventilates when she's about to make love? Why does this keep on happening to me? After the fifth time, she knew she wasn't normal, that something was wrong with her. So without saying a word, she would maneuver her way out from under his body, gather her clothes, and leave.

But tonight is going to be different, she told herself when they were rolling around in his bedroom kissing. *Tonight, no matter what, I'm going to go through with it and prove to him that I am a woman. None of this fingering shit or him giving me head. Tonight I'm going to have sex, and I'm going to enjoy it.*

"You ready, baby?"

Brooklyn looked down at him and watched as his manhood grew before her eyes. "Yeah, I'm ready."

He slipped on the condom. Brooklyn watched calmly, but that didn't really mean anything, because she was always calm at this point. She needed to allow him to enter her without hesitation. Then she would have made progress.

He looked down at her with skeptical eyes, and she knew he expected her heavy breathing to begin. But it didn't because she was more determined to do this then she'd ever been about anything in her life.

It was no longer about love or hormones. That had gone out the window after their second attempt to make love. Now it was solely about sex and proving to herself that she was a normal woman with animalistic needs. She had to confirm that there was nothing wrong with her, that she needed and wanted sex as badly as the next woman.

Steadying the breaths she was taking, Brooklyn closed her eyes in singular concentration. She felt the tip of him forcing its way into her opening until it was in as far as it was going to go. She was so happy that she wasn't reaching for her inhaler she didn't even notice the pain. Once inside her, he moved slowly, careful not to hurt her. Brooklyn knew enough about sex to know that she was supposed to gyrate her hips along with his strokes. Mechanically, she did what she knew was expected of her: moaning at the right times, screaming out his name when he quickened his pace, and shrieking out in ecstasy when he reached his pinnacle.

I did it, she remembered thinking when he rolled off her and onto the other side of the full size mattress. She was beyond delighted that she had overcome that hurdle successfully. Brooklyn didn't even notice that she was smiling from ear to ear until he asked, his chest heaving up and down, "Damn, baby, was it that good?" Small beads of sweat glistened over his skin.

She'd almost forgotten that he was there. "Uh, yeah." She pulled the sheets over her exposed breast and turned onto her side. "It was that good."

It wasn't until he fell asleep that Brooklyn really thought about what had just taken place. She had lost her virginity on prom night to the person she always intended to give it away to. She should be happy. She should feel joy or something. But she didn't. She felt nothing at all except pride at doing what she couldn't do before, and that had nothing to do with the man lying next to her. For all she cared, any ol' man would do the trick as long as she was able to say she'd had sex. That's when it happened. That's when Brooklyn realized that she wasn't normal. Something was wrong with her, and in her mind she wasn't a normal woman.

After that night, Brooklyn dodged her boyfriend's calls for weeks until they stopped coming. She refused any guy who asked her out on a date and focused all her energy on finishing high school. When she started classes in the fall at Northeastern University, nothing had changed. Still no interaction with the opposite sex. She was convinced that this was the way things needed to be until she figured out why she felt so unattached in relationships.

It was her junior year, second semester. Her English professor assigned the class Shakespearean sonnets to recite in class, in groups of two. Brooklyn was paired with her classmate Karen. They made plans to meet in the library to rehearse. Since Brooklyn spent most of her time in the school library, she was already sitting at a table when Karen, the only other black girl in her class, came waltzing in.

"What's up, girl?" Karen took the seat across from Brooklyn.

"Just getting some reading done, but I'm ready to crack open this Shakespeare." She pulled the paperback book out of her bag and flipped to the marked page. Brooklyn began reading sonnet twenty-one aloud with a tongue that made it obvious she knew what she was reading. She understood the language and felt the words as if she had written them herself. It wasn't long before a small crowd of people formed around her, but Brooklyn didn't notice. She was too engrossed in the text even to see anyone else.

"Shit," a boy exclaimed when Brooklyn stopped reading. He walked with a swaggering limp over to her, rubbing his hands together. "You sexy without opening your mouth, but damn, girl, you make a brother wish he knew something about whatever it is you over there reading." He licked his lips and winked at her. "Can I get your number, boo?" He rested one arm on the back of her chair and the other on the wooden table.

Brooklyn closed her book and took off her reading glasses. She was getting so used to turning guys down that the word no just flew out her mouth.

From the way he cocked his head back and twisted his face, Brooklyn could tell that he didn't hear that word very often.

"No? What you mean, no?"

Even if he isn't used to hearing the word, he damn sure knows what it means, she thought. "I mean exactly that. No. As in, you can't have my number."

He sucked his teeth. Apparently the admiration he'd had for her a few seconds ago was now replaced with displeasure. "Forget you, then. You ain't even that cute anyway," he screamed as he walked away, making a ghetto scene as if being black didn't cause enough attention.

She saw a few people laughing as the crowd dispersed but paid them no mind. She just went back to reading.

"That was the point guard for the basketball team. You know that, right?" Karen asked, seemingly impressed by what Brooklyn had just done.

Brooklyn pulled her eyes away from her book and placed them on Karen. "I don't care who he is, because I'm not interested," she said, all the while thinking, *that's what's wrong with women. We don't care how a man approaches his personality or us. We zoom in to the title that he carries and bingo, we immediately have a winner or a loser.*

"You're not interested in good-looking men?" The lines across Karen's forehead deepened.

"Nope. I'm not interested in any man." Brooklyn resumed reading in hopes that their meaningless conversation was over. But she could feel Karen's eyes still on her. Uncomfortable, she looked up again.

"What?"

Karen smiled. "You're really pretty. You know that?"

All of this was starting to confuse Brooklyn. She didn't know where that compliment came from, but she did know it would be rude if she didn't return it. "So are you, Karen," she responded.

"Hey, do you mind if I read along with you? I sort of left my book in my dorm room." Karen was already starting to make her way to the other side of the table

What the hell? Brooklyn asked herself. *Who comes to a study meeting without their study material?* "Yeah, no problem."

She moved the book in between the two of them and, with her index finger, pointed to Karen's part. "This is where I stop and you begin," she said, rotating her head up to Karen. Before her eyes settled, Brooklyn felt Karen's wet lips touch hers. She jumped back so far she fell out of her chair and onto the carpeted floor.

"What the fuck?" She wiped her lips with the back of her hand. But that wasn't enough, so she pulled her shirt up from her waist and used it to wipe her lips also. "What did you do that for?" She got up off the floor mad as hell and ready to fight.

Karen face turned as red as a brown woman's skin would allow. She was embarrassed. "Aren't you gay?" she whispered.

"No!" Brooklyn screamed. She didn't know why Karen's question pissed her off, but it did. "Strictly dick! I don't get down with other females like that."

"But you said you weren't interested in men. I've known you for three years, and I've never seen you with a guy. You sure you aren't just pretending?"

Brooklyn flopped down in her seat. She hated having her sexuality questioned. So what if she didn't go out on dates or jump in bed with every man who pursued her? That didn't mean she wanted to do whatever it is that gay women do. She was confused about her intimate problems with men and why she felt so detached, but she was sure she never had been and never would be sexually attracted to another female. It just wasn't her cup of tea.

"I'm not gay, Karen. And I don't appreciate you kissing me either. Even if I were gay, you were out of line."

Karen raised her hands above her head in surrender. "I'm sorry. My gay-dar must have been a little off. Look, Brook, it's not a big deal. We can just forget the whole thing happened." Karen's attempt to lighten the mood and bypass the situation flew over Brooklyn's head. She didn't care about Karen's apology or her stupid gay-dar. At first, her being celibate was cool. It was her business and hers alone. Nobody had to know why. But now people were getting involved. It wasn't that she cared about what people thought about her, but she also didn't want to have to go through something like this again. This was some bullshit. She scooped all her things into her arms and walked out of the library. It didn't matter that Karen was calling for her to return. She had bigger problems to solve.

Brooklyn tossed and turned in her bed, not wanting to reminisce any longer. It angered her that she was still unable to fix her issues with men. Nine years had passed and still no sex. She did eventually start dating, but no one ever grasped her interest to the point where she wanted to bed them. Sometimes she would get so fed up, she'd think maybe she actually was gay and just pretending. But she was smart enough to know that that wasn't true. She needed to figure this thing out fast because sleeping alone was getting old—and lonely.

The next morning Brooklyn woke up to her phone ringing loudly in her right ear. She tried to ignore it. Sleeping late was supposed to be one of the perks of not having to report to work. She had quit her job almost a month ago, and still she wasn't able to sleep past ten o'clock. Something always came up. Usually one of her sisters would need her to do something or other for them, and she would oblige.

Brooklyn balled up her fist and punched the mattress while screaming into her pillow. Whoever was calling would not settle for the voice mail. She reached for the phone, still with her eyes closed. "Hello?" Her voice was deep, groggy, and probably unattractive, but she was too tired to care.

"You 'sleep, Brook?" Leila's voice bellowed in her ear. She sounded as if she'd been up for hours. "It's, like, almost nine thirty, girl. You need to wake up."

"If I was sleeping then I wouldn't be talking to you, now would I Leila?" Brook was not a morning person, and she knew Leila was aware of that. She couldn't comprehend why her sister still bypassed that fact. "What do you want?"

"Oooooo, Ma used to say that you had a bad attitude when you woke up. Nobody even had to say anything to you when we were kids. You'd just snap at people because it was morning."

"Whatever. Don't be bringing Ma into this. I'm tired. I didn't go to sleep till late, so there you have it. I do have a reason." Brooklyn sat up in bed, accepting that her sleep was over. She rubbed her eyes, forcing the haziness away.

"Late night? Hot date?"

"Don't play. You know I wasn't on a date. I just had a hard time getting to sleep, that's all."

"You need a man, Brook. A boyfriend would fix all of that."

"I don't need anything but a cup of coffee and some inspiration to write." In one quick motion, Brook was out of bed and making coffee with one hand while holding the cordless phone with the other.

"Okay, but do you want a man? I mean, you got to get back on the horse eventually. People just don't give up on sex for no good reason."

"Leila, that's none of your business. I told you about my issue in confidence—and in a moment of weakness, might I add. Not for you to be throwing it in my face every chance you get. I'm not one of your patients, you know."

"No, but you're my little sister, and I'm worried about you. It's not healthy to box yourself off and ignore the crisis."

"Crisis? Leila, my not wanting to have sex is not a crisis. It's a personal decision. And if you want to talk about unhealthy, what about you and your fear of commitment? You want to talk about that?"

"That was a low blow. I can't believe you went there," Leila said, her voice sounding more like Brooklyn's.

"Had to. Now, was there a reason you called other than to piss me off? Because I have things to do."

"Dinner tonight, at my place."

"Is Raven coming?"

"Yes. She called this morning and said that we all needed to get together."

Brooklyn took a second to think it over. "Alone? I hate it when she brings Sean and you have Trevor because I always feel like the fifth wheel."

"Yes, alone. It will just be the three of us. Are you gonna come?"

"I'll be there. And you better not be lying to me either just to get me to come."

"One time. I did that one time. Damn, Brook, let it go!"

Brooklyn heard her sister whisper something to a faint voice in the background. "Look, my next appointment is here. Are you coming or not?" Leila asked.

"I said I would be there. Bye."

Brooklyn thought about her day's agenda. Breakfast, shower, library, lunch, writing, and now dinner with her sisters. Minus the dinner, this had been her routine for the last couple of weeks. She was living out her dream of writing her first novel, and this routine was the structure she needed to stay on track, since she was only giving herself a year to complete it. Her book was the only thing in her life she could truly call her own. Sometimes she wished things were different, that she didn't have to be alone so often. *It won't be like this always*, she told herself on the way to fix breakfast and start yet another predictable day.

Chapter Five

When I leave this earth, I'll be leaving my daughters with each other.
Loneliness they shall never know. —Wanda

"COME IN HERE, GIRL." LEILA said. She and Brooklyn stood on opposite sides of the door. Leila wore a pair of Seven Brand jeans with a teal tank under a looser white tank. With little makeup on her golden skin, she exemplified natural beauty. Her hair was pulled back in a loose, curled ponytail that called attention to her newly cut bangs, which hung right under her arched eyebrows. From head to toe the woman knew how to work with what God gave her, and by many standards, he gave her a lot to work with. "Why are you looking around like a criminal or something?" Leila pulled her sister by the arm and gently yanked her into the apartment.

The look on Brooklyn's face didn't disappear until she had taken a thorough look around the tastefully decorated home. "I was just making sure you weren't lying earlier, that's all." Now relaxed, she took of her jacket and hung it in the hall closet. "I don't smell any food. What did you cook?"

Leila picked up a folded piece of paper of her living room table. "I didn't. I ordered Chinese food. It will be here any minute." Brooklyn gave Leila a nod of approval before making her way to the kitchen, where Raven was leaning on the refrigerator talking on her cell phone. "I love you too, Tristan. Be a good boy for your daddy and eat all of your dinner, okay?" She waited a second for his response and then smiled before saying good night and repeating the same routine with her son Josiah. Over the next three hours, the sisters ate, drank, talked, told themselves that if they ate one more bite their stomachs would bust, and then did it all over again. Brooklyn and Raven got into a heated discussion about Tyler Perry and his films. The man was vastly making a name for himself in Hollywood with his movies based on the lives of southern black folks. He mixed comedy with tragedy and lined all his stories with the Holy Gospel. Basically, he was introducing greater America to a certain type of black American that Hollywood seemed to overlook. In Brooklyn's eyes the man was pure genius, but Raven saw his movies as "buffoonery and coonery."

"I just don't get why he has to make his most famous characters so damn ignorant," Raven said. "They don't speak proper English. He portrays them as idiots and expects us to applaud him?"

"It's comedy, Raven. Calm down and stop taking everything so serious," Brook said defensively.

"I'm sorry if I don't see the humor in a black man finally making it in Hollywood and choosing to put black brothers and sisters on screen acting foolish and ignorant, mispronouncing English words and feeding into the negative stereotypes that white people already hold to be true," Raven said. "All that man is doing is making it harder for black people who are trying hard to fight that negative image and display our people in a better light."

"That's the issue right there. Instead of watching these movies and learning about a culture of our own people that we didn't know existed, people want to act like they're made-up characters with no real premise. In fact, there are millions of us out there who can relate to Tyler Perry's characters. We've become so assimilated with white America that we tend to look down on anything that doesn't fit into that mold, even if it means turning our noses up at our own people. There was a point in history when blacks didn't know this language, and let's not pretend that we as a people still aren't working at grasping it every day." Brooklyn paused, hoping she was getting her point across to her sister, who never backed down from a debate. "I'm not saying everything he produces is gold, but I don't think we should criticize the man for making movies about us and for us. That alone is enough for me to show him some love."

"I guess you have a point."

Later they sat in Leila's den, sipping Chablis while some old-school Lauryn Hill played in the background.

"I love that photo of you." Raven pointed at the black-and-white shot of Leila that hung on the wall.

The photo captured her sitting on a bench in Franklin Field Park reading to three children who sat around her. It was part of her psychology program to intern at different places that could eventually help determine what field she might go into. Leila had always known she wanted to work with couples, so she used the opportunity to work with underprivileged children, most of whom were girls that belonged to the foster care system.

"You really look like Mom in that photo," Raven added in admiration.

The look on Leila's face softened. "You think? I always thought you looked more like her." She sipped her wine. "She was so beautiful, though. Even if it is just that photo, I'll take what I can get."

"You guys both look like her," Brooklyn chimed in, her voice resembling a child who had just figured out that she was cheated out of the bigger half of the candy bar. "You two have her eyes, big, bold, and beautiful. Her smile, natural and perfect. It took four years of braces to fix these teeth." She flashed a phony smile for the sake of her argument. "You guys even have her golden skin."

"Brook, you might not look like her, but you're beautiful. Don't ever doubt that about yourself," Raven said, shaking her head.

"I know, I know. I'm as gorgeous as they come," Brook said smugly, causing her sisters to laugh. "No, but seriously, it always bothered me that I never resembled you guys. No lie, I used to think I was adopted." This time Brooklyn had to laugh. It took her a few seconds to realize she was laughing alone. "What?" she asked, her eyes bouncing from one sister to the other. She began to feel nervous, as if they were hiding something from her. Maybe her words had struck a nerve.

"Wait, am I adopted?" she screamed, jumping to her feet, almost spilling her wine on the carpet.

"Brook, no." Leila looked up at her, telling her more with her eyes than her words that she was their blood sister. "You're not adopted." She said the words like they were ridiculous. "You don't look like us because we look like Mom and you look like…. him." She gulped down whatever was left in her glass and refilled it.

Brook sat back down slowly and carefully. In all her years she'd never seen a picture of her father. She had never known what he looked like. She had always assumed she was just the oddball because she was the last-born. Sometimes it happened like that, especially with black people. You never know whom your child would come out looking like. She remembered as a child asking her mother why she didn't look like her. Her mother had responded, "You look like my mother, and she was born and raised in Brooklyn, New York. I knew the second I laid eyes on you that you were going to have her features, so that's why I named you after the place she loved so much." After hearing that story, Brook had felt special, as if she had been given something her sisters weren't. But now, that feeling was destroyed by the unwelcome truth.

"You two remember what he looks like?" she asked guardedly, but she didn't know why.

They both nodded, but Raven said, "You look just like him. He had tight eyes, chocolate smooth skin, and thick, curly hair just like yours. You even have his dimples." She counted off their resemblances on her fingers with her eyes to the ceiling. "The man was evil but good looking nonetheless."

"I can't believe this. Why didn't you tell me this before? Don't you think I would've liked to know this stuff?" she said, her eyes bulging out of their sockets. "All this time I thought I was the oddball and lo and behold I look exactly like my daddy."

As soon as the last word left her tongue, Brook wanted to take it back.

Not only because it felt weird saying it out loud but because she'd made the mistake of saying it to her sisters. So many times as a child and even as an early teenager, she would lock herself in the bathroom, turn on the faucet, and face the mirror. She would be careful not to speak too loudly as she would say "Dad" or "Daddy" again and again. Watching the motion of her lips and tongue as they worked together to form the neglected words. When she was feeling really brave, she would pretend he was calling her from another room in their home and she would respond in a high-pitched tone, "Yes, daaadeee," just like she heard one of the girls in her class say one day when her father came to pick her up. Oh, how Brook wished she were in that bathroom right now. The faucet would have drained out that word, and her sister wouldn't be side-eying her right now.

"Hold up," Leila snapped. "The man gave you good genes. There is no reason for you to start dropping the D-word around like he gave you anything that actually caused him to get off his lazy ass and contribute to your life—or any of our lives, for that matter."

"Uuugg, I can't stand his ass." The look of disgust on Raven face was firm. "I wish he were dead," she announced with emotion.

"Raven!" Brook yelled. "That's really harsh."

"No. She's right. That man did some awful things to Mom. He damn near killed her on more than one occasion. He's a monster," Leila said. "Brooklyn, you've heard the stories, but you didn't have to see Mom sprawled across the kitchen floor unconscious from taking too many blows to her head and blood dripping from so many parts of her body we didn't know where she was bleeding. Your 'daddy' didn't do anything while Raven and I cried our eyes out screaming for Mom to wake up. He just stood there, blank faced, his tight eyes piercing down on us."

"Or what about the time Mom didn't do something or other exactly the way he told her to and he beat her so bad that her nose met her forehead?" Raven said at a snail's pace, the words bringing back the mental image.

"Or when—"

"Stop it! Stop it!" Brooklyn shouted in tears. All these images of her mother being beaten close to death were too much to handle. She wasn't familiar with that side of her mother, could never imagine her balled up in a corner covering her face with her hands, trying to protect it from the forceful blows coming from above. She hated knowing that her mother had endured so much abuse and that she wasn't there to help her. So many times Brooklyn had wished she could stand between her father and mother and take the hits for her. But she couldn't. What was done was done, and that's what hurt the most. "Why are you telling me all of this?"

"Because you need to know the truth. You need to know why you should never refer to him as 'daddy' or use any other term of endearment. He doesn't deserve that. Not only did he abuse Mom but also he left us. He left us without as much as a wave or a damn goodbye letter. He might be alive in this world, but he's dead to me." Raven's voice was sharp with anger, completely sure of her stance.

"Me too," Leila agreed. "Everything we overcame, everything we amounted to in this life is because of Mom and despite him."

She turned to face Brooklyn, who couldn't seem to stop the tears from rolling down her cheeks. "We're Wanda's girls, not his."

Brooklyn ran her hands down her face, capturing the moistness in them. This was all overwhelming for her. She was used to seeing her sisters laughing and having a zest for life. Never had she seen their faces plagued with so much anguish. "Have you ever thought about his family? Aren't you the least bit curious about the other part of your linage?" She posed the question to both her sisters.

"Hell the fuck no!" Leila retorted, the offense of the question seeping through her words. "They can all go to hell as far as I'm concerned. They know more about us then we know about them, and I can't recall one time—" She stuck her pointer finger in the air. "Not one time when anyone from his family made an effort to build a relationship with us. They pretended like we didn't exist, just like they pretended like Mom's black eyes didn't exist."

Brooklyn's whole body was experiencing heat flashes. Her hands were dripping with sweat, and her head was lighter than a helium-filled balloon. She had always known her sisters had a strong dislike for their father, but for the first time she could see and hear how deeply their hatred for him was embedded in their souls. Their father had been present for less than a fourth of their lives, but he had made such an impact on the women they'd grown to be. For the first time Brooklyn saw and heard those effects, and that's what pained her the most. Before tonight she'd had mixed feelings about him. She was always riding the fence and holding on to her childhood dreams. But now she was sure. Brooklyn hated Daniel Cartel, and she was sure of it. She wiped away the rest of her tears as well as any contradicting feeling she had ever harbored for the man.

Chapter Six

Don't just read books, little girl. Read people. —Wanda

THERE WERE FIVE LIBRARIES WITHIN walking distance of her house, but Brooklyn preferred taking the T to Copley. The library was huge and located in an effervescent part of the city. All sorts of people walked through the revolving doorway, mostly college students and homeless people looking for shelter for a few hours. If she sat there long enough she would learn the stories of some of these people. She studied sociology in college and became intrigued by how the social science enhanced her writing. Sociologists study people, and authors write stories about people in the most believable manner they can create. At the library, Brook was able to do both, and to say the least there was always inspiration to be found in the uniqueness that was Copley library.

When the train stopped, she waited in line to flash the conductor her monthly pass and then darting to an open seat before some other lucky person got there first. She was lucky enough to find a two-seater. Brooklyn took the inner seat out of train etiquette although she preferred the aisle seat. There was never enough leg room in the inner seat, and she hated getting stuck sitting next to some weirdo who smelled funny or, worse, found it appropriate to start a conversation with her.

When the doors closed and the train started to move, she took her notebook out of her satchel along with a pen. Something about the rambunctious sound of the train allowed her juices to flow. She'd written many poems and short stories on train rides over the years.

Like always, she allowed herself to fall into a trance and just permit the creativity to pour out of her mouth. It was how she wrote. First she thought about a word or a sentence and then she said it aloud, not caring if people stared. Then she wrote it down, repeated it, and started the process over again. This allowed her to feel the words as well as hear the way they sounded cohesively. Every writer had his or her thing, and this was Brooklyn's.

The train stopped. Passengers got off, and more got on. She moved her satchel off the seat next to her and onto her lap when she noticed someone eying the seat.

The train started again, and so did her creative flow.

"You know, people might think you're crazy if you keep talking to yourself." The passenger sitting next to her tapped her on the shoulder.

"What did you say?" She couldn't hear anything over the sound of the train moving over the steel tracks.

"I said, people might think you're crazy because you're talking to yourself," the passenger repeated.

"Not that it's any of your business, but I'm not talking to myself. Well, not really. I'm writing, and I like to hear myself say it before I put it down on paper."

"Oh, I see. So you're a writer?"

"Yeah. But if you don't mind, I really need to get back to this." She held up her notebook, the page marked with her unruly handwriting. She looked back down at what she'd written and tried to get back into her rhythm.

"No problem, Brooklyn. I didn't mean to interrupt."

Brooklyn froze upon hearing her name. She ran through the short conversation she'd had with the stranger. She just knew she hadn't introduced herself. She closed her notebook and stuffed it back in her bag. Her bag she pulled tightly to her chest. Her stop would come in a few minutes, and then, Brooklyn told herself, she would walk as far away from this psycho as possible.

"I'm not a crazy stalker or anything. I know that's what you're thinking. We met the other night at the poetry jam. Remember … we shared a moment?"

She tilted her head to examine him fully. Now she felt mortified. How could she forget such a handsome face that easily? But then she remembered his attitude, and it all came rushing back at once. He didn't deserve to be in her memory.

"How did you remember my name?" she asked, loosening the grip on her satchel, feeling more at ease.

He shrugged. "I always remember the name of a beautiful woman."

Fabulous bullshit, Brooklyn thought. *So he remembered my name and recognized me in a different setting. Quite impressive, but still not good enough.* "I'm beginning to think you keep paying me compliments just to hear me say thank you."

He smiled. "I'd much rather hear you say something else, but I'm working on that."

She didn't know if his innuendo was meant to be so inappropriate. There was something intriguing about this man that far exceeded his good looks. He had a definite swagger that was beyond sexy. Plus, he smelled really nice. "Excuse me?"

"I wanted to ask you out the other night, but you rushed off."

"Oh, is that what you called yourself doing?" She let out a sarcastic laugh. "Could've fooled me."

"I'm sorry about that. Usually I don't come off as suck a jerk. You should give me another shot."

"And why would I want to do something like that?" *This is the question that separates boys from men,* she thought. Boys stutter around searching their brains for a half-decent answer, but most of them end up saying something stupid that shows their immaturity, probably a sex joke thrown into the mix. Men—well, she had yet to meet a man who answered the question with enough poise to make her consider going out with him.

"Because I would like the chance to show you that I'm a good guy," he said with sincerity. "Really, let me take you to dinner and convince you of what I already know about you."

Not hating his response to her question, she asked, "And what is that?"

"I know that you're worth my time, and I want you to know that I'm worth yours."

She tried to hold back her smile but it was unsuccessful. He was cute and charming. The man was confident, but this time he didn't seem cocky. *Maybe he deserves another chance,* Brooklyn thought. It had been years since she had even considered giving out a second shot, but this man was different, and she was without a doubt interested. She couldn't quite put her finger on the intrigue. The attraction was deeper than physical. For some odd reason, this man was different then all the rest she'd met. That alone had to be worth something. "One dinner," she told him, still smiling but trying to be firm.

"I'll take it. When are you available?" He was already touching buttons on his phone. Probably going through his calendar, she figured.

"When do you want to take me out?" She sidestepped his question, not feeling comfortable giving him her schedule. He would have to tell her when, and she would then say whether she was available or not.

He searched her eyes, surprised that she was giving him so much control. "If it were up to me, we would be having dinner tonight."

"Ohhh ... well, uh, don't you think that's kind of quick?" She didn't like the way she tripped over her words, but his bluntness was unexpected. Normally she would take his words to mean that he wanted to take her out tonight in hopes of ending his day with some sex he hadn't expected when he hopped out of bed that morning, but she wasn't getting that vibe from him.

"No. Considering this is the second time we've spoken. Plus, I don't believe in wasting time."

"Fine." Brooklyn had said the words, but even she was surprised at herself. This was totally out of her character, but for some reason it felt right. "Tonight it is." She gave him her number and watched as he punched it into his phone. The conductor announced that her stop was next. Brooklyn stood and scooted past him, making her way closer to the door. She didn't have to look back at him to know that he was giving her the once-over, checking out all that she was working with, her thighs, long muscular legs, and plump ass included. She smiled inside, knowing he liked what he saw.

"I'll be calling you in a few hours, Ms. Brooklyn," he said as the train came to a stop.

"Okay." The doors opened. "Wait. Now I want to know the answer."

"Answer to what?" he asked.

"What's your name?"

"Jason. But my friends call me Junior."

Chapter Seven

JASON WAS EXCITED ABOUT HIS date with Brooklyn tonight. He'd called her around three to make plans to pick her up at eight. She hadn't picked up the first time he called, and he thought she had given him the wrong number. It turns out she had forgotten that he was supposed to call and she didn't usually pick up for numbers she didn't recognize. She called him back an hour later.

"Is this Jason?" she asked.

"Yeah, I was beginning to think you played me."

"My bad. You still game for tonight?"

"Of course."

Jason told her he wanted to take her to one of his favorite restaurants, but he wanted it to be a surprise. Brooklyn wasn't too excited about not knowing where he was taking her, but she told him that she would go with the flow. "I'm really hoping you're not a serial killer," he heard her say.

"I'm not," he assured her. She gave him her address before hanging up. By seven thirty, Jason was dressed in a casual suit and a green dress shirt with no tie. He looked through his bathroom mirror and wished he had gotten his hair cut. The tight curls were growing a little too long for his liking, but it was too late for that, so he put a small amount of gel in his hair to tame it. He ran his hand over his smooth jaw before turning off the light. He was heading for the door when his phone rang.

"Hello?"

"Hey, do you want to catch a movie or something?"

"Umm, Ice, I sort of have a date tonight." He felt guilty. Since her father's death, she had been depending on him a lot more, and he knew he needed to be there for her. Until tonight he'd spent every night with her. Eating, shopping, watching movies—anything to get her mind off of death. He was her person, and she needed him. "But I can cancel. I'll call her and say that something important has come up."

"No, no. You go and have fun. It's not polite to cancel on a woman, Junior," she said.

"Are you going to be okay?"

"Yeah, I'll be fine. But I expect a full report tomorrow."

"You got it."

On the ride to Brooklyn's house, Jason thought about Ice and wondered if he should still cancel his date and swing by her house. There was no doubt in his mind that he wanted to have this date with Brooklyn, but Ice was his best friend. And friendship trumps beautiful women.

Although "beautiful" really wasn't the word to describe Brooklyn. She was a few steps beyond any measure of beauty he'd ever seen. Like him, she had brown skin, but hers was radiant in the way her yellow undertone glowed. Her hair especially took him. Thick and full, it had been pulled back both times he'd seen her, but he could tell that it flowed well past her shoulders. "Stunning" was a more appropriate word to describe her. No, he wouldn't cancel on Brooklyn.

He parked directly in front of her house and was getting out to knock on her door when he saw her come out of the brick building, locking the door behind her. She turned and descended the stairs. With half his body out of the car, Jason stood over the hood watching her. She wore a black cocktail dress that fell right above her knees. Her hair was straightened and, like expected, reached the middle of her back. She came to the car, opened her own door, and fastened her seatbelt before saying, "Hello."

The drive to the restaurant was anything but quiet. Jason asked her questions about her writing and was impressed that she was in the midst of writing a novel. He also discovered that she was a huge sports fan—and not one of those girls who said they liked sports to impress a guy. She really knew her stuff.

Once they arrived at the restaurant, Jason watched as Brooklyn's eyes lit up. *She must be impressed,* he told himself. Since he had made reservations, they were immediately seated, and a waiter brought them menus. They each perused their menus, not saying much of anything. When the waiter came back to take their order, Jason decided on a sirloin steak, mashed potatoes, and broccoli.

"I'll have the stuffed chicken, but no tomatoes. I'll have red peppers instead. Oh, and can you have the chef put cranberries and mangoes in my brown rice?"

The waiter smiled at her, took her menu, and said, "For you, Madame, anything." And then he left.

Now it was Jason's turn to be impressed. "Looks like you have an admirer. There aren't many people who can request the chef to make a specific meal just for them." He sipped his wine as the waiter left.

"Who, John?" She tilted her head in the direction of their waiter, who was now tending to another table. "He's an old boyfriend. We just broke up last week, actually."

"What?" he asked as if his ears had deceived him. He didn't like the idea of Brooklyn's ex being too close for comfort on their first date. This was his time with her. Not the waiter's opportunity to win her back. "Do you mind if we eat somewhere else? There are plenty of restaurants on this street." Brooklyn held her lips together in a smile, and he could tell she was suppressing her laughter. Jason didn't see the humor, nor did he appreciate her making a fool of him. She looked up at his serious face.

"I was kidding." She unleashed her laughter. "Can't you take a joke?"

He laughed too, but more out of embarrassment. He felt silly for overreacting. "Apparently not. Sorry about that."

She waved him off. "It's cool. Good to know the lengths you'd go to make sure we had a good night, though."

He was glad she had found the good in what he'd said because he sure couldn't. "So, how did you get the chef to make the food you wanted?"

He was still curious. But if he had to guess, he would say her beauty got her pretty much anything she wanted.

"I have connections," she said, quickly adding, "But not those kinds of connections." She laughed a little more. And Jason couldn't help but admire the deep dimples that appeared on her cheeks whenever she spoke. It was then that he looked into her eyes. They were beautiful on her but also very familiar. He'd seen those eyes before.

Desperate to change the subject, he said, "So, what sort of last name accompanies the name Brooklyn?" While getting ready for their date, he realized that he had never asked her full name.

"It's just Brooklyn or Brook."

"No last name?" he asked, suspicious of why she was holding back.

"I have one, but it's irrelevant."

At first he thought she was playing, but the nonchalant look on her face told him otherwise. He had no choice but to accept her explanation. From their first meeting at the club he had realized she wasn't the type of women that complied. She was strong-willed in a very noticeable way but struck a balance with a calm demeanor. "Okay, so Brooklyn it is."

"Yes," she responded, and he could tell she was glad he hadn't tried to force the issue. "Junior or Jason, which do you prefer?"

"Ah, all my friends call me Junior, so you can call me that as well."

She nodded and sipped her white wine spritzer. When she lowered the glass from her lips, she said, "Do you mind if I call you Jason? I was never the type to follow the crowd." She took another sip.

"Sure. I like the way you say my name anyway." He gave her a wink.

The waiter returned with their dinner. Upon Brooklyn's request, they held hands and blessed their food before eating. This time she asked him a host of questions. Everything from his favorite color to his biggest fear. They talked right through dinner and were in the middle of dessert when Jason noticed a tall man with a chef's jacket approaching their table. The man stopped in front of Brooklyn, pulling her to her feet. The two embraced, and she kissed him on the cheek. All the while, Jason could feel the jealousy rising within him.

"Jason, this is the chef." She introduced the two men. Jason stood and took the hand that the man extended to him. So this was how she was able to specify her food order, Jason thought. She might not have dated the waiter, but she was a little too chummy with him. They were definitely more than friends, as Jason knew by the way Brooklyn was resting her hand on the man's chest.

"He's the reason I get exactly what I want. Trevor is my sister's boyfriend."

Jason didn't know if she could see it, but his whole body loosened after hearing that. He was glad he didn't let on too much about his suspicions. Forget being a stalker or a serial killer, she would surely think he had control issues. Jason usually wasn't so insecure. He knew he was a handsome man, and women didn't shy away from fawning over him. But Brooklyn was doing something to him. He needed to get it together, and fast, before he totally lost it.

"Nice to meet you, Jason," Trevor said.

"You too, Trevor. The food was delicious."

"Thank you," Trevor said to him. "Brook, can I speak with you for a second?"

Jason paid the bill while Trevor took Brook to the side to talk. He didn't want to be nosy, but he sensed that whatever they were discussing was important. He waited patiently by the front entrance for their conversation to end.

On the drive back to her place, he said. "I didn't know you had a sister. Are you two close?"

Brook smiled. "Yes, very close. She actually lives down the street from me."

Jason walked Brooklyn to her front door, not wanting the night to end. Their date had lasted three hours, but it felt more like three minutes. She had the type of personality that drew people in. At least it drew him in. He stood on her stoop like a puppy dog in the winter begging to be let into a warm house.

"Thanks for dinner, Jason. I enjoyed your company." She stuck her key in her door, turned it, and pushed the door open.

Jason stuck his hands in his pockets to keep them from touching her.

"Can I call you tomorrow? I mean, if you don't mind." Jason didn't know why he was acting so irresolute. Brook hadn't given him a reason to think she was high-maintenance in the slightest.

She let out a small laugh, and he knew she was aware that he was stumbling. "Yeah, you can call me, Jason," she said, turning and walking into her building. Jason stood there. He didn't move. Couldn't. Not until …

"Are you going to stand out here all night?" Jason didn't realize that she was still there, watching him watching her.

Embarrassed for the third time that night, he'd had enough. "No. I'm going." He began to walk. Then he felt Brooklyn pulling on his sleeve. She pulled him back to where he had stood before. She took his face in her hands and lightly pressed her lips against his.

"I don't believe in wasting time either." She kissed him again.

Jason was lost for words as he watched her disappear into her building. Everything about the woman amazed him. He walked back to his car satisfied and anxious. He had to see her again, and soon. Brooklyn No Last Name was a woman like no other.

Chapter Eight

Help people every chance you get. Period. —Wanda

RAVEN HELD TWO LOOSE SHEETS of college-ruled paper in her hands. She was reading each for the second time. Amused by the resemblance, she shifted her eyes from side to side. Ms. Mitchell and Ms. Jackson sat in the same seats as before. Only now their faces showed smiles and not frowns. When had Raven called them into her office, they had come in record time with lists in hand. Raven didn't know what she had expected, but it wasn't this. She hadn't expected to be reading two thorough lists of qualities they each were looking for in a man. Some people would think that the assignment Raven gave the girls was a bit mature, seeing that they were so young. But Raven knew otherwise. She understood these girls and what they faced in this unfair world. *It's never too early,* Raven thought, *to teach a girl how to be a productive and valued woman in society.*

"You both want a college-educated, working man with good credit and no children." She read off the similar attributes. "Oh, and I can't forget good-looking." That addition made both girls blush. "Sound about right?"

"Yes," Ms. Mitchell responded. "Is that too much to ask for?" She posed the question as if she actually thought she was demanding too much of a lifelong partner.

"No," Raven said. "Not at all. You want what you want. Never settle for less than what you deserve, ladies. Never." She rummaged through her desk until she found what she was looking for. She pulled out a notebook and tore out two sheets of paper. Grabbing two pens from the mug her husband had bought her when she first got this job, she handed them to the girls.

"What's this for?" Ms. Jackson asked. "We have to make another list?" She seemed less than enthused.

Raven sat back in her chair and nodded. "Yes. But this time the list will be about you. This time, write down everything you can offer someone else. Everything you can and plan to be able to bring to the table."

Ms. Jackson raised her hand. "For what? Are you going to give our list to some guys or something?"

"No. This is for you." Both girls gave Raven a look that said, "You're wasting our time, lady," so she decided to explain.

"Look. You, ladies, without a doubt belong to a small group of women your age. You know what you want. That's commendable, and I applaud you for that." She softly clapped her hands. "But that's not enough. You ladies want things that most women in your demographic will never be presented with. To get these things, you have to better yourselves. It's like economics: the larger the commodity, the larger the buying pool is. Do you understand what I'm telling you?"

"I think I know what you're saying," Ms. Mitchell said. "If we make sure we have substantial and valuable things to offer any man, then we will have a lot more men to choose from than these dusty ol' guys around here?"

"Yeah, something like that. But I'm not telling you to write people off just because they're from this neighborhood. There are a lot of good people here."

"I catch your drift, Mrs. T.," Ms. Jackson said over the loud bell sounding. It was fifth period now. Raven handed them the paper. "Make that list, ladies," she reminded them on their way out.

They each threw over their shoulder, "We will."

Four hours later, Raven was headed home. She felt good about her conversation with her students today. Being able to mentor girls was why she became a principal, and it was always rewarding when she got to do it face-to-face. She hoped that they each understood what she had offered as one of the keys to getting anything you want out of life, not just the guy.

For Raven, getting the guy hadn't been as hard as keeping him. From the beginning, she and Sean had been inseparable. He was the first man she had ever let get close enough that she felt comfortable sharing her thoughts with him. Sean listened to her when she talked, and he was interested in all the aspects of her life that made her the woman she was.

For the most part, they were a happy couple. It wasn't until Raven would question his whereabouts that their major problems erupted. It was almost uncontrollable how her mind traveled, thinking about all the possibilities, when she didn't know exactly where Sean was or who he was with. Her obsession became so bad that Sean couldn't take it. He told her time after time that he wasn't cheating on her and that he needed her to trust him. But hearing that just wasn't enough.

One night when Sean said he was working late, she called his phone and he didn't pick up. She got his voice mail three times. Next, Raven did the unthinkable. She told herself not to jump to conclusions, but that did no good. She drove up to his workplace and busted into his office like a madwoman, expecting to find her husband getting it on with his mistress. Instead, she found him in a staff meeting. As soon as Sean saw her, Raven read his glare. His eyes told her that this had been the last straw and he was done with her as his wife. She had completely embarrassed her husband and herself.

That night when Sean came home, he didn't say a word to her. Raven frantically tried explaining to him what she didn't even understand herself, but her words just sounded like jibber jabber. She pleaded with him not to leave, but he didn't listen. He just packed all his things and their son and left. Raven tried calling him, but he ignored her calls for over a week, only contacting her to let her speak to Josiah. Raven knew for sure that she'd lost him for good. She couldn't stop crying and hating herself for not trusting the man she loved. It wasn't like she didn't want to trust him, but something in her wouldn't allow Raven to be totally at ease. Never in a million years had she thought that God would have chosen her to be a wife. She was always thinking about ways that her marriage could go wrong and factors that could disrupt her dream.

After almost a month apart, Sean called her, and they talked for over five hours about her fear of losing him and ending up a single mother. It was the first time she had told anyone how much she feared ending up like her mother. Raven loved her mother for all the sacrifices she had made for her children, but she couldn't get past the lonely life her mother had lived. The only company she could count on was bill collectors and the people at the welfare office. Raven told Sean about the times when she would catch her mother crying herself to sleep and Raven just knew it was because she was tired of doing everything on her own. The doctors said it was a blood clot that killed her, but Raven and her sisters knew it was all the stress and lack of sleep finally catching up with her. Her mother's circumstances were different from Raven's, and she understood that. But she also knew that her mother hadn't asked for that life, nor had she planned to raise three daughters on her own. The way Raven saw it, marriage was like an intense game of musical chairs. You're safe until the music stops and you're the one left without a chair, no longer qualified to play the game. Raven felt like the kid who knew he was going to lose even before the game started; it was just a matter of time.

It was difficult, but she told her husband all of this. Sean suggested they get counseling, and Raven agreed. At that point she would have said yes to anything that would make him come home. Leila recommended a colleague of hers, and they began seeing her immediately. That was over two years ago, before her second son was born. Since then Raven had learned how to relax her fears and to lean more on trust. For the most part, she was doing pretty well.

Loud honks from behind her took Raven out of her daydreaming. She looked through her rearview mirror and sucked her teeth at the man behind her as he gave her the finger. Just for his gesture, she kept her foot on the brake for another few seconds. *Boston drivers are the worst*, she thought. A little tired and ready to see her children, she took the back streets home, avoiding the traffic but having to turn every few seconds on the short roads.

Once home, she greeted her boys at the door and relived her sister from her babysitting duties—but not before grilling her about the man she'd had dinner with the other night. Raven couldn't believe her ears when Leila called her and informed her that Trevor had run into Brook on a date at his restaurant.

"So, who is he?" Raven asked for the third time. She didn't appreciate Brooklyn evading the question by faking an important meeting she needed to be at.

"None of your business, Raye." Brooklyn reached for the door. "I can't do anything without y'all all in my stuff."

"If you just tell me what I want to know then I promise I will leave it alone. And I won't tell Leila, either." Raven knew she was lying. If she found out who this guy was, she would call Leila as soon as Brook left. It wasn't like they were trying to block or anything like that, Raven told herself. They were just concerned about their younger sister and wanted to be informed on new things in her life. For some odd reason, Brook had always been more private about her life than her sisters, and Raven always felt like she was pulling teeth when she inquired about Brook's life.

"You're a bad liar, Raven. It's sad. I love you, but you and your sister are both nosy." She opened the door, and Raven knew she wasn't getting anything out of Brooklyn that day. "See you later."

And before Raven could take another crack at it, Brooklyn was out the door and Sean was walking through it. Raven studied the distraught look on her husband's face. He walked past like a zombie and sat on the couch. His eyes were focused on the television even though it was not on. Raven thought he looked as if he'd seen a ghost.

"Baby." Raven made her way towards him. "What's wrong? Is everything okay?" she said, her voice trembling. When he didn't respond, she asked again, this time louder.

"Nothing, babe." He shook his head slowly, bringing his eyes into focus and looking at her. "Everything is fine."

"Then why are you home so early?" She brought her wrist to her eyes and examined her watch. "You don't usually come home for another three hours," she said, now sitting next to him on the couch, her legs folded under her body. She rested her arm on his shoulder.

"I just didn't feel so good, so I left a little early and came home." He flashed a practiced smile.

Raven placed her hand on his forehead and then moved it to his neck. "You don't seem to have a fever. Do you think you're coming down with something?"

Sean took her hand from his neck, brought it to his lips, and kissed her palm. He continued to plant kisses on her wrist and up her arm, settling on her neck and sucking gently, just the way Raven liked it. He pulled her into his arms, probing his tongue down her throat and caressing her body. Raven pushed him back against the cushion, allowing her to fall on top of his body. She enjoyed this position because it made her feel powerful and in charge. Sean opened the two buttons on her shirt that allowed him access to her breast, gently squeezing her nipples through her lace bra. Raven sucked in a small breath, searching for his belt buckle. With one hand behind his neck and the other on his pants, she maneuvered them open and lodged her hand into his boxer briefs, pulling out his erect penis and smoothing her hand up and down his shaft. She watched as he closed his eyes and desperately tried to hold on. Not until she saw his jaw tighten and heard a small whimper escape from his mouth did she release him. "How bad do you want it?" she whispered in his ear, taking the opportunity to nibble on his lobe. Now Raven knew she had him just where she wanted: at her mercy and feeling like she was the best.

In one swift motion, Sean flipped her onto her back, causing Raven to let out a yelp. He took both her small wrists and pinned them above her head while his other hand went to work between her legs. He grabbed her and started to massage her through her pants, causing Raven to squirm. With her hands immobile, she had no control, no way to please him in return. Her only option was to lie there and enjoy the pleasures her husband knew her body wanted. He lowered his mouth to hers and kissed her deeply, only stopping to ask, "How bad do you want it?"

Raven looked up at him, wanting to respond but not wanting to be the one to give in. So she gave him the "I can take way more" look. Sean let out a small chuckle, unzipped her pants, and pulled them down to her knees along with her panties. Scooting down the couch until his torso was between her legs, he took one long look at her before his head disappeared into her open legs, resting on her womanhood. First he licked gently, causing Raven to shudder just a little. Then he upped the ante, torturing her G-spot. Raven was really trying to control herself, but yanking on her shirt or the fabric of the couch wasn't doing the trick. Sean said he had left work, but as far as she was concerned he had come home and was going to work on her right now. His moans, accompanied by the occasional licking of his lips, were driving her to the edge. Raven knew she couldn't hold on much longer. Her mind wanted to, but her body wasn't getting the message. She would lose the competition and secede to her opponent; the end was nearing, and this race would soon be very much over. Palming the back of Sean's head, Raven screamed out his name as her body released its fluids into his open mouth.

"Damn, Sean," she panted, desperately trying to gain her composure. She yanked on his shirt, pulling him up to her. "I want it real bad."

Sean pulled Raven into his lap and held on to her round ass. They were skin to skin, both ready to make that move that would unite their bodies. Raven positioned her knees, spreading her legs to the max at the same time Sean lifted his hips to meet hers.

"Mummy! Can you read this book to me?"

It was Josiah screaming for her to come up to his room. Raven cursed out loud. She had forgotten that her sons were right upstairs in their room and could have very well come downstairs and caught their parents doing something that would surely scar them for life.

She slid off her husband and readjusted her clothes while he did the same. "I'm coming, Josiah," she said, tucking her shirt back into her pants. She whipped her head around to face Sean. "You know we should be ashamed of ourselves, don't you?" She smiled at him, making her way up the stairs to tend to their son.

Sean followed her, grabbing her around the waist. "The only thing I know is that this isn't over." He squeezed her butt, making Raven seriously consider a quickie.

"You're so bad, Sean Thompson."

"Only for my wife."

Chapter Nine

SEAN STOOD LEANING AGAINST THE windowpane in his bedroom, careful not to wake his sleeping wife. Their lovemaking had worn her out. That was the point, Sean told himself. After leaving work in a hurry, all he'd wanted to do was come home and make love to his wife the way a husband should. He glanced over at her, knowing that she was the most beautiful woman in the world. He turned back to the window, watching as the heavy raindrops fell down against it.

Sean walked to the bathroom, turned on the faucet, and splashed cold water on his face. He had to shake the awful feeling he was having. If he didn't, Raven would know something was up. Tonight he had used sex as a decoy, but he knew that wouldn't last long. Raven was far too intelligent and perceptive to be distracted time after time. He turned the water off and raised his head to the mirror in front of him, not liking the image that stared back. He was ashamed of the man in the mirror, and if Raven ever found out she would be too.

Raven was everything to him. From the day she walked into his office wanting to know if he would speak to her class for career day, he had known that one day he would make her his wife. He knew it was a long shot, her being so cultured and seemingly spiritual, that she would go out with a man whom most would consider worldly and money-oriented, but for some reason she had accepted his dinner invitation.

It was over dinner that he imagined what their children would look like. If they'd have her nose and his eyes. But it really didn't matter because he would love them all the same. He wouldn't care if his children were short or tall, skinny or fat. As long as he had the opportunity to be a father, he would be happy. Being a father was important to Sean because of the positive relationship he'd had with his own father. He was always there for him and his siblings, never missing out on important events and always taking a genuine interest in whatever they had to say. Sean wanted to be everything to his children that his father was to him and to be the husband to Raven that his father was to his mother. He always treated her with the utmost respect. Every Tuesday his father would bring home a dozen roses for his mother because they had met on a Tuesday afternoon and his father never wanted to forget the day his life had changed for the better. Growing up in their house, you wouldn't know how to answer the question, "Who is in charge here?" Both his parents shared the title of the boss. It was truly an equal marriage, and that's what Sean wanted for himself.

But now all that was in jeopardy. The respect, trust, and happiness would be stripped from him and he was the one to blame.

Sean had walked into work this morning just as he did every day. He parked in his assigned place, rode the elevator up to the seventh floor, and greeted the secretaries as he walked into his office. He had three meetings that morning, which went by at a snail's pace according to his grumbling stomach. He ordered some Chinese food and worked until it was delivered.

"Come in," he said once the delivery boy knocked on his door.

The door opened. He looked up, surprised to see not the boy but Natalie, another agent who worked at the firm. She was carrying his food in her hand and hers in the other and smiling thinly at him.

"Hey, I grabbed this from Zack. I knew it was yours, and he was all the way on the other side of the hall. By the time he made it down here, your food would've been cold." She walked into his office and placed his food in front of him. "Mind if I join you?"

"Sure," Sean said, digging into his Lo Mein noodles. Natalie was good company. She was smart and funny. Sean considered her a friend and didn't mind sharing his lunch hour with her in the slightest.

"So how's the new Jansen account going?" he asked her, motioning for her to take a seat.

"It's going well. We have a lot of ideas for branding that he really liked, so I think we're on the same page. Mr. Jansen isn't the type of guy who makes our jobs easy, you know?"

Sean sat back. "Yeah, I know. I've dealt with a hundred Mr. Jansens', and I can't say that I wish I were in your shoes."

"Yes, but I wish I were in yours. Aren't you doing the Sox wife?" she asked in a teasing voice.

"Jennifer. Her name is Jennifer. And yes, she is my client," he told her.

"You have an awful lot of female clients, Trevor. How does your wife feel about that?"

Her last question made him feel uncomfortable. Natalie knew he was married and had even met Raven on a few occasions, but she had never inquired about their relationship before. It felt weird even discussing Raven with a coworker because he knew she wouldn't appreciate it. But Natalie was not just a coworker. She was also a friend, and friends could discuss their spouses. Right?

"Uh, she doesn't mind me working with women," he lied. Although Raven was working through her issues, he knew she still didn't feel one hundred percent comfortable with him working with women all day long. But he wasn't about to tell Natalie all of that. Friend or not, that wasn't any of her business. "Raven knows I only want her."

"She must be some special lady. Not many women would be so understanding." Natalie licked the sauce off her top lip. "I wish I could find a man who understood that my job is separate from the rest of my life, but I haven't been so lucky."

"That's a shame. You're a good catch, Natalie," he told her. As far as Sean was concerned, it was the truth. Not many women could hold their own in a male-dominated firm and still pull in the amount of clients that

Natalie did. She had her own money and no kids—not to mention that she was easy on the eyes.

"Thanks, Sean. That really means a lot to me." Natalie gathered the rest of her food and placed it in the trashcan. I'm really glad we're friends." She walked behind his desk and gave Sean a hug, which he returned.

"Me too, Natalie," he responded, pulling back from the embrace and looking at her. It was the first time that Sean had actually taken the time to pay attention to her features. She was indeed pretty, with caramel skin and enchanting hazel eyes. She had a dimple right next to her left eye that never seemed to go away.

Natalie leaned in closer and kissed his lips tenderly, using her top lip to slowly divide his. She did this until both their mouths were open, ready, and willing to exchange tongues, and they did just that, kissing wildly like two teenagers behind the school building. But they weren't behind a school; they were in his office. And they weren't teenagers; they were grown adults. Sean knew all of this, but he couldn't bring himself to stop because what they were doing felt too good. It wasn't until an image of Raven flashed into his head that he pulled back. Raven, his wife, the mother of his children and the woman he loved.

"I'm so sorry, Sean." Natalie stepped back and wiped her lips with her index finger. "I don't know what came over me. I never meant to disrespect you or your marriage."

Sean stood feet away from her, not really hearing anything she was saying. The only thing he heard was the sound of Raven's voice when he told her that he'd kissed another woman. Or rather that a woman had kissed him—but he knew it wouldn't make a difference to Raven. His lips touching any woman that wasn't her would be all that mattered to her.

"Natalie, I think you should leave," he said calmly. As soon as Sean heard the door close behind Natalie, he packed his briefcase, threw on his jacket, and left work early for the first time.

He drove around the city for a while, thinking about what he had just done and why he had done it. He tried telling himself that he did it because he wasn't getting enough attention at home, but that was a lie. Raven had the same sexual appetite that he did if not bigger. She never held out on him. So he thought about the other aspects of their marriage, but still he drew a blank. Raven was a wonderful mother to their sons; she cooked, cleaned, and worked a full-time job, never complaining. He was married to the women of his dreams, and there was nothing wrong with their marriage. The only explanation he could come up with was that he had experienced a moment of weakness. A moment of selfishness where nothing else mattered but him and what he wanted. He was the one to blame. But Sean also knew that wasn't true. He would never have kissed Natalie in a million years. *She* had come on to *him*. She was the one who kissed him. Placing the blame on Natalie made him feel a little better. Now he would tell Raven what Natalie had done and she would be mad at her rather than him.

That was the plan until he got home and saw Raven with her sister Brooklyn. Seeing the two of them together made him think about all the stories Raven had told him in therapy about their childhood and why she was so obsessed with having a perfect marriage. She had opened up to him, and when she did, Sean had promised that they would be together forever. That he would never hurt her or ruin the life they shared. That was the problem when dealing with a woman who has already been hurt by a man far before you ever entered the picture, Sean thought. Every mistake you make is epic, every slip-up is noticed. For years he'd been paying for the damage done by her father, something he'd weathered with poise until now.

When he pulled up to his house and saw her standing in the doorway, he decided that there had to be a new plan. He would not tell Raven anything. It was just a meaningless kiss, and it would never happen again. He would make sure of that. A kiss wasn't worth his wife's losing faith in him. Because that was exactly what would happen. She would never look at him the same way. Instead of seeing the loving man who would give his own life to protect hers, she would see a deceitful, selfish man. Those were two qualities she used to describe her father. And Sean was nothing like the man he'd never met but despised with a passion. Sean couldn't allow the comparison to take place. He needed a new plan. The new plan was to go home and make love to Raven until he no longer remembered what had transpired hours earlier in his office.

He returned to bed, frustrated that the plan hadn't worked. Yes, they had made love for hours, and it was good. But as soon as it was over and she was asleep, his thoughts started to haunt him. She needed to know. He had to tell his wife everything. When he did, she would understand, he told himself. She would be mad at first, but once he explained that it wasn't his fault, she would get over it. He shifted in the bed and brought his hand right over her shoulder, ready to shake her out of sleep and spill his guts. But then he stopped, knowing that he was lying to himself. Telling Raven would only put him out of his misery and transfer it onto her. She wouldn't see it the way, but he pretended to himself she might. She would be beyond angry. To be honest, he didn't know how she would react, but he knew it wouldn't be good. No, he wouldn't wake her up tonight. Sean decided that he would never, could never, tell his wife what had happened. He would just have to suffer in silence, for her sake.

Chapter Ten

Life and death are inevitable. —Wanda

A GUN.

Leila decided that carrying mace wouldn't do the trick any longer. She would register for a gun and start to carry it as well. People seemed to be getting crazier by the day, approaching her like she was some sort of old, fragile woman. But she wasn't. She had never shot a person before—or anything, for that matter—but she would have no problem pulling the trigger on someone like Clark Simmons. Unfortunately, she didn't have that gun that she so badly needed right now. But he did.

Leila was in her office, just finishing up with her two o'clock and preparing for her lunch break before her four o'clock. She took off her heels and rubbed the bottoms of her feet, counting down the hours until she would soak them in a hot bath. She was in the midst of pressuring her thumb into the middle of her foot when she felt a presence behind her. She whipped her head to see who it was and smiled upon recognizing Clark Simmons standing with his hands in his jeans pockets, his eyes facing the floor. He looked disoriented, judging by the way he shook his head and swayed his body at the same time. She was sure that they didn't have a scheduled session today. She had, however, had one with Denise this morning, but her client had called to cancel at the last minute.

She slipped her feet back into her shoes and stood to greet him. "Clark, can I help you with something?"

"Don't fuckin' say another goddamn word!" he said through clenched teeth. His fists were now balled up at his sides. He slowly brought his chin up, revealing the evil glare on his face.

Leila stood, frozen in awe of how he spoke to her. The man obviously thought he was talking to someone else, perhaps his wife. She tilted her head at Clark, the lines on her forehead deepening. She tried to decipher if he was serious or not.

"Excuse me?" she asked.

"I said, don't say a goddamn word!" he said, louder than before. Clark took slow steps in her direction. "Why did you tell my wife to leave me?" He was now yelling, and Leila knew her assistant would be knocking down the door any minute, saving her from this crazy man.

"Answer me!" he demanded, now directly in front of her. He was so close that she could feel his body heat and his anger.

Leila had taken only one course in school on how to react in hostile situations such as these. She knew she wasn't to match his tone or his aggressive demeanor. That would only add fuel to his fire and further provoke him, elevating his anger. She would stay calm and talk him down. "I didn't tell your wife to leave you, Clark. I would never say something like that."

"Bullshit! You told Denise that I'm not a real man. You told her that she and my son would be better off without me!" He spat at her, saliva hitting her face.

Leila didn't know how to respond to that. She had never said those words to Denise because she knew better than to say them, but in her opinion, Clark wasn't worth a damn, and he was showing it right now. "If you would like to have a seat, Clark, we could discuss this. I'm sure that this is just a misunderstanding, and I'm happy to help in any way that I can." Leila used her mechanical monotone voice to match the mechanical smile on her face.

"I don't need to sit. And we don't need to discuss shit," he said. "You need to call my wife and tell her that you didn't mean anything you said. Tell her that I'm the best thing that ever happened to her and she would be crazy to leave a man like me," he said with his finger in her face, sweat beads dripping from his balding head.

"I can't do that, Clark. You and Denise are welcome to schedule an appointment and the three of us can talk this through, but I can't get involved in your relationship the way you are asking of me." She was stern in her stance.

Clark didn't seem too discouraged by her words. He just gave her a devilish grin. Although Clark was a black man, Leila could see him with his face painted white and bright red lipstick smeared roughly across his lips like the Joker The man before her was soulless. "Are you sure about that, Doc?"

"Yes, I am," she responded. "Now, please leave my office."

She pointed to the door. But Clark didn't take a step. Instead, he reached behind his back and pulled out a shotgun. He lightly tapped it against his other hand before bringing it up and pointing it in her direction.

"Does this change your mind, Doc?" He brought the gun to her left temple. "You're scared now, aren't you? Look at you. Always used to being in control and ruining other people's lives. Bet you never thought someone would ruin yours." He pushed the gun harder into her skin. "I used to like you. Thought you were a nice lady who was going to save my marriage because you seemed like the type of person who could do that." He rotated the weapon slowly against her skin, allowing Leila to feel the cold metal and picture the spot in which he would direct the bullet." But you didn't. Instead you turned my wife against me and convinced her that I ain't worth shit. You're an evil bitch, that's what you are!"

Leila didn't say a word. Not because she didn't want to but because she couldn't. Never in her life had she been that close to a loaded gun. She felt the cold metal against her skin. And she could feel the exact spot on her face that the bullet would rip through the second he pulled the trigger. She would be dead within minutes, and he would stand over her body as blood gushed from her head and not feel an ounce of guilt. He'd probably shoot her a few more times just for some extra shits and giggles.

"Cat got your tongue, bitch?" Clark's voice took her away from her depressing thoughts and brought her back to her devastating reality. "That's cool, 'cause I'm not finished talking. I want to know why you did it. And you'd better not try that psychobabble shit on me either, or I'll blow your fuckin' head off."

Leila knew she had to answer him. She had to find her voice to say, "Do what?"

"Don't act dumb. Why did you say all that stuff? My marriage doesn't have shit to do with you or how you run your life. You didn't have to say those things, but I have a feeling that you don't like men very much. Do you?" Using his other hand, he pointed to the photo on her desk. "I know that's your man in that picture, so I know you're not a lesbian or anything like that."

"I don't have a problem with men, Clark." She thought about reiterating that she had never said those words to Denise, but she figured that now was not the time.

"Sure you do. You got a good setup here. You pretend to counsel couples, but what you really do is persuade women to leave their men. I'm on to your little game." He lowered the gun and pointed it to her desk. "But I don't care about anyone else but Denise. Call my wife." He paused between his words.

Leila moved as fast as she could, but her legs felt like they weighed a ton. Every time she pulled her foot up, it felt like a sandbag was attached to it. Her body shook, but somehow she managed to get to the phone and dial Denise's cell number. She dialed, praying that Denise would pick up and come get her husband before he shot Leila. Then they could go live whatever life they chose to. That is, until Boston's finest came knocking at their door, ready to lock Clark's crazy ass up for a very long time. And when he was up for parole, Leila would testify against him and make sure he stayed behind bars for as long as possible. Clark thought she loved being in control. Well, he hadn't seen anything yet.

But Leila was getting ahead of herself. She had yet to hear Denise's voice on the other end of the phone. It just kept ringing. She looked up at Clark. He was standing at a distance, but still the gun was aimed at her. Leila knew he could hear each ring, and she saw his anger building.

Denise wasn't going to pick up the phone, Leila knew it. The way she saw it, she had only one choice. Clark was thinking and acting irrationally enough for her to be confident in the fact that he would hurt her. Just how badly she was uncertain. Still, with the phone to her ear, she thought about her sisters and Trevor. They were the three most important people in her life, and she couldn't imagine never seeing them again, allowing this man to take her life like it was his own to do with as he wished. She had worked too hard for it to all end like this, and she wasn't going down without a fight.

So now, listening to the dial tone in her right ear and the little voice roaring around in her head, she would make a run for the door. She was in closer proximity to it than before, and if she ran fast enough, swiftly enough, not letting fear slow her down, she would make it out alive.

Leila eyed the closed door that was her only way out the room. It would be a long shot. She only needed an inkling of a chance. That was enough to convince her that she could do it. Dropping that phone from her hand, not caring where it landed, Leila took long, fast strides toward the door. Clark's baritone screaming drowned out any other sounds in the room, including the cocking of the gun. She reached for the door, flung it open, and began to feel the sweetest relief until the loud sound of a gun releasing a bullet stopped her dead in her tracks. It was the excruciating, burning pain in her left arm that made her fall to the floor. She reached around her back and felt blood seeping through her clothes and staining her hands. She screamed for help as loudly as she could, grateful she was still alive and alert. From the floor she saw shoes running toward her and then the sound of the gun blasting again. Not once but twice, both bullets marked with her name. She felt them ripping through her body like a needle through a delicate piece of cloth. Memories of her childhood and her sisters flashed before her eyes before they closed, and Trevor's name slipped from her tongue for the last time. She was gone.

Chapter Eleven

BRANDICE WAS BEYOND DEPLETED OF all her energy. She hadn't left her house all day. In fact, she was still dressed in the sweatpants and tank top she'd worn to bed the night before. It had been a long day. Brandice had woken up at the crack of dawn and called every single one of her father's family members. She needed an address, the name of a mutual friend—anything that would give her a clue on where to start searching for her father's daughters. But she had no luck. Everyone said they couldn't help her for one reason or another. Her father was one of a dozen children, and not one of them wanted to give up any information. This frustrated Brandice, but she was determined to grant her father's last request of her, so she dialed her Aunt Sharon's number. Sharon was her father's closest sibling in age, being one year older than him. Brandice didn't see Sharon often, but she considered Sharon her favorite aunt because unlike most of her father's family, Sharon didn't seem to care that her brother had married a white women. She never treated Brandice any differently than her other nieces and nephews, and Brandice appreciated that. Sharon was also the mother of her cousin Kevin. Kevin and Brandice had gone to grade school together, and Kevin would protect his younger cousin whenever necessary. He and Brandice used to be really close until high school. When Brandice was in the ninth grade and Kevin in the eleventh, things got shaky. They hung out with two different crowds, Kevin with the black kids and

Brandice with the white kids. It wasn't that she didn't like the black people at her school, but Brandice always found it easier to get along with white people. While growing up, she didn't have the swagger that most black kids had. Just like dancing, it didn't come naturally to her. It wasn't until much later that she felt comfortable enough in her skin to relate to both sides. So she didn't rock the boat or use her whiteness when it was valuable or her blackness when it came in handy. For most of grade school she was known as the white girl who hung out with Junior. And she and Kevin were no longer friends or cousins. They were just two people who went to the same church on Sunday and just so happened to share the same blood.

"Hello, Aunt Sharon, this is Brandice. How are you?" she said upon hearing her aunt's voice on the other end.

"Hey, sweetie, I'm blessed. How are you?"

"Fine, Auntie. But I have a question for you. It's about my father's ex-wife and his two daughters."

"Oh, that was so long ago. I don't know too much about that situation."

"Yeah, Auntie, that's what everyone is saying. But I really need to know something. So if you can remember anything, it would really be of great help to me."

"Why are you so concerned about this, Brandice? Your father was a good man to your mother and a good father to you. You shouldn't concern yourself with things of the past. It's not healthy."

Brandice didn't know why her aunt was saying these things to her and speaking to her as if she were a child. "Auntie, I love Daddy, and he will always be wonderful in my eyes. He asked me to find his daughters for him. I'm doing this for him," she defended.

"Well, I can't help you. I don't know anything about them, and even if I did … Just leave it alone, Brandice. You always were too nosy for your own good."

Brandice took the phone away from her ear, not believing the words her aunt had just spoken to her. Pulling it back, she said, "Goodbye, Auntie," and hung up.

How dare she talk to me like that? She was way out of line, Brandice thought as she ran her hands through her hair, racking her brain for a new plan. Obviously, the one that involved family help wasn't going to cut it. Her own mother was unwilling to help. When Brandice had approached her about finding the women, her mother didn't hesitate to tell her that she wanted no part of the journey. Like Aunt Sharon, she asked Brandice to let it go. It was the sternest Brandice had ever seen her mother. She chalked it up to a woman not wanting to meet the family her husband had before her. It was a normal reaction for a woman grieving her husband's death. At least, that's what Brandice thought before she made over thirty phone calls and received the same standoffish response. There was a reason no one wanted to be a part of this, and Brandice knew that whatever it was it was the reason her father was unable to share this information with her while he was alive.

Brandice picked up her phone once again, ready to dial. Then she heard her doorbell ringing. A welcomed distraction, she decided, no matter who it was. Sliding across the wooden floor in her colorful fluffy socks, Brandice stood on the tip of her toes to look through the peephole. She opened the door with the first smile on her face all day.

"Hey, Junior." She gave him a peck on the cheek as he entered her house. While he stripped off his coat, hung it in the closet, and slipped out of his shoes, Brandice stood leaning against the wall with her hands on her hips.

Junior turned to her. "What?" he asked. "Why are you looking at me like that?"

"Oh, boy, don't play with me like that. I haven't seen you in two days, and that's just not natural. What have you been up to?" She let out a small laugh. "Or should I say who?"

Junior made his way further in the house, stopping in the small but nicely constructed stainless steel kitchen. He opened the refrigerator. "You seem to be in good spirits, Ice. I'm glad to see you're feeling better."

Brandice followed his voice, waving her hand in the air, "Yeah, yeah, yeah. Enough about me. I want to know about Ms. Thing who's taking up all of my best friend's time." She closed the refrigerator door. "You can eat after you tell me."

He hopped onto the countertop and nodded to the bowl of apples and bananas on the kitchen table. He caught the apple that Brandice threw him. "Ms. Thing," he mocked her, "has a name, and it's Brooklyn."

"Okay, so what is so special about Brooklyn that has you MIA?" This was the question she really wanted to know the answer to.

He bit into the Granny Smith. "Nothing much, you know. She's just beautiful, smart, funny, and loves sports. But no big deal or anything," he said sarcastically.

"Wow, it's like that?" Brandice asked. But she couldn't be too surprised. Junior was a relationship type of guy. Lucky for Brandice, he hadn't been in a relationship in almost a year. His last girlfriend, Renee, had moved to the West Coast after getting her dream job as a television producer. They were together for two years, but neither one was into the whole long-distance love thing, so they called it quits before either one got hurt. Junior said he was cool after Renee left, but Brandice knew that he was hurting for a long time. It didn't help that Renee had met someone else and gotten engaged a few months ago. Renee sent them both invitations to the wedding that would take place next year. A man's pride could only take so much. They had respectfully declined.

"Yeah, I can't even lie. Brooklyn is a certified ten." He flashed his hands in front of his body like he was on a game show or something. "I mean, first off, baby girl is fine, petite just like I like them. I saw her at the poetry club, and she was tight. She's a writer, a good one."

"Goodness, boy, does the girl have eleven toes? Bad breath? A sinus problem? Something that makes her human and flawed like the rest of us?" she teased.

"Ha, ha, very funny. But naw, the only thing about her that's strange is she's a very private person. It's like pulling teeth to find out things that people on dates normally just tell each other."

"Uh-oh, she might have skeletons in her closet. You better watch your back, Junior," Brandice warned him.

"No, Brook's not like that. She's just private, that's all."

Intrigued by the use of a nickname, she said, "First it was Brooklyn, which is a beautiful name by the way, and now it's Brook." She lowered her eyes. "Aren't we full of surprises today?"

"Whatever, Ice. As long as you don't call her Ms. Thang when I introduce you to her then it's all cool."

"Oh, I get to meet her? Little ol' peasant me gets to meet the princess?" She smiled wickedly. "Whatever should I wear?" she said in a joking manner.

It was good that Junior was moving on, and from the looks of it to a good woman, but a part of Brandice felt pushed to the side and replaced by a woman she didn't even know. The way Junior spoke so candidly and affectionately about Brooklyn made Brandice uncomfortable. She was used to being the woman in his life, and now she had to get used to sharing him again. Brandice thought about how this new girl would deal with Junior having a female best friend. Like the others, she would probably feel uncomfortable at first, but once she realized that they felt more like cousins then friends, she would warm up to the idea.

"You all right, Ice?" He asked in an alarmed tone. "Everything cool?"

Brandice pushed her concerns about Brooklyn to the back of her head and told him what was really on her mind. "I've just been trying to get some help from the family about finding my daddy's daughters, and no one will help me. Not even Auntie Sharon. I don't know who else to ask. I've looked them up in the phone book, but there weren't listed. At least not under the Cartel last name. They probably don't even live in Boston anymore. They could be anywhere."

That thought alone, that her sisters could possibly be living God knows where and she would never be able to locate them, was enough to tire her out all over again. There were 6.8 billion people in the world, and she had to find two of them single-handedly, since she wasn't getting any help from her family.

"Ever thought about hiring someone?" Junior asked. "Like a private investigator or something?"

"No, I didn't, but that's a good idea." Her eyes widened at the notion that all hope might not be lost after all. "Do you know a good PI?"

Junior shook his head. "No, but that's what Google is for."

The two sat in front of her laptop computer until they found the top recommended private investigator in the state. Brandice picked up her phone for what seemed like the hundredth time that day. "Hello, is this Tracy Atler? Good. My name is Brandice Cartel, and I'm looking for my sisters, Raven and Leila. Can you help me find them?"

Chapter Twelve

A woman's intuition about her man is hardly ever wrong. —Wanda

WHEN RAVEN WOKE UP IN the morning, she reached her arm over her bed and felt the cold sheets under her hands instead of her husband's warm body. She opened her eyes to find the room dark and the curtains pulled together. The only light in the room came from under the closed door along with the sounds of her two sons clacking metal spoons against her marble kitchen table. Her alarm clock hadn't gone off yet, so she knew she hadn't overslept. It must've been the good loving last night that pushed Sean to get the boys ready for day care this morning, since that was usually her area, Raven thought.

She leisurely got out of bed and into the shower. She took her time getting dressed in her business-attire pinstripe pantsuit, styled her hair in loose curls, and applied her makeup. Raven sauntered down the stairs to greet her family feeling better than ever. Her mind was clear and her body loose and well worked out thanks to her marvelous husband.

"Hey, baby, I missed you this morning," Raven said, kissing Sean on the cheek.

"Oh, I thought I'd get the boys ready for school so you could sleep a little longer," Sean responded, not taking his eyes off his youngest son, who was sitting in his lap as Sean fed him fruit loops.

Raven sat down next to Josiah. "You almost ready to go? Today your class is going to the children's museum, and you don't want to miss the bus."

"I'm ready now!" Josiah tilted his bowl and brought it to his mouth, gulping the color-stained milk. He wiped the milk mustache off with the back of his hand and jetted to the front door.

Raven reached over the table for her husband to hand over Tristan. "I'm going to get these boys to school. I don't want to get caught in traffic and have to drive Josiah all the way down to the museum myself."

"That's okay, babe. I'll take the boys to school this morning."

"Why? It's on my way to work, and I do it every day." Raven dropped her arms because apparently her husband wasn't going to hand over his son.

Sean brought the dishes to the sink, still holding on tightly to Tristan. "I want to spend some time with the boys and also give you a little break. I'm going to try to help out more around the house."

Raven surveyed his face before saying, "Hmm. Okay, Sean, what's the catch?"

He laughed. "Why does there have to be a catch? Can't a man just want to be a better husband and father? Is that a crime, Raven?"

"No. That's not a crime. But you've been acting funny since you came home from work early yesterday. And not that I don't love everything you're doing and saying, I just want to know what's up. Is that a crime, Sean?" She extended her hands once again, and this time her son came to her. She hoisted him onto her hip. "Is there something you want to tell me, baby?"

"Here we go again." Sean threw his hands into the air. "Raven, I thought you weren't going to do that anymore."

"Calm down. I'm not even going there, Sean. I trust you, and I know you wouldn't do anything to hurt this family. Something is bothering you, and I know it because I'm your wife and I know you. I saw you get out of bed last night, looking out the window like you were waiting for your dog to come home or something."

From the look on his face after hearing her revelation, Raven knew she had struck a nerve and that undeniably Sean was hiding something. Maybe it was work-related. Stresses from his new client might be getting the best of him, she figured. Sean was always driven by money, and his job meant a lot to him. This Raven was well aware of. But she wasn't used to him bringing those stresses home. That was one of the things she loved about him. So of course she would notice when Sean was acting out of character. "Did something happen at work?"

"No," Sean said coolly, looking her dead in her eyes. "I appreciate your concern, but you're reading too much into this, Raven. If you want to take the boys to school then that's fine. I don't want to fight about this."

"Who's fighting? I thought we were having a conversation." She handed Tristan back to Sean. Raven didn't want to fight either. Things were so good between them. She didn't want to push something that wasn't there. "Thank you for taking the boys." She kissed him on the lips, calling a truce. When he returned the kiss, Raven knew all was well in the Thompson household as they all left the house to begin their days.

Reviewing the stack of tenth-grade lesson plans on her desk, Raven couldn't get the conversation she'd had with Sean out her head. She replayed everything he had said from the time he walked into the house in the late afternoon until they said goodbye to each other that morning. She was trying to find a clue that would verify what she already knew: that something wasn't right. But her mind was drawing blanks. Sean might have been telling the truth. He could very well have been doing what he said this morning, trying to be a better husband and father. And that was believable; he was that kind of guy. "Stop being so damn paranoid," Raven said aloud. "I'm better than this. My marriage is better than this."

She convinced herself. Raven had just gone back to focusing on the papers in front of her when her secretary, Patrice, knocked twice before entering.

"Principal Thompson, there is a women out here who says she needs to speak with you immediately."

"Is she a parent?" Raven asked, pulling her eyes from her papers to address Patrice.

"No. She says her name is Natalie Fisher and that you would know who she was." Patrice rolled her eyes to the ceiling, obviously perturbed by the mystery.

That name didn't ring a bell to Raven. She knew a lot of people, but had only a few people she considered friends, and none of them had the name of Natalie Fisher. "Send her in, Patrice."

Patrice called for the woman. Raven noticed that the women had been crying. Her eyes were all puffy and red, her mascara all out of place. She sat across from Raven, looking at her quickly before dropping her head. "I'm sorry to bother you like this at work, Mrs. Thompson, but I really didn't see another option."

"No apologies necessary, Ms. Fisher." Raven handed her the box of tissues from the top drawer of her desk. "My secretary says that you told her we know each other, but I'm having a hard time placing your name and your face."

Natalie wiped her face with the tissue. "I work with your husband, Sean. We met at the Christmas party last year and the year before that as well."

"Right. Now I remember." Now that she knew who the woman was, Raven was interested in finding out why she was in her office crying. "Is there something you need to tell me, Ms. Fisher?"

"Please call me Natalie. And yes, there is something I need to discuss with you." She said softly, like a terrified child. "I'm so sorry for what happened. I don't want you to think that I'm that kind of woman, because I'm not. I don't usually go around kissing people's husbands, and I understand why you thought it was best for Sean and me not to work together any longer, but I really need my job. That job is all I have. It means everything to me," Natalie ranted. Her words smashed together because she didn't bother to take a single breath until she was finished saying her piece.

"What did you just say?" Raven asked, clearly in disbelief. Her ears were definitely playing tricks on her, because she thought she had heard this woman say she had kissed Sean. And that was impossible, because he would have told her if something like that happened. Wouldn't he? "I'm not in the mood for practical jokes, Ms. Fisher, but for your sake I hope you're joking right now," Raven said querulously.

Natalie shook her head. "I know I was wrong, and I apologize for that. I understand that you were upset when Sean told you what happened between us, but if you could find it in your heart to tell him that I can keep my job, I promise I will stay as far away from him as possible."

It took all the self-respect and inner strength that Raven had to keep her from jumping across her desk and strangling this woman until she felt her last breath escape her limp body and then dropping her dead body to the floor for the janitor to come clean up. She wouldn't do that. She would compose herself for as long as possible because she needed to know every little detail and by the looks of it, Natalie didn't mind sharing. "Sean fired you today?" she asked plainly, peeling the hatred off her voice.

"He said after he told you about the kiss yesterday, you demanded that he fire me." Natalie lifted her head, illuminating her eyes, which were clouded over by the tears rolling out of them.

"Natalie, was yesterday the first time you and my husband became that close?" Raven asked the question she wasn't sure she wanted to know the answer to. Never mind, she did want to know. There was nothing appealing about being oblivious in this situation. No matter how hard the truth stung, she wanted to know.

"Yes, and it was a mistake on my part. I kissed him," she restated through light sobs. "I don't know why I did it. I'm embarrassed by my actions."

The phone rang, but Raven let it go to voice mail. She was in a daze right now. This was a lot of information to take in all at once. A part of her knew she wasn't wrong for being skeptical of Sean from the beginning, and the other half of her was in full agreement. Men couldn't be trusted, including Sean. He had cast Raven as the fool. She could've kicked her own ass for playing the part so well. Not only did he not tell her about kissing Natalie but he also used her as the reason why he fired the woman. *What a piece of shit*, she thought. The man Raven loved and called her husband was not the person Natalie was presenting her with right now. The man she was referring to was a complete stranger. The same stranger who sexed her brains out last night and lied to her face this morning.

The phone rang again. Raven picked it up this time and slammed it back down in one swift motion, never taking her eyes off Natalie, who was waiting for Raven to tell her that she would ask tell Sean not to take her job away. But that was the last thing on Raven's mind. She couldn't care less about Natalie's damn job—or her life, for that matter. The trick admitted to kissing her husband but had the nerve to ask Raven for a favor in the same breath. The nerve of some people, to ask about a silly little job when Raven's whole life was about to be altered. She couldn't even think straight; images of Sean's lips on Natalie's clouded her head. She saw them touch lips gently at first, the way Sean did to her when they first started dating. Then she pictured him wrapping his arms around her waist, pulling her body into his, and thrusting his tongue down her throat as they each squeezed the other's ass. Loud moans of devilish pleasure could be heard until he bit on her bottom lip, softly telling her to quiet down before someone caught them. Yes, that's what Raven knew had happened between Sean and Natalie. While she was home tending to their children, Sean was busy trying to create one more.

If only she had listened to her gut feeling when Sean asked her to be his wife. She should have said no right then. Saying no would have ensured that she wouldn't be having this dreadful conversation right now discussing Sean's infidelity. She wouldn't be sitting in front of her husband's mistress as the oblivious wife who somehow held the power in a weird way.

"Principal Thompson!" Patrice screamed as she burst into the office. "Your sister Brooklyn has been calling you. She says to get over to Mass General Hospital. Leila has been shot."

The nurse led Raven straight to the room where Leila was being treated. Brooklyn had told the nurses that Raven would be arriving shortly, and one was waiting for her. She ran beside the nurse as she hoped and prayed for the best with each step she took. The closer she got to being with her sister, the more rapidly her heart was beating. All she knew was that Leila had been shot. She didn't know where it happened, who did it, why, or if she was going to be okay. The latter being the only important fact at the moment. Leila had to survive this. If she didn't, Raven wouldn't know how to handle losing her, and she certainly knew Brooklyn wouldn't be able to think of life without her sister. They were used to life throwing surprises and obstacles in their paths, but they were just as used to dealing with those obstacles together. Every piece of the trinity was vital to their survival in this cruel and unpredictable world. That Raven was sure of. Finding a way to keep living life after the sudden death of their mother was proof that there was indeed a God. That was the only way the three sisters could explain how they were able to deal with their loss. It had to be Jesus and a million of his angels watching over each of them. At one point, right after her memorial service, they had all thought they'd never be able to laugh again or find the will to want to live without their mother. But God … that's it. Nothing but God.

The nurse stopped at room number 1203 before pointing towards the door. "Right here, Mrs. Thompson."

Raven stood outside the door for lonely minutes after the nurse had disappeared down the busy emergency room hall lined with empty gurneys. She said another quick prayer before opening the door. She exhaled deeply seeing Leila lying in a bed with her arm bandaged up and sitting in a sling. Aside from the bandages and the IV attached to her arm, Leila didn't look harmed at all. In fact, she was laughing at whatever Brooklyn was saying to her. The sight was nothing like what Raven had expected, but then she thought about when they were kids and Leila broke two of her fingers while playing volleyball with some neighborhood kids. Leila had just shoved her fingers in her other hand, not saying a word, until one of her teammates missed the ball and the game ended with Leila's team losing. It wasn't until the other team started their victory celebration that Leila started to cry out in pain. The doctor said her fingers were broken in two different places and that if it were him, he'd be crying just as loud. But Leila didn't fool Raven,

Brooklyn, and their mother. Of course she was in pain, but more about losing a competitive game of volleyball than her broken fingers.

"I thought you were dead!" Raven rushed to Leila's side, touching her arm and causing Leila to scream out in agonizing pain.

"Damn, Raven!" She swatted her sister's hand away. "I'm not dead, but that bastard shot me in my shoulder. He's lucky he only got me once. Do you know he tried shooting me three times?" Leila pushed her body up using her one mobile arm. "Dumbass couldn't even shoot straight. I mean, that Negro really could've killed me."

Brooklyn waved her hand up and down over Leila's face. "Earth to Leila, I think that was his point." She rolled her eyes in Raven's direction. "She's been like this since I got here."

"Well, his bitch ass missed twice, and I'm going to make him pay for this shit," Leila continued on her rant.

Raven dropped into the seat next to the bed. She pressed her thumb and pointer finger in the small crevice between her eyes, closing them for a second. "What the hell happened, and who shot you?" She could care less about what her sisters had been saying to this point. For some reason they were taking this incident too lightly. Sure, Raven could see that her sister wasn't in too much pain, but that didn't negate the fact that someone had tried to kill her. Her life had almost ended today, and she didn't seem fazed by that in the slightest. But that was Leila, Raven thought. She was invincible in so many ways, always feeling that there was a way to trump someone who wronged her. Never doubting her abilities but finding ways to strengthen them. And Raven knew Brooklyn admired that quality in their sister. In fact, almost everyone who met Leila felt the same exact way. It was pretty much mesmerizing, the drive and determination she had when she set her mind to something.

"Okay, so one of her patients came into her office like a madman," Brooklyn answered. "He said Leila ruined his marriage and demanded that she fixed it. He shot her when she tried escaping from the office." Raven asked, "How bad is it?"

"Bad enough that Clark's ass is going to prison," was all Leila offered, lightly tapping her wounded arm with a twinkle in her eyes.

"Stop it!" Trevor screamed from the corner of the dark room. Raven spun her head around. She hadn't noticed her sister's boyfriend was even in the room. She was so focused on Leila nothing else mattered.

"Stop acting like this isn't as serious as it is." Trevor shoved his hands in his pockets. "I usually don't get involved in your antics, but the three of you can't honestly be for real right now."

"Trevor, calm down," Leila said. "We're just finding the humor in the situation."

"No! There is no humor. You almost died today. Someone shot you, Leila," he said, holding his hands in fists at his sides. "I almost lost you, the woman I love, and I can't figure out for the life of me why you don't see that."

Trevor looked at her, his eyes searching for an ounce of what he was feeling reflected in his girlfriend. He wanted to know that after all that happened, she recognized how short life could be and knew to cherish the people who loved her the most. He wanted her to realize that he loved her beyond reason. That being his wife was something she wanted now. But he saw none of that. Instead it was like staring at a brand new person, someone he had never met before. Someone who didn't know him.

"Trevor, I do see that."

Trevor shook his head and walked to the door. "Do you really, Leila? Because I don't think you do."

Leila called after him, but Trevor walked out, not responding to her pleas.

"What the hell is his problem?" Leila posed to Raven, who in turn shrugged her shoulders. Seeing Trevor and hearing him proclaim his love for Leila reminded her of Sean and Natalie and her own messed-up drama. She had left Natalie in her office when she rushed to the hospital, not caring about either her or Sean when she thought her sister might have been dead. But now, seeing Leila alive and well, her mind swarmed with those thoughts again.

"Trevor loves you, Leila," Brooklyn spoke up. "You don't give him enough credit for everything he does to make you happy. I know I'm the last person who should be giving you dating advice, but I wouldn't be a good sister if I didn't warn you. You're going to lose out on him because of your selfish attitude."

Raven gave Brooklyn a sideways look. "Don't listen to her, Leila. Keep doing what you're doing. Don't let him pressure you into marrying him just because that's what he wants. Trust me, it will blow up in your face."

"What do you mean by that?" Leila asked. "What's going on with you?" She had *worried* written all over her face.

"Nothing, but I need to get home to Sean and the boys." Deciding not to tell her sisters what transpired today, Raven gave them each a hug and kiss. She had to talk with Sean. Anger was building inside her, and he needed to be her target. "I'll call you guys later tonight."

Raven arrived at home faster than usual. It was almost seven o'clock, way past rush hour, so there was light traffic on route nine. She'd texted Sean at the hospital to tell him she'd be home late and to feed the boys, which he didn't mind doing since he was "doing more round the house." He'd texted her back asking if she wanted him to do the laundry since he knew she planned on doing a few loads tonight. She'd texted back, yeah, thanks.

All the way home she thought about how she would approach Sean. She wondered if she would spring it on him out of nowhere or ease into the subject. If she would be able to control her emotions and speak calmly, as if he hadn't hurt her as badly as she knew he had. Or would she roll in her house like a mad black woman and raise hell, scarring her children without a doubt and introducing Sean to a new side of her as well? All of these were viable options. She thought about how in minutes her life would really change for good. Right now Sean had no idea that she was on to his lie, and she had the power to keep it that way. To make him believe that his attempt to pull the wool over her eyes had been successful. He would never know anything, and their lives could remain the same. But Raven couldn't do that. If she did, she wouldn't be the woman she claimed to be. She wouldn't be able to look herself in the mirror and truly be satisfied with the image before her. By keeping this information from Sean, she would be doing to him what he did to her. She would be a deceitful, lying bastard. And why should she have to live with that title when she hadn't done anything to hide?

Raven didn't get two steps into her house before noticing that something had changed. The house had been cleaned from top to bottom. The floors were spotless, the kitchen immaculate and smelling of Pine-Sol and Windex. In the words of her mother, the house was spic and span.

Sean appeared from the kitchen with a glass of Moscato in his hand. "I talked to Trevor. He said that Leila is going to be fine." Sean handed her the glass of sparkling wine. "I know you must have been worried out of your mind."

She took the wine, sipped it, and placed it on the coffee table. "Are the boys sleeping?"

"Yeah. Josiah was worn out from the field trip, and Tristan fell asleep with him in the car ride home."

Raven nodded. She was amazed by how serene he seemed. The fact that he was an adulterer didn't seem to weigh down heavily on his conscience. "Did you clean the house?"

"Yes. Do you like it?" Sean smiled approvingly. "I think I did a good job."

Scanning as much of the house as she could from where she stood in the living room, she agreed. "Yes, you did," she said, looking into his eyes again. "You did a good job, baby."

Sean wrapped his arms around Raven, pulling her chin up with his finger. He bent his neck to meet her lips and kissed them tenderly. Raven draped her hands behind his neck and pulled him farther down to meet her. She kissed him with all the passion she could muster. Twirling her tongue in his mouth like the pro she was, she knew she had him when she felt him growing against her stomach. Sean was ready for the red light special; his moans told her so.

It wasn't until he began undressing Raven that she pulled away, pushing him lightly in his chest. She watched as Sean's eyes questioned her. "Can I ask you a question, babe?" She wiped her lips with her thumb, not changing her sexy tone.

"Sure, you can ask me anything. You know that," Sean said, looking a little baffled.

"Am I a good kisser?"

"What? What kind of a question is that?"

"I mean, like, on a scale from one to Natalie, where do I fall? She said smoothly, like it was a normal question a wife would ask her husband. She watched as the expression on Sean's face changed drastically from loving to surprised. But then again, that was the point. "I asked you a question, Sean."

Sean gave her a sorrowful look, his face now looking deflated. "What are you talking about, Raven?"

Raven sent him a hardened glare. "Don't play me stupid, Sean. I asked you a damn question, and sadly you know the answer, so answer me, dammit!"

"Raven, it's not what you think. Nothing happened between us. We were eating lunch, and she just kissed me. I don't know why she did it. I didn't send her any signals that I was interested in her because you know I only want to be with you. I promise you, I didn't have sex with her, baby, you have to believe me."

"You lying motherfucker!" she said through clenched teeth.

"I'm not lying to you, Raye. She did kiss me, but we didn't have sex," Sean said, desperately wishing he could prove his innocence. He didn't know how she knew about Natalie, but that didn't matter right now. All that mattered was getting her to understand his side.

"Fuck her, Sean. I don't give a damn about that bitch!" Raven could no longer suppress her rage. The fact that Sean didn't see what he had done wrong made her blood boil. "This is about you and me. You lied to my face, Sean. When I asked you what was going on you told me nothing. Not once but twice you told me I was overreacting. You knew if you brought up my jealousy issues I would lay off, so that's what you did." When Raven said those last words, she realized that was where her anger was brewing from. Sean was supposed to be her knight in shining armor. The man who pioneered her new way of life. A life that didn't include having to constantly watch her back and guard her feelings. He was supposed to be the man that she used to dream about (the one from television, because that's the only place that type of men existed). Sean was supposed to be better than this. He was supposed to protect her heart, not wait until he had her loving him more than she had ever thought possible to break it into tiny little pieces and piss all over it. He wasn't supposed to be her father.

"I wanted to tell you, Raven. For real, I did. That's why I came home early yesterday. But then I punked out when I saw your face." He walked closer to her, but Raven took steps back. "I didn't know how to tell you. I knew you would react like this."

She cocked her head back in bewilderment. "React like what? Like a wife who has to find out that her husband had his lips all over another woman from the other woman? Is that right, Sean?" When he didn't answer her, she said, "I should slap you for even saying some dumb shit like that."

"If you want to hit me, Raven, go ahead." He spread his arms, opening his chest. "I deserve it."

She pushed his hands down to his sides, turning down his offer. She had thought she would want to hit him. She had imagined herself slapping him in the face multiple times, punching his chest and gut until he curled over. But she didn't have the urge to do any of that. Instead she looked at her husband with dismissive eyes. "You're not even worth it, Sean."

This time Sean wouldn't take no for an answer. He pulled Raven into him, not caring that she was twisting her body to break free from his grip. "What do you mean I'm not worth it?" He shook her forcefully.

"Get your hands off of me, Sean!" Raven screamed. "I swear to God I will call the police if you don't release me right this second."

And that wasn't a threat; it was most definitely a promise. It wasn't that Sean was hurting her, because he wasn't, but she would be damned if she let him think that putting his hands on her was acceptable. No matter the situation, he needed to know she wouldn't stand for that. Sean let her go gently. "What are you trying to say, Raven?"

Raven stepped away from him again, tears spilling from her eyes. "I'm saying I can't trust you. You might not have initiated the kiss with Natalie, but you lied to me about it. You looked me in the eyes and lied to me like it was nothing. Like it was so easy."

"It wasn't easy, Raven. It was the hardest thing I ever had to do. But I thought I was doing the right thing," he tried explaining. "I didn't want to burden you with unnecessary drama."

"Drama? I'm your wife, Sean! You should be able to tell me anything. At least that's what you said to me when we got married."

"I know, and I'm so sorry I lied to you. It will never happen again, Raven, believe that."

"I wish I could, but I can't." She folded her arms under her breast. "It's too little too late."

Sean turned his back to her, and Raven could hear him whispering to himself. She couldn't make out exactly what he was saying, but then again she didn't care too much either. When he turned back to face her, Raven saw the tears in his eyes. This was only the second time she had witnessed him cry, the other being at their wedding ceremony. He'd cried while saying his vows to her, promising to love and cherish Raven for all of eternity, through sickness and in health, and vowing to always be there for her. Any doubts she'd had about their future—and she had plenty—went out the window when she stood before him that day listening to his words, knowing they were lined and dipped in solid gold truth. "I can't lose you, Raven. I love you so much. I love our family, and I'll do whatever it takes to regain your trust."

"If love means you kiss another female, lie about it, come home kissing me with those same lips, and then try to cover it all up by firing your little mistress, then I can live without the type of love you're dishing out," she spat.

"Just let me make it up to you. Let me prove to you that this will never happen again."

"It won't work."

"Why not? We can get through this; I know that we can make this work."

"No, Sean. It won't work because I don't want it to work."

"What?"

"I don't want to put my trust in you that you won't do this again. I won't be your fool, Sean." Raven wiped the tears from her face. She didn't want to cry, at least not now. He didn't need to see the tears that he was causing. She would save those for later when she was alone. It was something her mother taught her. She said, "Never let your man see your weakness. It's unattractive, and he'll never allow your strengths to outweigh that. Suck it up and wait until you're alone. You can console yourself far better than any man could. Always remember that, because a black woman's strength is her foundation. Without it everything else in her life will crumble."

It was too late for that. Raven had already shown Sean too many of her weaknesses. He had used one of them against her today, something she never thought he'd do. "You can either leave now or I will."

"No. I'm not leaving you or this family. We need to talk this out. I'll sleep down here for tonight while you cool down and we can discuss it more tomorrow, but I'm not leaving."

"Fine. You stay and I'll leave, but I'm taking the boys with me." Raven rushed to the staircase, but she didn't make it far before Sean was grabbing at her again, this time only tightly enough to interrupt her strides up the stairs.

"Don't take my sons," he said in a tone that was more asking than demanding.

Raven slid his hands off her body and continued up the stairs. Sean shouldn't have a say in the matter. Why didn't he see that? Why didn't he see that this was his entire fault? He had nobody to blame but himself. He was asking her to do something he wouldn't do. And she knew this, because when Raven had messed up, Sean had taken their son with him. "If I have to go, then they're coming with me. You decide."

Sean shoved his hands across his chest and under his armpits. He took a few steps back and then, too fast for Raven to stop him, he threw his body into a swing that landed his fist in the wall, shattering the plastered pieces to the floor. She jumped. His knuckles began dripping blood, but that red didn't match the fire in his eyes. Raven ran past him and into the kitchen. She returned with an ice pack wrapped in a dishtowel along with a wet towel to wipe the blood. She took his hand in hers and gently secured the ice pack in it.

"I'll leave, Raven," Sean whispered timidly, like a child. "I'll go to my brother's house for the night. But I want to come back and talk to you tomorrow or the next day. Whenever you're ready."

Raven let out a sigh of relief. She would have done it if she had to, but she didn't want to take her boys and leave their house. They didn't need to suffer because their parents were having issues. But she knew that Sean wouldn't go easily. It was one thing to tell him that she didn't want to see him, but to tell him that she would be taking the boys was something she really didn't think he'd go for. Even knowing that he was the cause of all this, Sean would suffer if she ripped the boys away from him. She was relieved that he hadn't put up more of a fight. Perhaps it was because he thought that if he did what Raven asked, she would sooner allow things to go back to normal. But that was far from the truth and far from the decisions she'd made already.

Leaving Sean, Raven began her journey up the stairs for the third time that night. "You can come back whenever you would like, Sean. To get your things. But I don't think there is anything else for us to discuss."

"Raven!"

She reached the top of the stairs and opened their bedroom door. "I want a divorce," she said before closing the door on her husband. On their love. On their marriage. On their family.

Chapter Thirteen

Anything is possible. —Wanda

THIS WAS NICE, BROOKLYN TOLD herself as she sat on the couch with Jason, his legs sprawled apart and the back of her head resting on his chest. Never in a million years had she thought she'd feel this comfortable with a man. Let alone a man she had only been dating for the last few weeks. But boy, those weeks had been fun, to say the least. She didn't know when she had started thinking about Jason every night before she went to bed and when thoughts of him sprang to her mind when she awoke in the mornings. It could've been the afternoon after their first date, when he called her inquiring about the next time he could see her. Or when they went bowling and Jason patiently taught her how to hold the ball and strategically roll it down the lane to hit a strike. (Something she was never able to do in the past.) That was one of the things she liked so much about him. Jason was the most patient person she had ever met, never pushing her to say or do things she wasn't ready for. Even when he asked her questions about her family, which he did quite often, he didn't push for more information than she was comfortable giving.

But it was more than just thinking about Jason. Brooklyn couldn't pinpoint the precise second or the hour or the day that she began to fall for the man. But she definitely knew she was falling, and for the first time in her life, she didn't mind allowing herself to feel such feelings. She enjoyed the way her heart fluttered every time her phone rang and she hoped it was him calling. No, she didn't know how or when she'd gotten to this place, but she was glad to be here ... with Jason.

She wasn't quite sure, but it seemed that he felt the same way. They had spent every day together since their first date, and he was usually the one orchestrating their outings. "You're the best part of my day," he'd say. The first few times she'd responded by smiling, but now, she'd counter by kissing his lips and saying, "And those are the best part of mine."

It was stuff like that; feeling comfortable enough with Jason to speak vulnerable affirmations and kiss him without reservation that frightened her. How was this happening so fast and without warning? How was he able to get her to do things like that? It was all so new to Brooklyn. Not just some of it, all of it.

Take the other day, for instance. Jason had cooked for her. He actually went online and printed off the recipes for some of her favorite foods. He went to the grocery store, picked up the ingredients, and cooked for her in her kitchen. When she asked if there was something he needed help with, he said, "No, my girl doesn't need to lift a finger tonight."

My girl? Now that was the first time anyone had ever called her that. Plus, Brooklyn wasn't aware that she was his girl. Didn't really know what that meant, either. Were they in a relationship? Was Jason her boyfriend? She had no idea. The last time she was someone's girlfriend was almost a decade ago, back in high school, when boys would ask you out by writing a love note on a piece of paper, folding it up into some sort of origami, and slipping it into your locker. The girl would respond either yes or no by repeating the whole process over. But this was now, and Brooklyn didn't have a note to answer her questions for her.

"Your girl?" she asked, raising her eyebrow and smiling at him.

Jason continued to stir the contents on the stove. "Yeah, my girl. What? You don't like that? Should I call you my woman instead?" he asked nonchalantly.

"What does that mean ... me being your girl or woman or whatever?"

Brooklyn asked more innocently than she noticed. But Jason did. He instantly sensed what she was asking him. It wasn't just the title that she was concerned about. It was the definition behind it.

He stopped stirring and walked closer to Brooklyn, who was leaning against a kitchen chair. "It means that you're the only girl I want to be spending my time with." He kissed her. "The only one whose lips I want to be touching." He hugged her. "And the only one whose hips I want to be holding. Is that okay with you?"

She looked at him, not really thinking because thinking would cause her to say or do things she was used to, like rejecting any form of commitment from a man. She didn't want to do that anymore. So today she would step out on faith and try something new. "Yeah, Jason, that's okay with me."

Everything was just too good to be true. She kept waiting for the ceiling to cave in and come crashing down, destroying this dream she was in. But whenever she would look up, all she saw was Jason smiling down on her, holding her close. And that's when she would tell herself, *whatever, this is nice.*

"So, do you think you can make it?" Jason said, tapping her on the shoulder. The movie they'd been watching was over, the ending credits rolling across the screen.

"Excuse me?" she said, dragging herself out from her daydreaming. She turned around to face him. "I didn't hear what you said."

"I want you to meet my best friend, Brandice. Do you think you could fit it into your schedule?"

"Brandice, huh?" She playfully nudged him. "Might Brandice be a beautiful young lady with thick light brown hair, petite, with bluish-gray eyes?"

Startled by her correct description, Jason said, "You know her?"

"Am I right?" Brooklyn laughed a little, knowing she was freaking him out.

"Yes. But how did you—"

"Remember when you took me on our first date, to my sister's boyfriend's restaurant? While you were paying the check, Trevor told me that he'd seen you there on a few occasions and that usually you were there with a woman who I just described to you."

"Trevor told you all of that?"

"He thought I'd want to know. He's like a brother to me."

"I get it. I would've done the same thing if it were Brandice—who, by the way, is like a sister to me," he clarified. "Our parents always discouraged us from even thinking about being anything more."

She sat up, leaning her arm on the top of the couch. "Well, I would love to meet her. I think it's cool that your best friend is a girl. Maybe she's responsible for you being so amazing."

"That could very well be true." Jason pulled her back into his body, placing her head under his chin so he could stroke her hair. "Tell me, who is responsible for making you the uniquely special lady that you are?"

And that was just as smooth as Jason always was. He knew the right amount of compliment to mix in with the inquisitions. Usually she would find some way to change the subject tactfully, without seeming rude. But for some reason Brooklyn felt like sharing. "My mom. She gets all the credit. Whenever I thought something was impossible, out of my reach, my mom would show me that anything could happen. She was a writer too, you know. That's where I get it from."

"Sound like a wonderful woman. Can I meet her one day?"

"No. She's dead." Brooklyn felt his hand stop moving on her head, felt the breath of the deep sigh he let out on her forehead. She expected that reaction. She knew Jason was probably beating himself up inside for even asking. "It's okay," she told him. "I miss her every day, but I know she's in heaven."

"I had no idea, Brook. I'm so sorry."

"Don't be. I might have only had a mother for a limited time, but I had the best there was, and for that I'm grateful," she said truthfully. It had taken Brooklyn a long time to get the point where she could speak of her mother without feeling sad and just be appreciative of all the memories and life lessons she would always have courtesy of her mother. She still had her sad days, days when she doesn't want to get out of bed because she knew she wouldn't be able to hear her mother's voice or feel her hugs. But she had learned how to handle those days with prayer and the belief that her mother wouldn't want to see her wallowing. She'd say, "Wallowing is good, but not for too long. You'll miss something excellent if you're busy living in the past."

"What about your father?"

There was a pause. Unlike the warm feeling that she experienced when talking about her mother, Brooklyn felt a surge of immense anger at the mention of her no-good father. "I don't have one."

"What do you mean by that?" he said, a disturbed look on his face.

"I mean, I don't have a father. Never met the man. Don't know anything about him except that he wasn't a nice person in the slightest."

"Is he—"

"Can you tell me about your family?" Brooklyn cut him off. She no longer wanted to answer questions about Daniel Cartel. Partly because he was the scum of the earth but also because she didn't feel like explaining why she didn't know her father and how horrible a person he really was. She'd told Jason all he needed to know. All there was to know.

"What do you want to know?" Jason asked, keyed up. Brooklyn could tell that he was enjoying their sharing time.

Equally energized, she sprang up to the opposite side of the couch. Folding her legs Indian style, she said, "I want to know everything. I bet you're an only child, aren't you?"

"I am. Lucky guess. My parents only wanted one child, and I have to say I enjoyed growing up being the only object of their affection."

That explained a lot. The way he attended to Brooklyn, so fully, he must have learned from his parents. "Are they still together, your mom and dad?"

He nodded. "Of course. When you meet them you'll see that they are madly in love. They're soul mates."

"Soul mates, huh?"

"What? You don't believe that there is a soul mate for everyone?" he said, reaching for her hand and pulling it to his lips before releasing it.

Brooklyn nibbled on the skin of her lips. "I think love is a lottery. Everyone rolls the dice, but only a few hit the jackpot. Those people interpret their luck as soul mates while the rest just keep on playing until they either find someone they are content with and leave the table with their earnings or run out of chances, throw their hands in, and leave with nothing."

Jason let out a nervous laugh. "Damn, girl, tell me how you really feel."

She shrugged. "You asked me."

"Tell me this, do you believe in true love?"

She peered at Jason. That was a loaded question, and she knew it. She silently scolded herself for walking right into this trap. Boy, did she wish he hadn't asked her that question. Did she believe in love? Yes, she believed in love. She loved her sister with everything in her body. Would jump in front of a bullet for either of them without thinking twice. Would even give them everything their hearts desired if she had the power. But that wasn't the type of love Jason was talking about. He was asking her if she accepted as true the intimate love between two people. And that she was unsure of, being that she'd never seen it firsthand. Never witnessed a lasting marriage, never seen two real people practice the things she would do for her sisters: sacrifice, unconditional care, loyalty, respect. Without an example of that, how was she to honestly say she believed it to be true? In her mind and heart she knew what love wasn't, but for the life of her, with all the knowledge she'd acquired over the years, all the books she read, all the things she observed, she still had no idea what true love looked like, felt, smelled, sounded, or tasted like. How incredibly sad.

"You're not going to like my answer, Jason," she whispered, disappointed in herself for once again not being able to go along with the flow. The story of her life.

"Ever been in love, Brook?"

"No."

"Do you think you could be? One day, you know, if you roll the dice and you win big?"

Good question. "Like my mom would say … anything is possible." She gave him hope, wanting to believe her mother's words, especially now. If only she could force herself to not be so freaking pessimistic right now.

But she knew that was a long shot. Her pessimism wasn't an accessory she liked to wear because it matched the color of her eyes. It was a learned way of life. Experience. Anything is possible. "One day, maybe."

"Do you mind if I love you?" Jason inquired, examining her face for a response.

"Excuse me?" Brook said choking on her words. "Come again?"

"Not that I can control the fact that I love you, but if it makes you feel uncomfortable, I won't say it to you," he said, allowing her the physical space she needed. If only she could get some mental space then maybe she could steady her heartbeat back to normal.

"How can you love me? We haven't even been intimate yet!"

This isn't about sex, Brook. This is about me knowing that my feelings for you are real. I want them to grow because I want us to grow. I tell you all the time that you're the best part of my day, but you're more than that. You're the best part of my life," he told her, not skipping a beat or blinking an eye. "I. Love. You."

Brooklyn paused, waited a tactful few moments. Maybe something she didn't know about herself would be revealed in those seconds and she would be able to return the kind words Jason said to her. But the seconds rolled by, and still nothing in her mind had changed. It was so aggravating being able to think everything through fully, analyze the words Jason had said and how he said them to her, but still feel void of any true emotion.

It was just like in high school, when she felt anesthetized after losing her virginity. The day she discovered she wasn't a real woman. "You deserve better than me, Jason. I don't deserve your love because I wouldn't know how to reciprocate it. You know exactly how you feel. You know how to express those feelings in words, and I'm still trying to wrap my head around being in a relationship."

He held up his hands and flashed a reassuring smile. "I know this is overwhelming for you. I'm not asking you to do or say anything that you don't feel. I'm just asking you a simple question, that's all." This time he moved towards her, erasing that physical space. "Do you mind if I love you?"

There was that question again, forcing its way into the conversation and determined not to leave until it was answered. And she wanted nothing more than to do just that. Like Jason said, he wasn't asking her to do anything. Wasn't forcing her to rush into something. But still she felt like she was on the Senate floor about to pass a new law or something. Like the rest of her life was dependent on how she handled this situation right here and right now. She could see the flashing Vegas lights, hear the roaring voices, and feel the warm, edged dice in her hands. She pictured herself blowing on them for good luck, tossing them round and round in her sweaty hand. It was time. She relinquished the dice and in doing so relinquished everything she was secure in. All to play the lottery of love, in hopes that she'd be a big winner. "I want you to love me, Jason."

Chapter Fourteen

Actions speak louder than words. —Wanda

LEILA LOOKED AT HER PHONE for the umpteenth time that hour. She checked to see if the ringer was on. It was. She checked to see if the battery was fully charged. It was. She checked to see if she had missed any calls, text messages, or voice mails. There were none.

She was waiting for Trevor to call. It had been one week since she left the hospital. And almost every day was a challenge for them because things were changing. It didn't take a rocket scientist to see that Trevor was purposefully distancing himself from her. In the mornings he would leave early before she awoke, and he came home late, around eleven or so, from the restaurant, complaining that he was tired and falling asleep instantly. He was slick, though. When she would ask him something he'd respond normally, without a hint that something was bothering him. He didn't call her throughout the day, but when she would call him, he'd answer affectionately, "Hey, Sweetheart," and then rush her off the phone by saying he was needed in the kitchen or something along those lines.

This was enough to drive Leila crazy. It was all she had to think about since she wasn't to return to work for the next few weeks (doctor's orders). Trevor's actions were out of the ordinary for him. He was definitely taken heed to the saying "Actions speak louder than words." In her thoughts she'd already gone down the list of psychological terms to describe his behavior, theories that would back up her diagnosis, but she pushed those thoughts to the back of her brain. As hard as it was, Leila tried not to psychoanalyze her own relationship. Not because she didn't find it useful—she did—but because for some reason it annoyed people, especially Trevor. He said she hardly ever spoke from the heart. That he couldn't tell if it was her speaking or Sigmund Freud. His comment, aimed as in insult but taken by Leila as a compliment, was duly noted. From then on she tried her hardest to separate the two.

She looked at her phone one more time. Trevor hadn't said that he'd call. She hadn't asked him to either. But that was neither here nor there. The point was he should want to call. Should want to hear her voice and hear how her less-than-exciting day of lounging around and watching television was going.

But the sad fact was, Leila knew Trevor wasn't going to call. Her common sense told her that much. He was making it clear to her that he wasn't happy with her. Well, not really her, but the way she chose to run their relationship. It wasn't like she was a dictator, demanding that things be done her way or no way at all. She wasn't a mean person. At least she didn't think of herself as one.

It was actually quite simple. In Trevor's mind, Leila controlled their relationship because she cared the least about its progression. Because she was content in the way things were and he was not, she held the power.

Contrary to Trevor's belief, she didn't feel that way by any means. No, she didn't want to get married, but Leila did care about where their relationship was headed. She loved him and wanted things between them to get back on track.

Especially right now.

This was new. Trevor had never been distant with her before. It was almost as if he didn't care anymore. Whether their relationship sank or swam, he had mentally given up and checked out. Leila could tell by the lack of affection in his kisses and how he didn't grab hold of her waist and caress her thighs while they slept. Even the way he looked at her lacked that certain oomph she was used to seeing.

She thought back to a time when all those factors were present in her relationship, when she didn't feel like the love of her life was slowly slipping away. Leila fingered through her memory like a file cabinet, coming up empty handed. How had she let this happen? How did she let her relationship get to this point? And then there was the question about what Brooklyn had said earlier at the hospital. "You're going to lose out on him if you continue to be selfish."

"What did she mean by that?" Leila asked herself out loud. Those questions she didn't have the answer to, and she figured it was a waste of time to sit there and do nothing. She placed her arm in the sling the doctor had told her to wear whenever she left the house and grabbed her coat and keys.

It was chilly outside. Leila pulled her waist-length black leather jacket around her body tightly with her one arm. She was waiting in the cold for Trevor. She had called him a moment ago to let him know she was outside his restaurant and she wanted to talk to him.

This might not be the best time or the most thought-out plan, but it's all I got right now, Leila thought.

Trevor walked toward her, noticed how cold she looked, took off his coat, and draped it over her shoulders. He took her ears in his hands and rubbed them gently, warming them. "To what do I owe this pleasure?" His voice alone warmed her soul.

Leila looked up at him smiling down at her. She wondered if she had imagined the whole thing. If things in fact had not changed and she was worrying for no reason. But then she saw the blankness in his eyes and knew she wasn't imagining it. The truth was staring her dead on. She half smiled. "Mind if we talk in my car?"

"Sure."

They both got into her Lexus RX 470 and sat there listening to each other breath for some time. Leila let her eyes wander listlessly, noticing that she needed to get some gas soon. She began counting the cars that passed by before, finally saying, "Trevor, I know something's up with you. You're isolating yourself from me gradually. Like you don't want to be with me anymore." She turned to him. "Is that true?"

"I love you, Leila, and I want to be with you. You know that." Trevor gave her a long, reassuring look.

"Then why are you treating me like a distant cousin or something? You don't talk to me anymore. We haven't had sex in weeks, Trevor. I know something isn't right, so just tell me, please. So we can fix this and get back to how things used to be."

"That's just it. I don't want things to be how they used to be. I want to move forward. I want us to grow." He sighed and rested his head against the seat back. "I want to get married."

Leila felt the contents in her head start to spin, causing a migraine to emerge between her eyes and shoot across her forehead. She wondered how many times they were going to fight about the same thing. She turned her body until her knees hit the built-in cup holders between them. "Trevor, you know how I feel about that."

"I do. And that's the problem." He looked out the window. "I don't know how much longer I can do this. I used to tell myself that you would change. That one day you would want all the things that I want for us. That if I were patient, you'd come around. But I can't keep lying to myself. You want what you want." He turned back to her. "I can't be mad at you because you told me in the beginning, before things got too deep, how you felt. I'm mad at myself for not believing you and for thinking that I could make this work because I love you. But I can't. I can't live my life loving a woman wholeheartedly but knowing that she doesn't feel the same way."

How insulting for him to question her love for him. She felt as though she was on trial for a crime she didn't commit. "But I do, Trevor. I love you so much. I don't know what else I can do or say to make you believe me."

Trevor didn't skip a beat. "Say you'll marry me."

Heavy silence. When she didn't answer, he said, "That's what I thought."

"That's not fair, Trevor." Leila fought to keep her composure, but she felt herself losing it. "You know that I love you."

"Yes, but not fully. Something is stopping you from fully loving me. I have as much of your heart as you're willing to share, but that's not enough, Leila. Not for me."

She sat, digesting his words, feeling like the doors of the car were closing in on her. Leila didn't work well under this type of pressure, nor did she feel the need to prove Trevor wrong by giving in to his desires. All the room she once had felt as if it was disappearing within seconds. "You can't force me to marry you," she told him. Waiting for the car to expand.

"Not trying to."

"Then why are you doing this, Trevor?" She shook her head. "Why are you making me choose between what you want and what I'm ready for?"

He took her face in his hands and held on to her cheeks. "Will you ever be ready? If you tell me right now that there is a chance—it could be the smallest chance—that you'll one day want to marry me, then I'll stay, Leila. I'll stay right here and wait," he told her.

She blew out hot air causing her lips to flutter. He didn't get it. He just didn't get it. "I can't, Trevor!" she yelled. "I can't," she repeated softly.

Her eyes closed. Neither her heart nor her mind was willing to say otherwise. Leila was sure that this was the way things had to be. She had made that silent promise to her mother and to herself so many years ago, and she was doing so well keeping it. Trevor wouldn't understand how important this was to her because he was too busy being self-focused. It was all about him and what he wanted. She couldn't count the number of times her mother had warned her about selfish men and said to avoid them if possible. But those were her emotions speaking. The analytical part of her knew that this had very little to do with Trevor and everything to do with her.

"I know psychology. I know how to work hard," she began. "And I know how to do my job. I listened in class. I followed the right examples because I knew that if I did those things, success would come to me. It was just up to me to put in the work. A singular effort for the most part. I know my abilities, Trevor. I know how far to push myself. I know I can always depend on myself. I'll never give up on myself. Never stop loving me." She pressed her pointer finger into the middle of her chest forcefully. "Never turn my back on me."

"You can depend on me."

"I'm not weak, Trevor," she said, ignoring him. "You can't just punch me around, expecting me to roll over for you."

"Is that what you think? That I want to marry you so that I can take all of that away from you, Leila?"

When she didn't answer, he asked again, "Is that what you think?" This time he spoke angrily. "Answer me!"

She peered at him, shrouding the doubt within her and replacing it with a confident tone. "That's what I know. Like right now, you're trying to control me by giving me an ultimatum. Is that what I have to look forward to in marriage? You trying to control me until I don't have a voice anymore?

Trevor snorted out a sarcastic laugh, though he didn't find a damn thing funny. "No, Leila, you don't." Trevor opened the car door, letting cold air into the already freezing atmosphere. "You don't have anything to look forward to, because I'm done." He opened his mouth and then closed it. He rolled his eyes. "After all this time, you still don't get it. I'm not a monster. I'm not your father, and you're not your mother."

Now he'd crossed the line. If Leila weren't so against domestic violence, she would have pulled him back into the car and strangled him until he took back what he said. "Don't you dare bring them into this!" she snapped.

"Why not?" He shrugged. "You do. You carry every negative thing that happened between your parents into your life. You're so scared of being like them you don't even notice what you've become. Bitter."

His words stung. She glared at him, telling him with her eyes that she didn't appreciate the comparison because she knew she'd just be wasting her breath if she said another word. Trevor had made up his mind that he wanted to leave. Their relationship was over, and although she didn't want it to be, she would accept it. She wouldn't ask him to stay where he didn't want to be. She wouldn't become the weak woman who went against her word for the man she loved. "Leave me alone, Trevor."

"That's all you've ever wanted to be. Alone." He stepped out of the car, slamming the door behind him.

Leila woke up the next morning around four. She was fed up with trying to put herself to sleep every thirty minutes just to find herself wide eyed, staring at the ceiling, in the next ten. As expected, Trevor hadn't come home the last night, and since the apartment was originally hers, she knew it was only a matter of time before he came by to pick up his things. He'd probably crashed for the night on one of his boys' couches and would stay there until he found a place of his own.

For a quick second, before she carried herself to bed, Leila had a thought that maybe Trevor would come home and they would talk this thing out the way they'd done so many times before. He would get everything off his chest, and so would she. They would argue, shout, and holler until there was nothing left to say except "I love you," which is what always happened. No matter how heated their arguments got, it always came down to their love for one another.

Needless to say, Trevor didn't come home, which is why Leila was now up and about, energized off a pot of coffee. She was busy filling boxes with Trevor's belongings. She'd already packed his clothes and shoes and was now in the kitchen wrapping his expensive top-of-the-line cookware in the Sunday *Globe*. Next were his cookbooks and then his extensive DVD collection. By eight she had all his stuff boxed up and stacked neatly by the front door. She looked around her apartment. It was void of any signs of Trevor, but still she could feel his presence. She looked in the kitchen and saw how many delicious meals he'd cooked for the two of them. The couch where they watched Christmas movie marathons. Even the fifth step on the staircase—Leila could hear Trevor's feet pressing against the loose wood, causing it to creak. Leila rubbed her eyes ruthlessly in dire need of a new image, an image that didn't include Trevor. During her attempt to get some sleep the previous night, Leila had convinced herself that her life would be better off without the eventual heartache that her relationship with Trevor would bring. It was better this way. Now she had more free time on her hands to focus on her work and her sisters. What God has for you is for you, and Leila told herself that Trevor wasn't for her.

It was now day ten, and that jacked-up logic had gone out the door three days prior. Leila waited for the time to come when every waking thought wasn't about Trevor—something he did, said, or made—but that day was dodging her with the skill of an athlete. Her days became longer and her nights shorter with the constant absence of sleep. Leila tried desperately to escape her own thoughts, but there was no distraction tough enough for that job. Not even alcohol. She tried.

On day three, her doorbell had rung. Leila felt her heart drop to her stomach when she opened the door to face Trevor. She let him in with a half smile, closed the door behind him, and went to her room while he loaded his things in his car. She watched from the upstairs window as, box by box, his presence disappeared. It pained her to see the man she loved walk out of her life. In the two years they'd been together he had been her best friend in every definition of the words, but still Leila knew she couldn't give him what he wanted from her. She couldn't be his wife, and that was that. She closed the curtains and crawled into bed, falling asleep instantly upon hearing Trevor's voice. That was the thought that played over and over in her mind day after day, and it was starting to drive her crazy. Leila needed to get out of that house and do something productive, but that wasn't going to happen due to her lack of motivation to do anything other than soak in the hot tub and sift through her cable channels for a holiday movie.

Plan B: call Renee.

Leila had met Renee in high school. They were both in the same homeroom in ninth grade. Some way or another the two had become close friends, although neither of them really remembered how it happened. One day they didn't know each other and the next they did, simple as that. Leila liked Renee because she was smart. Not just book smart but street smart. She could see a sucker come from a mile away and an asshole from two miles. She didn't take shit off anyone, but she wasn't cocky about it. She called it liked she saw it—nothing more, nothing less.

Leila and Renee were like two peas in a pod when it came down to almost everything except for men. Renee, an attractive brown-skinned woman from Dorchester, the first to school anyone on "black facts," who knew more about the civil rights movement than those who actually lived through it, was totally and wholeheartedly against dating black men. Renee was one of those women who believed in statistics and studied history. She calculated the odds of her having a happy and lucrative life with a black man versus a white man and that was that. Renee was raised by her mother, didn't know her father or her grandfather, and had no uncles, but despite all that she loved black people with a passion. She loved everything about being a black woman except the lack of productive black men to choose from. Renee didn't see any reason to delve into a situation when the risks far outweighed the rewards. Statistics and history were all she needed.

Leila was popping the corks off the bottles of Moscato when Renee knocked on her door. "Come in," she bellowed.

Renee pushed the door open and made herself comfortable in the living room. "Don't tell me you called me over here because you're sulking about Trevor leaving."

Leila rolled her eyes at her best friend the certified cynic. "I called you because I need to talk to you. Do you think you can quit the sarcasm and just be a good friend for maybe an hour?"

"Oh, stop being a drama queen and tell me what's going on. And please don't start talking about how Trevor doesn't understand you and how it's hard for you to trust people, because we've had this talk a million times."

"I know we have, but it's still true, and I still can't let it go. Believe me, Renee, I've tried to stop being this way and to just relax and let things flow naturally, but I just can't."

Renee cocked her head back in disbelief, and Leila knew she was in for an earful. "Leila, who are you fooling, girl? You and I both know that you don't try to do anything that you truly don't want to do, which is why you and Trevor will never be together. You can't see past yourself. It never crosses your mind that maybe he's different and can change the way you look at men. Instead you feel obligated to live in the past and to make every man out to be the same person. A bad one."

Leila heard what Renee said, and she couldn't believe her ears. "You're one to talk, Miss 'I don't date men with too much melanin in their skin.'"

"See, I don't know why you want to make this about me. I'm comfortable with my decision to live my life like this, and I'm not complaining. But you, on the other hand, love being who you are until the consequences of you come back and bite you in the ass. That's your problem. All I'm saying, Leila, is if you want to shut everyone out and live privately—and lonely, might I add—than cool, do that. But don't start acting surprised when you get exactly what you asked for."

"Damn, Renee, why do you have to be so mean?" Leila hissed.

"Because you need to hear this."

"I'm scared, Renee."

"I know you are, but life is about conquering your fears, not living in the shadows of other people's."

Chapter Fifteen

IT HAD BEEN THREE AND a half weeks since Brandice called Tracy Atler in regard to finding her sisters. The two had met on four previous occasions, going over all the information that Brandice was able to offer, which wasn't very much. But Tracy was confident that she could dig up some clues to uncover the mystery.

The first time she left Tracy's Newton office, Brandice felt rather confident in the woman's skills. The way she studied every detail and analyzed every bit of information was enough to make anyone want to rent a James Bond movie. But that was two weeks ago and still nothing. Not one lead about where either sister was located. Brandice was beginning to think that all hope was truly lost until Tracy called and asked Brandice to come to her office as soon as possible. She said she might have found something.

It wasn't until getting that call that she felt her heart stabbing away at her chest in a nervous, anxious way. Until now she had been leaning on pure hope, persistence, and chance. Now that she had professional help, Brandice was beginning to feel that she might actually get what she set out for: to find her sister and relay her father's message. She showered and dressed quickly, her hands shaking uncontrollably all the while. Brandice could hardly think straight because her mind was clouded with endless possibilities and scenarios about how her two sisters would react to seeing her. She was willing to bet that they didn't know she even existed, and she hoped that their mother, Wanda, wouldn't get in the way of what she had to do for her father. Brandice had told Tracy that Wanda was the name of her sisters' mother and that her father and Wanda had gone through a less-than-amicable divorce. Tracy seemed pleased with the little bit of information Brandice was able to offer, and now she knew why. Brandice was on her way to find out exactly who Leila and Raven were and where she could find them.

"I thought you were going to tell me good news," Brandice blurted out in frustration. The gusto she'd had before walking into Tracy Atler's office was now gone. "This is terrible."

"The first thing I do as an investigator is to find out if the people I'm investigating are even alive, Ms. Cartel. I know this isn't what you were looking for, but I assure you that finding out that the mother, Wanda Desotelle, is now deceased is actually making progress in the search for your sisters."

It took a few moments for her words to settle into Brandice's consciousness. For some reason she wanted to cry. This woman, her father's first wife, was someone she hadn't even known existed until a few weeks ago, and the little she did know about the woman had been the few less-than-positive words her mother said about her. But none of that mattered because Brandice knew how much pain losing a parent caused. So she wept for her sisters.

"Ms. Cartel," Tracy interrupted, "would you like me to postpone the search until you can handle the results of whatever it is we find?"

Brandice quickly shook her head. Now, more than ever, she knew that this needed to be done—and soon. Life was short, and who knew how much time she had left to put the pieces of her family together. Brandice was beginning the see that she had more in common with her sisters than she had thought. And then there was that small, selfish thought that was making its way to the front of her head. Maybe her sisters could help her get over the loss of her father, walk her through the grieving steps and back to living a healthy and happy life. Leila and Raven were her sisters who now represented survivors of tragedy. Coming together would be beneficial for all of them. "No, Tracy, do whatever you need to do to locate my sisters. I need them."

Chapter Sixteen

You can't cover a volcano with a bottle cap. —Wanda

"SEAN, I THOUGHT I TOLD you that I would drop the boys off at your brother's house," Raven said after opening her front door expecting to find the delivery boy but instead seeing her soon-to-be-ex-husband. This was beginning to be way too much for Raven to handle. Together she and Sean had both decided that she needed her space to figure out exactly what she wanted to do. Even though in Raven's mind she'd already decided. Time after time Raven had told Sean that she wanted a divorce, but he was convinced that she just needed more time and space. He had agreed to give her just that, but even that wasn't working. Every day, Sean found some excuse to come over unannounced. Yesterday he had needed his special running shoes, and last Wednesday he had stopped by to kiss the boys good night. Sean thought he was slick, but all this was beginning to get on Raven's last nerve.

"I know, but I was in the neighborhood, so I thought I'd give you a hand."

Raven rolled her eyes. "Sean, you have got to stop doing this, okay? I know you want things to go back to the way they were, but this isn't the way."

Sean looked past Raven and into the house. "Are you expecting company?" he asked.

Raven looked behind her and then back at her husband. "Why are you asking me questions you already know the answer to?"

"I was just making sure." He smiled. "Can I come in to get the boys?"

Raven moved to the side to let him in. She watched his eyes as they roamed the house, taking note of all the changes that she'd made. The couch was now closer to the bookcase, and the flat-screen television that Sean praised like a deity was now tightly sealed in a box in the basement. Those were just a few of the changes that Raven had been more than happy to make.

"You like?" Raven decided to ask even though she knew he didn't.

"It looks good," Sean lied. "You look good. How have you been, Raye?"

That was the million-dollar question that everyone had been asking her since the separation. And she would tell Sean the same thing she told everyone else. "I'm hanging in there, you know?" Raven walked back to the kitchen, where she had been marinating pork chops for dinner. She had to do something to keep busy because, unlike everyone else, Sean knew her too well. He'd know she was lying.

Sean followed her into the kitchen. "Is this easy for you, Raven?"

"Sean, don't—" She gave him the side-eye.

"No, really. I'm over here going out of my mind wondering if I'm ever going to be allowed back in my house. If I'm ever going to be able to make love to my wife again. I can't sleep. I can't concentrate at work, and I'm driving my whole family crazy because all I do all day long is obsess over how much I love and miss you. Then I come over here and you appear to be in the highest of spirits, as if this whole thing isn't affecting you at all."

Raven waited a few seconds, searching for the decorum she needed to engage in this conversation. "Are you asking me how I feel or are you telling me how I feel? Because you really don't have the right to even be approaching me at all after the stunt you pulled with your little girlfriend." Raven regretted those words as soon as they left her lips. It was never her intention to make this about the kiss. She knew Sean wouldn't have willingly kissed another woman. This was about him lying to her face, and she needed him to understand that.

Sean opened his mouth and closed it again, tight. He just looked at her as she diced onions. This wasn't a conversation he wanted to have with Raven because he knew how much he'd hurt her, but he also knew that they had to do this. They had to get everything off their chests if any progress would ever be made.

"Raven, I don't know how many more times I can apologize for this, but here it goes again." He moved around the kitchen island to face her. "I'm sorry."

"I know you are, Sean," Raven said, not pulling her attention away from the knife and vegetables in her hands. This is exactly why she had wanted to drop the boys off; then she would have been able to make up some excuse about having to be somewhere, and she wouldn't be having this conversation right now. Raven didn't mean to come off so smug, but the reality of the situation was that although she was hurting over their separation, she had halfheartedly expected something like this to happen one day. It wasn't that Sean wasn't a good man, because she knew that he was. But as much as she wanted to have a good and honest marriage, she had known that somehow, some way, things just wouldn't work out. It was something Raven had come to terms with years ago. She knew that disappointment was one factor that shaped her life. When people let her down or broke promises, it centered Raven and for the most part made her stronger in herself. Disappointment always brought her to realize she should never get too complacent while resting on the backs of others. "Sean, you know me, and you know that I'm not going to sit here and fall apart just because our marriage isn't going to work out. I can accept that things will change, but I don't think that makes me a bad person."

"Did you ever really love me?"

Raven dropped the knife and closed her eyes slowly. She shook her head a few times in utter disbelief at his nerve. She'd spent years giving him all she had to offer, and when she had felt like that might not be enough, she had dug even deeper within, pulling love and affection from her past lives to give her husband. "Are you serious right now?" She opened her eyes. "After all these years of marriage and two children later, you're asking me if I loved you?" Raven picked the knife back up and began chopping with determination, the quiver in her bottom lip moving as fast as her hands. "I never once gave you any indication that I wasn't here for the long haul, Sean. I have been loyal and faithful to you since the day we met. Love was never our issue. It was and still is trust." She walked to the refrigerator and ducked her head deep into it. Raven wasn't about to let him get the best of her right now. She let the cold air dry her wet eyes. "The boys are upstairs. Please go and get them and then leave, Sean."

"I'm not going to leave here until we figure this thing out. I can't keep doing this. I need to know what is going to happen with us."

"I don't have any answers for you today."

"So, can I come back home then?"

"No."

"Why?"

"Because I can't trust you. I don't know if I want to even be married to you anymore, and I'm not about to give you false hope."

"You know what? This is some crap. You've made mistakes in this marriage too. You are definitely not perfect."

Raven slammed the refrigerator door. " I know, but thank you for reminding me."

"Oh, you know what I mean."

Raven rubbed the sides of her head. This was not how she had expected to spend her Saturday afternoon. *How much more of this can I take?* she silently asked herself. Raven didn't know when their relationship had moved from easygoing bliss to her feeling like she wanted to punch something every time she was in his presence.

Gathering what strength she had left, Raven asked, "I'm tired, Sean, and I don't want to have this conversation with you today. You said you would give me some space, and I have yet to receive it. Can you at least give me that much?" She spoke in a much calmer tone, but the frustration was still there. "I can't think with you over here all the time."

"Oh, so me being here is bothering you?" He didn't wait for her to answer. "I'm going to give you exactly what you want, Raven. I won't be bothering you anymore," Sean said, clearly annoyed by his wife's words. "I'm going to get my sons and I'm gone." He walked out of the kitchen and through the living room and was on his way up the stairs before Raven called out to him.

"You're not going to take my children when you're clearly upset. They don't need to be around you when you're like this," she said. "You can come get them for church tomorrow."

Sean descended down the few steps he had managed to climb. "Who do you think you are? I'm their father. I can take my boys anytime I feel like it."

"Sean, no."

He let out a soft chuckle that was filled with disbelief yet understanding. "You know what?" He reached into his pocket and took out his keys. "I don't even have time to argue with you. You think you're superwoman and you can do everything by yourself, so here you go." He held up his hands as if to secede. "You can call me when you need me. Until then, you won't be seeing or hearing from me."

Chapter Seventeen

TREVOR EXITED THE HYNES CONVENTION Center train station and took a deep breath. The smell of fresh coffee and doughnuts from Dunkin' Donuts was indigenous to the city of Boston and a smell he enjoyed immensely, but today it had absolutely no effect on his mood. The effects of living without Leila were just now settling, and it amazed Trevor just how much a part of his life she was. The midday phone calls that he used to look forward to didn't come any longer, but that didn't bother him as much as not being able to come home to her every night. He loved reaching their house and seeing the bedroom light on and her car parked on the street. The comfort of knowing that she was just there whenever he needed her was what he missed the most. There were so many nights he found himself parked down the street from her house, just hoping for a glimpse of her. He wanted to see her, to talk to her and hold her, but he knew that would be detrimental to his stance. Leila wasn't willing to give him what he needed from her, and that was it. He couldn't be in a relationship with a woman who only gave him half of herself no matter how much he loved her. Trevor loved Leila with every bone in his body, and he tried to show her this every chance that he got. He never lied to Leila, and he had never once cheated on her or done anything to cause her pain. He had tried so hard to be the man that she needed and deserved. Trevor knew the day would come where he would become exhausted with his efforts going unnoticed, but a small part of him thought that Leila would one day open up her eyes and see that they had a really good thing going. What hurt Trevor the most was knowing that Leila didn't see in him what he saw in her. She didn't feel the same security and unconditional love that he felt every day they were together.

So here Trevor was, walking into his restaurant, which was yet another place the reminded him of Leila. He was immediately greeted by the afternoon maître d', Langston.

"Hi, Chef." Langston came from behind the table where he stood.

"How are you, Langston. How big of a crowd are we expecting tonight?"

Langston didn't have to look at the reservation book to answer Trevor's question. He memorized everything that was in it every day, which was one of the reasons Trevor appreciated having Langston around. He was very efficient. "We have a full house tonight, Chef."

Trevor smiled; at least something would bring joy to him today. He began his walk to the back of the restaurant to prep the rest of the chefs and cooking staff before Langston asked to speak with him in private for a moment. Trevor took Langston to his office and closed the door before they both sat. "What can I do for you, Langston?"

"I have some bad news, Chef. You know that young lady and her father who always come in on Tuesdays for lunch?"

Trevor nodded his head. He'd seen the pair from time to time.

"Well, the father passed away a few weeks ago from a stroke. The daughter came in today for the first time in over a month. I asked her if she was waiting on her father to arrive and she just broke out into tears." Langston let out a heavy breath. "I told her that we are all very sorry for her loss and that today's meal would be on the house. I know I don't have the right do make that decision, but I didn't know what to do. You know how it is when a woman starts to cry?"

"I'm happy you did what you did," Trevor assured him. "I just wish we could do more." He got up from behind his cluttered desk. "Is the young lady still here?"

Langston stood as well. "Yes, Chef. She's at her usual table, but she hasn't ordered yet. I think she's still trying to get herself together."

"Okay, Langston. I'll take it from here." Trevor led the young man out the office and back onto the main floor, where he saw the young woman sitting at her usual table. He watched from a distance as she used the cloth napkin to dab her eyes and looked out the long glass windows at the taxis honking and people with shopping bags darting through traffic. Trevor slowly approached her, not wanting to alarm her. After all these years, he had never learned her name.

"Excuse me, miss," he said as he reached the table.

She turned around, clearly surprised by his voice.

"I didn't mean to scare you. I just want to offer my condolences about your father. I didn't know him very well, but he seemed to be a nice gentleman."

She smiled. "Thank you very much. And yes, he was a very nice man."

Trevor pulled out the empty seat across from her and sat. "I know this isn't much, but being a chef, I believe in the power that good food can have on a broken spirit. I would like to make you whatever you would like to eat today."

"Oh, no. There's no need to go out of your way. I know you're extremely busy preparing for the dinner rush."

"I insist." Trevor took out his pad from the top pocket of his chef's jacket. "This is the least I can do."

Trevor could sense that she was intrigued by his offer. When she accepted, he was elated to be able to do something for her. He listened intently as she told him exactly how she wanted her food. He was impressed with her culinary knowledge as well.

"Okay, I can have this out to you in about twenty minutes. Is that fine?" he asked, still searching for her name somewhere in his memory bank but still coming up empty. "I'm sorry, but what is your name?"

"Brandice." She extended her hand across the table. "Nice to meet you, Trevor." She pointed to the bottom of the menu where his name was printed.

Trevor shook her hand. "That's an interesting name. What does it mean?"

Brandice laughed. "Nothing, really. My dad has a sister named Brandy and a sister named Candice, thus the name Brandice," she explained.

As she talked, Trevor's mind was busy making connections, "You know what I just remembered? Your friend, that guy that comes in here with you sometimes—what's his name?"

"Junior?" she asked back.

"Yeah, I think that's his name." He snapped his fingers in accomplishment. "He's dating my girlfriend's sister. Well, my ex-girlfriend."

"Brooklyn?"

"Yeah, you know her?"

"No. But I've heard so much about her. I'm supposed to meet her really soon. She seems like a really amazing person."

"She is. Wow, the world really is a small place." He got up to leave. "Give me twenty minutes, Brandice. I promise it will be worth the wait."

When Trevor came back nearly an hour later to retrieve her plate, he was pleased to see that she'd eaten all the roast beef, mashed potatoes, gravy, and seasoned corn that he had prepared. She had even finished the coconut sweet potato pie he brought out for dessert. "Can I take it that you enjoyed the food?"

Brandice patted her stomach. "It was delicious. I don't think I'll be able to eat for another three days, though. I'm so stuffed. Thanks again, Trevor."

"No problem. Come by anytime."

And she did just that. Being in that restaurant where she'd shared so many good times with her father made her feel good inside. She always sat at "their table," and it felt as if his presence was there with her. It didn't hurt that Trevor had made it a routine to prepare her favorite meals every week. When she revealed to him that she'd always wanted to go to culinary arts school, Trevor started letting her come to the kitchen when they weren't too busy to learn a few things. Trevor enjoyed Brandice's company. She was funny and smart and made him feel like she needed him. But it wasn't a romantic thing in the least. Trevor was beginning to see Brandice as a little sister. He knew she was going through a difficult time, and he didn't mind being there for her.

Today, he was busy teaching her how to properly cook a filet mignon. Trevor stood over the stove as Brandice watched from a distance. "You think you can handle it now?" he asked, pleased with his teaching methods.

"I'm sure I can," Brandice responded. It was clear that she was an active learner. She was tying the strings of her apron around her waist when her cell phone rang. "Brandice Cartel," she answered before engaging in the conversation. She hung up and walked over to the stove, ready to cook.

"Did I hear you say Brandice Cartel?" Trevor asked, trying to shroud his inquisitions.

Brandice kept her eyes on the food. "Yeah, that's my name."

"That's not a common last name, you know. I know a woman with that same name." That got Brandice's full attention. "Really? Who?" she asked, wide eyed with anticipation.

"My ex-girlfriend. Remember, the one I told you about?"

Brandice moved away from the fire. "You never said what her first name was." She slightly shifted her body to face him. "Is her name Raven?"

Trevor gave her a strange look. "Raven is her sister. My girl's name is Leila. And how do you know Raven?" This was all getting to be a little weird for Trevor. The look on Brandice's face was enough to alarm anyone. He ran to the sink and got her a glass of water. Her face was beginning to turn pale. He watched as she drank, still waiting for an answer. Brandice finished the glass and motioned for another. She drank that as well, holding her chest and leaning against the stainless-steel countertop.

Trevor knew something was terribly wrong. He told his sous chef to take charge and took Brandice into his office. They both sat, and he could see the color starting to reappear in her face.

"What's going on, Brandice?" Trevor asked. "I want to be able to help you, but I can't if you don't tell me what's wrong.

Brandice looked at him. She tried speaking, but she couldn't find the words. She tried shaking the confusion from her head. As best as she could, Brandice explained everything to Trevor about her father and his two daughters whom she had never met. She told him about the letter and the private investigator she'd hired to locate Raven and Leila.

Now Trevor needed a glass of water. If he'd heard her correctly, Brandice was telling him that she was Leila's sister and that the man for whom Trevor had cooked meals for over the last five years or so was Leila's father. The man she never knew but who was responsible for her cold disposition toward men and committed relationships. But it wasn't just Leila. Trevor had known the Cartel sisters for quite some time, and as far as he could tell, Brooklyn and Raven were just as screwed up as she was. Leila hardly ever spoke about her father, but when she did it was never in a positive way. Trevor tried to recollect just one time when Leila might have mentioned him without venom in her voice, but he knew that was a waste of his time. Leila hated her father.

"Trevor, I need to see my sisters. Where do they live? Do they live together? Do they look like—do I look like them? Did you know their mother? Can you call Leila today? Is Raven married? Do they have kids?" Brandice asked all in one breath.

"Calm down, Brandice," Trevor told her with his eyes as well as his words. "I wish that I could help you, but I can't. This situation with your sisters and their father is much deeper than I think you realize. And I really don't think it would be a good idea for me to get involved." Trevor wanted to tell her more, but he knew that it wasn't his place. Even though he and Leila were no longer together, Trevor had too much respect for Leila than to do this to her now. Then Trevor glanced at the woman sitting across from him. The look of disappointment that was plastered on her face made him want to think twice.

"Look, Trevor. I'm not sure what you're hinting at, but I have a feeling that you're not going to tell me either." She waited for his response, which was a simple nod of his head. "My daddy wanted me to find these women, and nothing is going to stop me from doing just that. If you won't help me, then I'm just going to ask Junior. He wants me to meet Brooklyn anyway."

Trevor felt his temper spike. It was clear that her stubbornness was a Cartel trait. Trevor knew that Brandice meant business, but he also knew what information like this could do to her sisters if delivered in the wrong way by the wrong person. Especially Brooklyn. There was no way for Brandice to know that Brooklyn was a delicate person, and if Brandice hurt Brook, Raven and Leila would be ready to break her face. Brandice's chances of winning over her sisters were already very low, and Trevor didn't want to see them completely dissipate. He knew that going through Junior to get to Brooklyn would be the wrong move.

Trevor thought about Raven but quickly released her as a viable option. He'd spoken to Sean just last week, and their separation was all Raven needed to handle right now, Trevor thought. "Brandice, they might be your sisters, but it's obvious that you don't know them at all. I want you to remember that." Trevor knew that there was a huge chance that he would regret what he was about to say, but he didn't see any other options. Brandice was a nice girl, but he'd have to feed her to the wolf. "I'll help you, but we're going to have to do this my way. Agreed?"

She said, "Yes."

"Leila is the one you need. We'll talk to her first." Trevor didn't like the sour taste that stung his tongue as he spoke. It was selfish and he knew it, but Trevor couldn't help but wonder how he could make Brandice and her optimism go far away. He still had an ounce of hope that one day Leila would be able to work through her issues and see that not every man was as awful as her father had been to her mother. He'd worked hard on laying down the foundation, and Brandice was going to mess it all up and drive Leila even further away from marrying him than she was now. As hard as it was, Trevor pushed those thoughts out of his head and reminded himself that this wasn't about him or his happiness but about the four women whom he'd grown to care about.

Trevor made Brandice promise not to tell Junior about any of their recent discoveries. She was reluctant at first to agree, seeing that Junior was the first person she wanted to tell. She agreed anyway, eager to finally be able to fulfill her daddy's wishes. With his eyes, Trevor smiled at Brandice, but he knew that whatever joy she felt in her soul now wouldn't match the heart-wrenching pain that she was about to experience.

Chapter Eighteen

Sometimes it's okay to cry over spilt milk. —Wanda

WITH A HOMEMADE CARAMEL CRUNCH apple pie in her hands, Brooklyn mustered up the courage to ring Jason's doorbell. She'd just spent the last two hours picking out the perfect outfit and hairstyle for the big day. Last week, Jason had insisted that she make time to have lunch at his apartment to meet his parents.

"Are you sure you want me to meet them now?" Brooklyn had asked as she picked up another card from the deck. She knew she wouldn't be able to avoid this very much longer. Last time Jason had asked, she had told him that Raven needed her to babysit—which was true, but Leila had offered to babysit as well. And the time before that, she had told him that she had to go to the DMV, which would take all day, and she didn't want to make plans she couldn't keep.

Jason looked at Brooklyn over the five cards he held in his hand. "Yes. I'm sure, and I don't want to hear any of your tired excuses, either." He laid down his card. "This is important to me, and my mother is already starting to think you're avoiding her."

"I'm not avoiding anyone," she lied. "And they weren't excuses, they were explanations." Brooklyn laid her card down. "Tell your mother that I am very excited to meet her and your father."

"So, you'll come to lunch then?"

"Yup. But under one condition."

Jason dropped all his cards to the table. "Name it."

"You have to have dinner with my sisters. They think something is wrong with you because I've been hiding you from them for so long."

Jason pulled all the cards together and began to shuffle. "You've been hiding me?"

"I don't think so. I'd like to think that I've been keeping you to myself for a while—which is a good thing, believe me. Once you meet my sisters you will understand. They can be a lot to handle."

"Well, if they are anything like you, then I'm sure we'll get along."

Brooklyn laughed knowingly. "They are nothing like me," she pointed out. "But in a good way."

She took the cards from him and cut the deck. "I'm not going to spoil the introduction, but I will warn you: Be prepared to be amused."

He dealt. "Meeting the family is a big step, don't you think?"

Brooklyn felt her stomach start to turn in that nervous way. He'd taken the words right out of her brain. Things between them were great. Jason was good to her, and she had strong feelings for him, but a part of her wondered how all this would change once they added more ingredients to the mixture. Brooklyn loved her sisters, but she knew they could be a lot to handle at times, and she had no idea what to expect when meeting his parents. She knew they would ask her questions and the polite thing to do would be to answer them with enthusiasm, but she didn't feel comfortable sharing certain aspects of her life with new people. For goodness' sake, there were some things she didn't even discuss with her sisters. She was nervous about how the encounter would flow. Would his parents pressure her about information that she hadn't even shared with Jason? Would they want to know about her upbringing? Because that was not something she wanted to discuss. "Maybe we should wait a little bit longer."

"Brook." Jason said her name with patience.

She exhaled. "You're right, you're right. Saturday it is." She had to start somewhere. "Is Brandice going to be there?" After all this time she still hadn't met the woman.

"Actually, no. She said she had something to do and backed out yesterday." Jason glared at his cards a second before tossing them aside.

"How're you just going to do that?" She asked in awe. "The game isn't over."

He stretched his arms over his head before bringing them across his chest. He grinned. "I want to play a new game." He came around the table and reached for her hands as she stood. Jason lightly kissed her forehead and then both her cheeks. Holding her small waist, he planted butterfly kisses down her neck and ears. The way Jason expressed his love for her was something she definitely enjoyed. Wanting to get in on the action, she took his face in her hands and kissed him avidly on his lips. Seconds, minutes, hours went by—Brooklyn didn't know the difference. Her only concern was feeling the pleasure he was providing and giving it back.

Jason's hands moved expertly over her body as he deepened their kiss. Brooklyn felt his cold fingers move under her shirt and glide over her belly before she jumped back, moving away from his reach. "I'm sorry, Jason," she whispered at the floor. "I'm just not ready yet." She fell quiet in her thoughts and aggravation. The thought of losing Jason because she couldn't win this internal battle she'd been fighting for years was relentlessly on her mind. And quite frankly, Brooklyn was becoming fed up with herself. Jason didn't deserve to give her so much and yet consistently watch her deny him of something so beautiful, so natural. Or so she heard. "I'm so sorry, Jason," she began.

"I don't know how to explain this … but I really am sorry," she pleaded, not really knowing if her pleas were for him or for herself.

He shortened the distance between them. "Shhh, sweetheart." He hugged her, which was meant to comfort Brook but really just made her feel even more childlike than she already was. "You don't have to apologize. When you're ready, then I'm ready."

She pulled out of his embrace. "I know you must think I'm crazy by now. I swear I'm not."

"I don't think you're crazy. I get it. You want to take things slow. I'm fine with that."

Brooklyn couldn't tell if he was saying that because he truly felt that way because it was what he thought she wanted to hear. Either way, this situation wasn't okay with here. She was so over feeling inadequate. It was a different story when she was alone and no one else knew she was crazy, but standing having this conversation with Jason disgusted her. She could only imagine what she looked like in his eyes. Probably an insane woman with way too many mental problems for even a trained psychologist to sift through. She imagined that when he looked into her eyes he saw all her insecurities and weaknesses. But what she wanted him to see wasn't the person that she obviously was but the person she so badly wanted to be. Fun. Able to love. Passionate. *Normal.* "I'm tired, Jason. I think you should leave," she told him.

Jason sighed. "It's no big deal, Brook. I'm not trippin'."

"Jason, seriously. I really am tired." She didn't want to discuss this anymore.

Jason said, "Talk to me, Brooklyn. You need to tell me what's going on. I've been patient and careful not to overstep my boundaries, but I can't take this anymore. You're so secretive about everything. It's like pulling teeth trying to get you to have a meaningful conversation with me." He paced the carpeted floor. "I can't keep doing this with you, Brook."

"If you don't want to be here, than leave, Jason! Nobody's making you stay," she yelled at him out of frustration. What happened to everything he was saying before, about always being there for her? It must've all been bull.

"If you want me to leave then I don't know what to tell you, because I'm not going anywhere until you talk to me." He took his sneakers off for good measure and sat on the couch.

Brooklyn rolled her eyes. This was one time that Jason's persistence got under her skin.

"I need to take a shower. I'll be back in a few minutes." She didn't wait for his rebuttal, just ran up the stairs, taking them two at a time, until she was safely in her room with the door locked. She stripped off her jeans and shirt, pinned her hair up, and made her way into her bathroom. The plan was to take a longer-than-usual shower, maybe twenty or twenty-five minutes. She just knew Jason would catch her drift and leave, assuming that she had no intention of returning.

Brooklyn made it a thirty-minute shower, just to be safe. *This is so pitiful,* she thought as she watched the sudsy water roll down her legs and into the drain. After a few minutes of mindless thoughts, she felt the pain in her jaw of self-inflicted tears, but she successfully shook it away. More than she hated not being able to be with Jason, she hated feeling sorry for herself. Brooklyn didn't know how she'd let things get so bad or why she couldn't reverse the damage, but for some reason it controlled her, immobilized her. Like a caged animal, she felt trapped—not in a box but in her own thoughts, fears, and doubts.

She took her time drying off and moisturizing her body before dressing in a tank top and cheerleader shorts. She quietly opened her bedroom door and walked on her tiptoes to the banister, where she leaned over to see if Jason was still there. Brooklyn mouthed a silent curse. There he was, sitting on her couch reading one of her *Essence* magazines as if he had all the time in the world. Clearly out of options, Brooklyn made her way to the living room. "You're still here?" she asked casually.

Jason didn't bother to look up from the article he was reading. "I'm not rude like you. I wouldn't leave without saying good-bye."

"Oh, so I'm rude now?" She made sure to keep her distance by sitting on the recliner adjacent to him.

"Yes. You stayed up there that long because you didn't want to face what was down here waiting for you, even though you knew it was me waiting. That's rude. Don't you think?"

Brooklyn didn't mean to hurt Jason, but she knew that's what her selfish action had done. It was the way his lips curled that told her she'd gone too far. "I apologize for that. But I don't want to deal with this tonight, or any night for that matter."

Jason laid the magazine on the table. "Ideally, I would like it if you would tell me something. Let me in a little. But I know you, and I know you won't. So I'm just going to dig here."

Brook tossed a throw cover over her body and snuggled in it.

"Are you a virgin, Brooklyn?"

"No."

The look of relief on his face didn't go unnoticed.

"Has it been a long time?"

She cleared her throat and said softly, "I suppose it has been." Brook could sense that this conversation was heading in a dangerous direction, but she was out of excuses as to why she wouldn't talk. Her last response had slipped out before she had a chance to lie. And even though she wanted to, she knew that lying was the sin that had put her in the position she was in now.

He asked, "Can you tell me exactly how long?"

She waited a few seconds before telling him about her high school boyfriend. She decided to leave out the part about making a complete fool of herself time and time again. She also told him that before he came along she didn't do much dating.

"Did you enjoy it?"

"What?" His question honestly threw her for a loop. It was so simple, yet for her so complex.

"I mean, do you enjoy sex? Is sex something that you like? Something that you crave?"

That was the first time Brook had ever been asked to think about sex as an enjoyable act. She recognized what it meant to the world, but never had she internalized how she felt about sex. She took a few moments to think but couldn't grab hold of her own opinion. "Honestly, if I told you yes, then I might be lying, and if I said no, that too could be a lie."

Even though this was the most she'd ever shared with anyone and Jason was making her feel comfortable, it was still hard for her to get the words out. They'd been locked inside of her for so long. Brook was afraid that if she opened that door, she might not ever be able to close it again. And she needed to be able to close it for her own sanity.

Ancient thoughts began to flow through her head, and that's when silent tears began to form in her eyes and slowly make their way down her face. She sat frozen as the tears dripped from her chin and into her lap.

She felt the stinging sensation in her eyes, so she blinked over and over for relief. Her mind raced. Past her college graduation, her sixteen birthday, the seventh-grade science fair that she placed first in, and the time she had to have her tonsils removed at the age of nine. She began to remember everything. Her body began to shake, and her cries became loud.

Jason said fearfully across the room, "Baby, what's wrong? Brook?" She didn't respond, just kept crying more and more loudly. Jason looked around the room, spotted her cell phone on the table they'd been playing cards on, and grabbed it. "Who should I call? One of your sisters?"

That's when she screamed, "No! No! No!"

Jason ran back to her side, dropping the phone en route.

Through her heavy cries, she was able to say, "I ... don't ... want ... them to ... know about this."

He pushed the table aside and bent down to his knees. Jason placed his hands on the arms of the chair she sat in. "What don't you want them to know, Brook? Can you tell me?"

She pulled the cover over her face and tried to control her emotional display. The tears subsided, but she couldn't manage the shaking. "I begged him to stop! I did, over and over. I promise I did."

"Who, Brook? Who did you beg?"

"But he wouldn't stop."

"Who?"

"My hands were too small to get him off of me, but I tried, I really tried."

"Who, Brook?" Jason yelled in anger, causing her to jump a little. "Who?" He repeated, whispering now.

She used the back of her hands to wipe her now red and swollen eyes. She inhaled, exhaled, and repeated. "I was six years old. My family went to a free clinic because my mother was sick and we didn't have insurance. She told us to sit in the waiting room until she came back, but I had to use the bathroom. I tried to hold it but I couldn't, so I walked to the restroom. I didn't know he was following me."

"What did he do to you, Brook? Tell me what this man did to you."

She felt the tears again, "He ... he ... molested me. I was six years old, and he didn't care. I cried for my mother and my sisters. The man laughed at when I started screaming for my daddy. 'You don't have a daddy, little girl,' he said. 'Now shut up.' So I just laid there because he said if I stopped crying it wouldn't hurt as much."

"No, no, no," Jason cried out, throwing aimless punches in the air. He pulled her into his arms and held her as tight as he could as she cried out her pains. "I'm so sorry this happened to you."

"I need you to go get my inhaler out of the drawer in the kitchen," she told him, holding her chest.

Jason reluctantly left her for a second and returned with the inhaler in hand. He watched as she pumped the medicine into her lungs and began to breathe easier. For hours he held her as she cried, and he listened whenever she offered more information, though it was minimal. And that's what Brook needed. After all these years of keeping that secret locked within her, she felt relief in letting it go. She had no idea why or how it happened, but the lightness she felt in her heart and head was soothing in an unfamiliar manner.

"Please don't tell anyone about this."

He bent his head to kiss her forehead. "Am I the only person who knows?"

She nodded. After that dreadful day she never felt the same again. Brooklyn never told her mother or sisters anything about what happened in that bathroom. Instead, she focused all her energy on convincing herself that maybe it was all just a dream and never actually happened. For years her strategy of avoiding men altogether and keeping a low profile had aided her efforts. Even at the young age of six, she knew that what happened wasn't normal, so she felt ashamed of it all. Once, a few years ago, she had tried telling Leila, but the words just didn't seem to come out. So, instead, she repressed the memories in hopes that one day they would no longer haunt her day and night. "Promise me, Jason."

"I promise."

Brooklyn took in the fresh air as she waited at Jason's front door, realizing that if she wanted to make a run for it, now would be the time.

"You made it." Jason greeted her with a hug after opening his door and taking the pie out her hands. "Come in. My parents are waiting for you." He took her hand in his. "Are you okay?"

Jason had been asking her that same question every hour for the past couple of days. Brooklyn knew he meant well, but she didn't want him treating her like she needed round-the-clock attention. "Yeah, I'm fine." She smiled.

Lunch went a lot smoother than she could have imagined. Jason's mother was kind and sweet toward Brooklyn and seemed genuinely interested in her writing. His father was nice too. He listened more than he talked but still managed to appear involved. And Jason. Brooklyn had never seen him so happy before. It was obvious that he needed his parents' approval on the decisions he made in life, and that included who he decided to spend his time with. Brook admired the dynamic among the three, the closeness and respect they displayed for one another. The afternoon flew by, and when Jason's mother invited Brook to a girl's lunch in the near future, she gladly accepted. Things were beginning to look up for her. Brook was finally entertaining the thought that for once, maybe, good things would be in the cards for her. No more worrying all the time, and the constant feelings she had about being inadequate could fade into the background of contentment.

Chapter Nineteen

Sometimes the cause is the cure. —Wanda

"YOU CAN CALL ME WHEN *you need me. Until than you won't be seeing or hearing from me.*"

Those were the last words Raven heard from Sean. True to his declaration, she hadn't seen him in weeks. Two weeks and five days, to be exact. He hadn't called her, and of course Raven wasn't going to be the one who gave in first. At least that's what she kept telling herself whenever she had the urge to call her husband. Which was almost every day. Mentally, she missed having someone to talk to about anything and everything. Physically, not being able to connect with him on an intimate level was beginning to stress her out. And emotionally, Raven thought she was falling apart. Everything in her world seemed complex. Even simple, routine actions like putting her boys to bed became exhausting.

Raven felt herself changing. She was always tired and just plain unhappy. And Sean was to blame for all of this. His selfish ways, she thought, had caused her life to change, and he had the audacity to call his actions "teaching her a lesson." That's what pissed her off the most. *I haven't done anything wrong*, she told herself. *Why am I the one suffering?*

Raven had decided that Sean was being childish in his vindictive ways. Last weekend he had sent his brother to come get the boys for their Saturday trip to the aquarium. Raven was in the kitchen packing lunch boxes when she heard the front door slam followed by the laughs and cheers of her boys.

"Sean," she called out.

Tristan ran into the kitchen. "Mummy, Uncle Eric's here."

Raven picked up her son and placed him on her hip. She walked out the kitchen and came face to face with her brother-in-law. She knew what was going on. "Eric." She kissed his cheek. "How are you?"

"Good, Raye." They embraced. As if he had read her mind, he added, "Sean was running a little late, so he asked me to come get the boys, but he'll be the one taking them out today."

Raven told her sons to run upstairs to make sure they had everything they needed. She waited until she could no longer hear their voices before she said, "Sean has you doing his dirty work, huh?" She motioned for Eric to follow her back into the kitchen. "That man is a trip."

Eric leaned on the countertop. "How's Brooklyn doing? She still looking fine?"

"Why is he doing this, Eric? And don't tell me that you don't know anything, because you know I'm not stupid."

"He's mad."

"Mad? Mad at what? I'm the one who should be mad."

"True. He messed up and he knows that, but you have to admit you might be taking this separation thing a little too far, Raye."

She couldn't believe what she was hearing. There was no way in hell any sane person could look at this situation and make her out to be the bad guy. Anger began to boil within her. She had always liked Eric. He was a good man, and her sons loved him, but he was two seconds away from getting slapped.

"I'm not going to admit a lie, Eric, and neither should you," she said acidly. "I'll tell you one thing: I'm not about to play these games with him. All I asked for was a little space, and he wants to go and make a production of it." Raven placed a few juice boxes in the boxes and shut them. She heard her sons stomping down the stairs. "I love you, Eric, but Sean needs to be the one who drops our sons back off." She handed him the two Spider-Man lunch boxes and briskly moved past him, not allowing him to respond. Raven kissed her boys and walked into her study.

It made Raven cringe when Sean still had the nerve to have Eric drop the boys off. She had to give it to him, Sean was sticking it out. But if he thought she would call him begging, he had another think coming. Raven didn't want to, but she could play this game better than most.

It was Friday afternoon. Raven's secretary had just reminded her that the annual school board meeting would take place that night. Things were so hectic at home that she'd completely forgotten. She needed someone to watch her sons. Raven called Leila. "I need you to watch the boys tonight. Can you do it?"

"You know I would love to have my nephews but I have physical therapy. It's my last session before they let me take this sling off my arm."

"All right. Good luck."

She called Brooklyn next but only got her voice mail. Raven knew that when Brook was writing she usually turned her phone off, so she didn't bother texting her. Raven had twenty minutes to pick up the boys from day care and be back at school, and she still didn't have any idea what she would do with the boys. This was something she never had to worry about when Sean was around.

She pulled into her driveway with her cell phone attached to her ear. "Raven," she answered.

"Yo, Raye." It was Trevor. "Is Leila with you by any chance?"

"No."

"Damn."

"She's at physical therapy. Try her on her cell in about an hour."

"Okay, thanks. How you been?"

"Tired."

"You sound out of breath. Are you running?"

"No. I'm trying to find somebody to watch the boys for a few hours because I have to go back to work."

"I wish I could do it but I'm working tonight also."

"Thanks anyway, Trevor. I hope we still see you from time to time."

"Me too Raye. Bye."

Raven was unstrapping a booster seat when she saw headlights approaching her car. She opened her door and stuck her head out. It was Eric. Again. He jogged toward her holding a video game. "Josiah left this in my car. I thought I'd bring it by on my way home."

Raven took the game. Josiah had been looking for it all week. She was actually glad that it had "mysteriously disappeared," as Josiah had put it. He was too attached to the thing.

"Thanks, Eric."

"No problem." He pointed to the other booster seat. "Need some help?"

"Please."

Together, they got the boys into the house and out of their coats and shoes. Raven was now running five minutes late. "Do you think you could stay here with the boys for a few hours? I have a meeting to get to, and my sisters can't babysit."

Eric looked pensively. It was clear he was torn. But in the end he said, "Of course."

Raven yawned as she stuck her key in the front door. "Exhaustion" was too soft a word to describe how she was feeling. She walked into her living room, kicked off her shoes, and walked past the man sitting on her couch.

"You're going to act like I'm not here?" he said.

She didn't respond, just began checking the rooms on the first floor.

"Raye, I'm talking to you."

She turned to face him. "Ahh... really? Because I thought you told me that unless I called you, I wouldn't being seeing or hearing from you," she said with thick mockery. "Yet here you are. In the flesh."

"You had my brother over here watching my sons when you knew I could have done it. Why didn't you call me?"

He was mad, but Raven didn't care. "Because I didn't need you," she reiterated. "Plus, how was I suppose to know that you were available? I haven't heard from you in weeks."

"I know taking care of this family alone is hard on you, Raven. You can pretend if you want, but we both know being a single parent isn't a walk in the park."

And those were the words that she hoped Sean would never say but they were also the source of his tactics. He thought that if he stayed away she would see how much he did to make their family function. Instead, Raven was beginning to see that with him things were easier, but without him she could still survive. That hadn't always been clear to her. "I'm looking at you now, Sean. I see my husband, but I don't understand you anymore."

"Don't do this, Raye. Don't throw away everything we have over one mistake," he pleaded.

There were no tears, but she could tell that Sean was reaching his breaking point. It was killing her to see him this way—the red in his eyes, the heaving of his chest. He was her husband. A good, attentive one who had never intentionally tried to hurt her.

But Raven knew that something was missing from what they shared, and the part of her that had tried ignoring it for years wasn't so small anymore. She wanted to tell him how she felt, to lay it all out hoping that maybe he felt the same way. But those eyes told her something different. Nothing had changed with him. Sean was still the same man she fell in love with and agreed to marry. Sean just wanted to be a family again, and after everything he'd done for her, didn't he deserve for Raven to be a good wife? The man had chosen her to be his wife, and he had no intentions of ever leaving her alone. This Raven was sure of.

Raven couldn't help but think about what she wanted. Five years ago it was this, but she wasn't sure anymore. She wanted a husband and children and to be happy, and even though she'd always equated the three, she felt the latter slipping away from her grip.

"Sean." She walked toward him, still contemplating.

He reached out and pulled her into his embrace. She rested her head on his chest, feeling his heartbeat. And she felt it. Security.

"I can't let you go," he said, barely above a whisper. He held her closer. "You mean the world to me."

She decided. Maybe two out of three wasn't that bad. "I'm tired. Let's go to bed."

A few days later, Sean had moved back into the house, and things returned to usual. They ate dinner as a family, both put the boys to bed, and stayed up taking care of the household chores together. Their intimate relationship even resumed. Raven had missed that, and by the measure of Sean's response to her body, he'd missed it also. Things felt nice. No more drama. Limited confusion. Just the way Raven liked it.

But it was different now. She found that she had to force herself to feel good about this. The bubbly feeling that she used to get every time she pulled into the driveway was replaced by an annoying anxiety, and she hated herself for feeling this way. Everything she'd ever asked for, she had. Who was she not to be satisfied? She prayed to God that no one had noticed the change in her because she really was trying hard to disguise it. Raven always smiled and laughed a lot whenever someone was around. And when she found herself giving in to her own conscience, she did everything in her power to distract herself. This effort alone was taxing.

Raven was relieved when her sister Brooklyn called her. *A welcome distraction.*

"Who is this?"

She expected to hear Brook's smart mouth, but instead it was Leila's loud laughter on the other end. "I said the same thing when she called me."

"Whatever. You two are so silly," Brook said. "Is it okay that I'm calling you guys at work?"

"Yeah. I'm just happy to hear your voice."

Leila agreed. "What's up? I feel like we haven't seen each other in forever."

"I've been so busy with work, the boys, and Sean," Raven said. "I need a break."

"Well, I'm just now getting back to work. I've had my break," Leila said.

Brook said, "I want you guys to meet Jason."

"It's about damn time," Leila chimed in. "You've had him all cooped up. He probably thinks we're crazy or something the way you've been dodging us."

"You are crazy, Leila, but he doesn't know that yet. Can we all do dinner?"

"When?" Raven asked.

"Tomorrow night."

"Cool," Raven replied. "Leila, did you ever call Trevor back?"

"Don't start with me, Raven. I was having a good day."

"I'm just saying, the man called my phone looking for you. It must've been important."

"When did all of this happen? You told me you hadn't spoken to him since the breakup," Brooklyn asked.

"I haven't."

"Then what's going on? Are you guys getting back together?"

"Oh, Lord, here she goes," Raven mocked. "He just called Brook, that's all."

"Can we change the subject, please?" Leila asked. "Things working out with you and Sean?"

"Yup."

"That sounds convincing," Brook said sarcastically. "Y'all are a mess."

"Oh, shit," Leila bellowed. "Look at little baby Brooklyn. She thinks she has all the answers just because she got herself a man now. What's this, relationship number one?"

"It's two," Brook snapped back. "And don't be jealous, Leila, it's not cute on you."

"Have you had sex with him yet?"

"Mind your business."

"That's what I thought. I'm warning you, Brook. Don't get to comfortable with this man. Watch your back. Right, Raven?"

"Just make sure you're happy, baby sis."

"I am happy."

"Make sure." Raven used the tone their mother used whenever she wanted to drive a point home. It was something that seemed to come naturally with motherhood. "You hear me?"

"Yes."

"Tomorrow night it is, ladies. I have to get back to work now. Love you, Brook. And Leila, try not to get shot today."

Now it was Brook's and Raven's turn to laugh.

Chapter Twenty

Let it go, girl. —Wanda

"No, I won't be taking any patients for the rest of the month," Leila said to her receptionist after handing over her appointment book. "I have too much paperwork to catch up on."

Which was half true. She did have a pile of manila folders stacked on her desk, but she could breeze through those in a full day if she skipped lunch. The whole truth was that Leila didn't think she could handle seeing patients right now. The whole shooting incident kept running through her mind. She couldn't get Clark's words out of her head. Even though she was convinced the man needed psychiatric help, she wasn't blind to the fact that he was convinced that Leila wanted to ruin his marriage and his life. And that she just couldn't understand.

And then there was Trevor and his opinions about how her cold-blooded personality didn't correlate with her profession. She was starting to analyze every negative thing that people had said about her. Before, Leila had just internalized it as ignorance, but that didn't suffice any longer. Leila thought highly of herself and how she carried out her duties as a relationship counselor. Sure, she wasn't naive enough to believe that she held all the answers, but she was well-educated and qualified to do this job.

But still, having one of her patients carry around so much disdain for her that he decided to take her out by murdering her was a lot to bear.

Clark thought she was evil. Trevor was under the impression that her heart was made of steel. And for the first time in years, Leila was unsure of herself. Every time she looked in the mirror she saw something different. It might have been a self-fulfilling prophecy, but she wasn't admiring herself so much these days. The previous night she had watched an episode of *Oprah* that she had saved on the TiVo. The guest lineup included people who'd survived near-death experiences discussing how they maneuvered through society now that they had a "new lease on life." People were talking about how now, they gave more of themselves to the community and took more risks. One lady learned how to fly a plane at the age of sixty because it was her childhood dream. Leila listened to their stories, all the while wondering how come she didn't have an "Ah-ha" moment after her near-death experience. Why hadn't she felt changed and renewed or ready to conquer her dreams or fears? All she had felt was anger, and then after a while, as with all mishaps in her life, she had dismissed it and kept moving. In college she had studied Harlow's attachment theory. It argued that children needed to develop healthy relationships with at least one of their parents or caregivers in order for social and emotional development to occur. Infants tend to find comfort in people who respond to their needs. Once a bond is secure, the child looks to that relationship for security. Any form of separation that breaks this bond may cause the child to form unhealthy attachment patterns in ongoing relationships.

In her early years of practice, Leila had memorized this theory inside and out, and she'd even referred to it while helping numerous clients. But it wasn't until now that she thought about how it could relate to her own life. As a child she was extremely close to her mother. Leila adored her so much, and she liked to think that she was her mother's favorite child. When her mother died, Leila was heartbroken. To this day she would give anything up to have her mother back. But it didn't take long for her to realize that there was absolutely nothing she could do about it. There was no amount of therapy, money, love, or prayer that would bring her mother back. Leila would have to learn how to live without the only constant she'd ever known. It was the hardest thing she had ever had to force herself to do, living the same life but changing everything it represented. When she finally mastered the skill of coping with death, Leila discovered that she didn't need anyone else. If she couldn't have her mother, then she would pass on the prospect of leaning on someone else for that feeling. And for years that was how she had maneuvered through society.

This needs to stop, Leila thought, *right here and now. Bitter.* That had been the word Trevor used, and now she was beginning to see why. It was hard for Leila to live her life the way she did. She was always thinking and cautious about every little thing she couldn't control. But it was even harder for her to fathom changing. That would mean letting go, taking risks, and allowing other people into her mental space. Just the thought of that was enough to make her heartbeat increase. *Relax, Leila. You can do this*, she told herself in semi-confidence.

But where would she start? How could she pioneer this new Leila? It was uncharted territory, but she was determined.

Leila told herself that she would seize the first opportunity that emerged for her to try to be more open-minded and passionate. No more cynical pessimism. From now on she would be open, adventurous, and accepting.

At least, that was the plan.

Chapter Twenty-One

JASON CHECKED HIS REFLECTION ONE last time in his rearview mirror. Tonight was extremely important, and the butterflies in his stomach were a constant reminder. He'd spent almost an hour getting ready and still wasn't absolutely satisfied with his attire. He couldn't decide on the black dress shirt or gray sweater, so before he left his apartment he called Brooklyn.

"Which one do you think I should wear?"

He heard her familiar giggle. "Are you serious right now?"

"Yes. Now please, which one?"

"I'd go with the black dress shirt under the gray sweater. That'll be hot."

He held up the combination over his chest and smiled. He liked it. "Thanks, babe. I'm on my way."

Now Jason was parked outside of Brook's house. He could see though her windows the silhouettes of three women walking around, engaging in conversation. He knew which one was Brook by the way she walked, and the other two had to be her sisters. Brook had made such an effort with his family; Jason wanted to do the same for her. Even though she was extremely private, Jason had managed to get a few stories here and there out of her about her childhood, and all of them included her infamous older sisters.

From the corner of his eye Jason saw someone peering through the window. It was Brooklyn. She was waving him in. He walked up to the door that flew open before he could knock. Brook greeted him with a kiss. "Don't be nervous," she whispered in his ear. She took his hand and led him further into her home.

Before him stood two beautiful women who wore welcoming smiles on their faces. It was weird; Jason had expected them to look like Brooklyn, but they each had very distinct features.

"These are my sisters." Brook held out her hand.

Jason greeted the first sister with a handshake. "Nice to meet you."

"Nice to meet you as well, Jason. I'm Raven Thompson."

"She's the oldest," Brook chimed in.

Jason could sense that. Raven had a motherly aura about her. He immediately felt warm in her presence. His eyes shifted to the other woman. She was a bit more standoffish. Jason got the feeling that she was sizing him up. The smile on her face morphed into a small grin.

He extended his hand. "Jason Washington Junior." He didn't know why he had spilled his whole name, but she looked like the type of person who required it.

Her smile returned, this time accompanied by the rising of her eyebrows. "Dr. Leila Cartel." She gave him a hug, which threw Jason off. And by the look on Brook and Raven's faces, it threw them off as well. "We've heard a lot about you, Jason."

"Did you say Raven Thompson and Leila Cartel?" Jason asked in a state of confusion. *Cartel? That's Brandice's name, but Raven and Leila? Why do I know those names?*

Leila nodded. "Raven's married."

"Oh, okay," he said. Jason couldn't pinpoint it, but something wasn't right. He thought back to all the conversations he'd had with Brooklyn, but he couldn't recall one in which she had actually mentioned the names of her sisters.

"What's wrong?" Jason heard Brook ask him. He was so far in his thoughts that he'd forgotten where he was or what was happening

"Nothing, I'm fine." He noticed that her sisters were busy chatting in the kitchen, probably about him. He took Brook to the side. "Is your last name Cartel also?" he asked, trying not to call attention to the beads of sweat that were forming under his hairline.

"Yes. But I don't use it."

"Why not?"

"Because." He watched her give him a funny look. "Are you sure you're okay? You're definitely acting weird."

"I'm fine," he told her again. "But why don't you use that last name?"

She shrugged. "I just don't."

And just like always, that was all she offered. Jason cursed under his breath. The mysterious Brook was usually sexy as all hell, but tonight it annoyed him beyond measure. He needed her to be straightforward with him and soon. But he wouldn't pressure her now. Not in front of her sisters. Jason had to get it together.

Dinner was interesting. Just as Brook had warned, he was absolutely amused by her sisters. They were extremely opinionated and quick with their wits. Dinner discussion ranged from sports to politics, and these women had something to say about it all. Where Raven was the motherly figure of the trio, Leila was undoubtedly the sister with all the answers. Jason was so used to being around Brook alone that he was surprised at her relationship with her sisters. With him she was independent and rambunctious, but around them she took on the baby sister role, allowing her older sisters to take care of her. It was a side of Brook he hadn't known existed. What a surprise.

"They love you," Brooklyn shouted, slamming the door behind her.

Dinner was over. Jason had decided that washing the dishes was a safe escape from the sisters, who'd retreated to the front porch. Jason rinsed the last plate and laid it out to dry. "And how would you know that?"

"We just had a twenty-minute conversation about you outside." Brook sat at the table. "Leila even said you were cute."

Jason feigned shock. "I must be a pretty good catch than."

"We seem to think so." She winked.

Jason scanned the bottom level of her house so that Brook could see him do it. When he noticed the questioning look on her face, he asked, "Why don't you have pictures of Raven and Leila around here?"

"I do," she replied, pointing to the ceiling. "Upstairs."

Jason had never been upstairs. That was yet another part of Brooklyn's life that she kept private.

He couldn't pretend any longer. Jason had put the pieces of the puzzle together as soon as he heard the name Cartel come out of Leila's mouth. *Ain't this some shit*, Jason thought. He knew the information he held had the power to do much damage. The woman he'd fallen in love with was the same woman his best friend had been searching for over the last two months. He knew how important meeting her sisters was to Brandice, but if she only knew what it would mean to them. Tonight Jason had witnessed three women who shared a past and knew each other so well they finished each other's sentences and grabbed food off each other's plates. Brandice would never be "one of them." Jason knew that. He also knew that Brandice didn't need or deserve to be shut down by her own flesh and blood, no matter the degree of separation.

And then there was Brooklyn, the woman who had his heart deep within her possession. Jason still found it hard to believe she had survived so many heartaches and still had such a beautiful spirit. He would never want to see her hurt again. He was beginning to feel it was his responsibility to make her happy. A sharp pain ran through his chest because he knew Brandice's appearance would disrupt that.

He had to find a way to stop this. Daniel Cartel was a man of many secrets, and now Jason knew why. Too many people were liable to get hurt if his secrets came out. Jason decided the Cartel women would be better off if things stayed the way they were. And he would do whatever it took to keep it that way.

Chapter Twenty-Two

BRANDICE WAS NO FOOL, AND she resented the fact that Trevor took her for one. She might be young, guarded, and a bit clumsy, but a fool she was not. The look in Trevor's eyes when he made her promise to keep their secret was all the proof she needed to confirm her gut feeling that he would try to sabotage her reunion with her sisters. That was the part she didn't get. Why would Trevor want to do that? Brandice contemplated numerous scenarios, but none of them justified what she considered to be inexcusable behavior on Trevor's part.

After leaving the restaurant and Trevor that day, Brandice drove straight home and powered up her laptop. After a few spelling errors, she was able to successfully Google Leila Cartel. Brandice found Leila's bio on her website. It wasn't lengthy and barely offered any personal information, but that didn't bother Brandice because all she needed was to see the huge picture of her beautiful sister that accompanied the bio. Her smile, Brandice decided, was mesmerizing. She digitally enlarged that photo, trying to find similarities in their features, and was disappointed that there were very few if any. Where Leila was brown, Brandice was barely tanned; Leila had a wider nose where Brandice's was longer. It was disappointing, but she found joy in one thing, the Cartel ears. Leila's chocolate ears were deeply folded around the edges with unattached lobes. Brandice couldn't explain the feeling in her chest, but she knew it had everything to do with the fact that she had an image of a sister that shared the same father as her. She knew she was one step closer to making her father's dying wish come true, and that truly excited her.

After cementing the photo of Leila to her memory, Brandice closed the computer and made a decision with little thought. She texted Junior.

BRANDICE: *I need to talk to you about something.*

JUNIOR: *I need to talk to you too. I'm about to leave Brook's and I'm on my way.*

Brandice didn't have enough time to come up with a proper approach for her conversation with Junior before he was knocking on her door.

"Come in," she said. "It seems like I haven't seen you in ages."

He kissed her forehead and headed for the living room. She followed.

"What's up, Ice? You seemed anxious in your text."

"Oh, yeah. I just need to talk to you about my father, but I didn't mean to take you from Brooklyn. How are things going with the two of you?"

Brandice watched Junior's demeanor change as he fidgeted. "She's good. What about your dad?"

"Damn, Junior, that's all you have to say? She's good? Why are you acting secretive?"

"I'm not. I just want to hear what you have to tell me about your father because I know that's why you wanted to talk."

Junior was in a mood that Brandice couldn't ignore. Part of her wanted to dig deeper and find out what was bothering him, but it wasn't as large as the part of her that needed to get to the point of his visit.

"I think I might have a lead on locating my sisters." Brandice watched as Junior's eyes lit up. "In fact, I'm quite sure of it."

"What do you mean you have a lead? When did all this happen?"

Brandice searched his face for an explanation. His tone disturbed her, as did the overwhelming look of fear on his face. "It happened a couple of days ago. The private detective I hired was able to find a few promising leads." The lie just slipped out. She didn't mean to, but telling Junior that she'd struck up a friendship with her sister's boyfriend and together they'd put the pieces of the story together didn't seem like information she needed to share, especially since she could tell Junior was hiding his own information.

"In fact," Brandice said, moving from the couch where she sat beside Junior to the opposite side of the room, "I was able to see a photo of my sister, Leila, and I have her address. She's a marriage counselor right here in the city. Oh yeah, and the other child my father had, you know, the one he didn't get to meet? Well it turns out that it was a girl, and her name is—"

Junior sprang from the couch, causing her to stop midsentence "Oh my God! Brandice, you know?" He crossed the room to where she stood. "You knew all this time that Brooklyn was your sister and you didn't think to tell me?"

"What? I just found out a few days ago. I'm not the one in the wrong here, Jason. I can't believe you knew how badly I wanted to find my sisters and here you knew where they were and didn't tell me." She was livid.

"Ice, I just figured it out too, and I didn't know what to do. This thing is a lot more difficult than you think."

Brandice could tell by the bags under his eyes that her best friend hadn't slept in days. He had a heavy heart, and it was weighing him down. She didn't want to add to his stress, but it was apparent that she would.

Jason told her how and when he'd made the discovery. Brandice listened as he spoke about meeting Leila and Raven, all the while envious of the picture of the four of them eating dinner and laughing together. It was the scenario she'd envisioned for the four of *them*.

"I get that you really care for Brook, Junior, but I can't pretend I don't exist just because they don't know about me yet."

"It's more than that, Ice. You don't know everything that those women have been through. They didn't grow up like we did. I could tell you some stories that would make you cringe."

She'd heard enough. Brandice resented hearing that. "My father died, Junior. He's gone, and that's not something I can ever change. Maybe I didn't grow up like they did and maybe we have different journeys, but I wouldn't call losing your father to a stroke a walk in the park!"

"I didn't mean it like that, Ice. I just think you should know that this could be very painful for both you and them. Think about it. Who would that benefit?"

"Me, Jason! This is what my father asked me to do, so that's what's going to happen. But it is clear to me that you don't give a damn about what I need right now. You're supposed to be on my side, not your little girlfriend's."

Jason grabbed her arm and pulled her into him. "I've always cared about you, and having Brooklyn in my life doesn't change that. It just means now I care about two women." He pulled her back to the coach. They sat in silence for more than twenty minutes, both supporting their heads with both hands, before Jason continued. "I'm begging you, Ice, please don't do this. Not yet, not without more thought."

The desperation in his voice was clear; there was a pleading look in his eyes. Brandice took it all in. Jason was the best friend she'd ever had, and he'd made more sacrifices for her than she could count. All he was asking her to do was to consider more factors than what she could see with her own vision. That wasn't too much to ask, considering he was more acquainted with her sisters than she was. Brandice was aware of all this, but it meant very little. She'd sacrificed enough already.

"I'm sorry, but I have to do this for my father."

"You're making a huge mistake, Ice."

"Maybe I am, but I couldn't live with myself if I didn't at least try."

Without a word, Jason stood, gave Brandice a hug, and left her home. She watched from the living room window as he got into his car and sat there for a few minutes before starting the engine and driving off. Brandice felt agony about hurting him as she had, but in her heart she knew that he had to see that delivering her father's message to his daughters was vital in her grieving process.

Brandice grabbed her phone, dialed, and waited for an answer. "Hey, Trevor. Junior knows everything, and before you start getting pissed at me, I didn't tell him. He figured it out. Do you think I can talk to Leila today?"

"Today? Probably not. She's not returning my phone calls."

"Well, I'm not sure, but Junior might tell Brooklyn if we don't get to Leila first, so you might want to try harder."

"Dammit, Brandice. Let me see what I can do. I'll call you back."

"I know how to get in contact with her, Trevor. I found her information online." Brandice wanted him to know that she wasn't as oblivious as he might have thought. She wanted to talk to Leila, right now. "Jamaica Plain, right?"

"Be outside your house. I'm on my way."

Chapter Twenty-Three

SEAN STOOD BEHIND HIS DESK, preparing to head home a little earlier than usual. He had no work left to do. He'd even gotten a head start on the work he had delegated for later in the week. That was after he'd sat in silence playing game after game of computer solitaire. Sean had wanted to go home hours ago, before the sun had gone down, but something had stopped him every time he attempted to make his way out the door. Sean felt sick to his stomach because as much as he tried to ignore the truth, it haunted him every minute of every day.

His marriage was in trouble. Sean could sense in the foggy spring air that things were about to change drastically and he wouldn't be able to control it. What pained him the most was knowing that without the opium of love, people changed from willing to heartless, and he knew that Raven was turning into the latter. It was in the way she moved. He could see that she was constantly thinking about life, questioning their marriage and whether it was worth staying in. Raven was good at disguising this. She was lively and still fun to be around. She even made sure to please him when making love, but he knew her. Sean knew that Raven was a pro at hiding her feelings when she wanted to. She held things in until she had made a decision, and then she stated her declaration. Raven would lay all her burdens on the table along with a plan to relieve them, and at that point it was virtually impossible to convince her otherwise.

It wasn't like she was doing it blatantly, but it really didn't matter because he could still see the emptiness in her eyes every time she walked through the front door and plastered that generic smile on her face when she kissed him. It was like it took all of her energy to pretend that she didn't have anything left within her. Seeing his wife that way, so depleted of happiness, almost depressed, made Sean want to throw up because he knew he was the cause.

Weeks had gone by since he'd moved back home. Their normal routine had resumed, and Sean did everything in his power to show his wife that he appreciated her and needed her in his life, but not even making dinner, doing laundry, and showering her with flowers seemed to bring any legitimate emotion out of her. The agony was enough to make Sean contemplate not returning home for a few days. Maybe then Raven would miss him, come to her senses, and show a little appreciation for everything that he did for her and the kids. The longer Sean sat there, thinking, the angrier he grew. He came to the conclusion that Raven didn't have the right to act as she had been. He was a good man, a man whom plenty of women would jump at the opportunity to be with, and his wife was acting like he could be replaced easily. He thought about how many times he'd turned beautiful woman down because he didn't want to hurt his family, about the restraint it took to be the black man that every woman swore didn't exist. Raven would have to be set straight, Sean decided.

Grabbing his coat, he made his way to his office door once again, this time being stopped by the vibration of his phone in his pocket. He reached into the breast pocket of his jacket and flipped the phone open after seeing Trevor's name across the screen.

"What up, bro. How you been?"

"I'm glad you picked up, man. I really need to talk to you."

"What's wrong? Is everything okay?"

"Not really. Where are you? Can I meet you somewhere?"

"I'm downtown at the office."

"Cool, I'm on my way."

Once again, Sean stood behind his desk, this time trying to grasp the words that Trevor had just said to him. But no matter how many times he replayed them in his head, it still sounded like something from a movie and not a part of his life. He asked Trevor to repeat himself twice and still it was hard to believe.

"What are we going to do, man?"

Sean turned around to answer Trevor's question. "You have to bring that girl to see Leila. If you don't, it sounds like she will do it herself. You know Leila. She's gonna ask how the girl found her. Your name will come up, and Leila will trip. We both know forgiveness isn't too high on her priority list."

"I'm on my way to get Brandice right now, but I can't help but wish that I hadn't gotten dragged into all of this. You know, I want to be the person that Leila leans on, not the one that that causes her the pain. I thought I hated their damn father before, you know? Because of him and the way he treated their mother, the only woman I loved doesn't have it in her to love me back. He's already done so much damage, and now even in his death, he finds a way to fuck shit up," Trevor said, throwing his head back.

"I feel you, man. Those Cartel woman are so messed up in the head, we could part the Red Sea and they still would doubt us." Sean released a pitiful laugh.

"You ever think about just walking away from it all?" Trevor asked quietly. "It doesn't have to be this hard. I know for a fact that with other women it isn't."

Sean knew how Trevor felt. He'd been in the same state of mind countless times before when Raven's past was too much for him to handle. On the outside she appeared to be a strong, happy woman who could handle anything that life threw at her, but once he got closer to her, Sean was bombarded with the reality that she was inundated with grief, hatred, and a bunch of other things that stopped her from being the woman she tried to portray to the world. He was the one who had to deal with it, the one who had to convince her that not all men were as evil as her father and that she didn't have anything to worry about when it came to their marriage. Sean dealt with her insecurities as well as he knew how to, even when they caused him to want to walk away time and time again. He was still there, by her side, like the husband he knew she needed him to be, and Sean thought that his actions deserved acknowledgement.

"Yeah, I've thought about it. But I love Raven, and I can't do that. It would destroy her."

"So, you telling Raye?"

"Hell yeah. I learned my lesson about keeping secrets from my wife." Sean walked around the desk and reached his hand out to Trevor. "Let's get out of here and do what we have to do."

Raven was sitting on the couch reviewing what Sean assumed to be school files when he came home.

"How was your day?" he asked, bending to kiss her lips.

She kissed him back. "It was long and stressful. We're getting ready for statewide testing, and we really need to perform well in order to get more funding next year."

Sean sat next to her on the couch. "I'm sure your school will do great. You always do." He tried to comfort her, but it felt unnatural, like anything he said wasn't what she needed to hear. "Are the boys upstairs?"

"Yes, they're playing video games." She went back to her files. "Dinner will be ready in about an hour."

Sean got up, sensing that now wasn't the best time to tell her about her long-lost sister, though he would have to tell her soon. "I'm going to jump in the shower real quick. Do you want to join me?"

Sean watched Raven's eyes dart back and forth from her work to him and then back to her work. He stood patiently, waiting for her response.

"Sure." She closed the folders and stacked them in a neat pile in the middle of the coffee table. "I would love to."

He knew that wasn't true. Raven would much rather finish what she was doing, but because she was trying to be a good wife, he knew she would oblige him. It had been that way since the day they got married. It was pitiful, and Sean knew it, but he loved his wife and would do anything to spend time with her, even if it meant using a little manipulation. So he took his wife's hand and led her to their bedroom.

He didn't want to ruin the good mood Raven was in. They'd taken a long shower, taking turns washing each other and making love. She was smiling. He knew it wasn't real, but at least she was smiling. Sean knew all this would end soon, but it had to be done.

She sat on the bed pulling a shirt over her head. He stood leaning on the dresser across the room, preparing to explain what Trevor had told him hours earlier, but Raven's words stopped his thought process all together.

"I feel dead inside, Sean," she said, not looking at him or even facing his direction. "I think it's us." She turned to face him, leaning her back against the headboard. "I can't explain it. All I know is that I'm not happy and this isn't working."

Sean had thought he wouldn't feel this way, since he'd kind of seen this coming, but the jolt of pain that shot through his chest was as strong as ever.

She'd finally cracked. Her thinking was complete, and he knew that a plan would be the next thing out of her mouth. One that would make her comfortable, never mind how he felt—or anyone else involved.

"Raye, please don't do this to me. I'm willing to do anything you ask of me. Just don't leave me, baby. Please don't leave me." He knew he shouldn't beg. It was so doglike that woman didn't find it attractive, but he was desperate.

"Sean, I don't want to leave you. Believe me, this has been weighing me down for months. You're a good man, and you deserve better than what I give you. It doesn't make sense the way I treat you. I can't figure out why I'm having these feelings, but I can't deny that they're there."

"Is it because of the kiss, Raye? I thought we were past that."

On her knees, she carefully slid to the foot of the bed. "No. It has nothing to do with that." She got off the bed and slowly walked toward him. "Honestly, it's about me, you, the way I feel about us."

"How *do* you feel?" he managed to say through the bulk of air that was trapped in his throat.

She hesitated. "Not good. I'm not happy anymore."

Sean hated how easily her words seemed to flow out her mouth. It was like she didn't feel his pain at all. She said she was hurting too, but he couldn't tell, not by the dryness of her eyes or the steadiness in her voice. It was enough to make him want to put his hands on her. He imagined snatching her up, throwing her across the room, and pounding on her the way she was pounding on his heart right now. He wouldn't stop until she screamed out for mercy, begging him the way she had allowed him to do minutes earlier. Maybe than he would stop, when she looked as lifeless as he felt.

"Are you sure about this, Raven? I'm not going to be here when you come to your senses and figure out that I'm the best thing that ever happened to your dysfunctional life." The words came out before he had a chance to think about them, but even then he continued. "You're so ungrateful it makes me sick. For the past five years I've had to hear you bitch and complain about how hard it is to find a good man or how you can't trust men because you didn't have a damn father. All this bull about how you can't imagine how a person could leave his family after making a commitment and here you are doing the same damn thing. You're a hypocrite, Raven."

She hopped off the bed, charging at him. "You don't mean that, Sean. You're angry, and I get that. You have the right to lash out, but you're going too far right now."

Now he really wanted to strangle her. How dare she try to handle him right now as if he were one of her damn students.

"Fuck you, Raye. You don't get to justify my words. I meant every word I said, and I hope you know that."

Now the tears started to fall from her eyes. Sean felt no remorse. She deserved to feel hurt. What kind of woman was so damn unforgiving, like she was without sin or something. No matter what, they were supposed to stay together. Sean had proven that he was in it for the long run, but as soon as things weren't going her way, Raven was ready to walk. He was in disbelief that she wasn't trying harder.

"I'm so sorry, Sean."

"Whatever." He waved off her apology, tired of hearing her voice and seeing her face. "If you want to leave, then go ahead and leave. I'm tired of you dictating everything. You have two sisters who probably need you more than we do. Go stay with one of them because I'm not leaving." He pushed passed her, flopping his body down on the bed as if to mark his territory.

She looked at him, and Sean knew she saw that he was dead serious about not leaving their house. As far he was concerned, she wasn't moving fast enough.

Her arms crossed, she rolled her eyes. She studied him for a moment before saying, "Fine, I'll leave tonight."

He watched her reach under the bed and retrieve a packed overnight bag. This threw him over the edge. For the first time in his adult life, he truly wanted to call a woman a bitch, but he suppressed the urge. Calling her outside her name wouldn't hurt her enough. She was a tough woman. In order to draw blood he would have to cut her deep, long, and slow.

"Trevor came by the office today because your deadbeat father remarried and had another daughter whom he loved very much. He died recently, and she needs to deliver a message to you and your sisters from him. She's probably on her way to see Leila right now. She seems like a nice girl … hmm."

Sean watched the color in his wife's face change as her body began to shake a little. She was in shock, blindsided, and it was the reaction he wanted. Now, with her mouth open and her heaving chest, she looked as defenseless as he felt. And Sean didn't have to lay one hand on her to bring her there.

"Sip on that." He walked past her and back into their bathroom, closing the door behind him.

Chapter Twenty-Four

Just because it's the truth doesn't mean it's your business. —Wanda

LEILA HAD NO IDEA WHY she picked up the phone. It wasn't the first time Trevor had called her this week or even today. Her plan was to ignore him until she figured out how to make things right between them. She wanted to apologize for whatever she had done to make him feel like she didn't appreciate him in her life. Over the last few weeks, Leila had come to the conclusion that she didn't need Trevor in her life to be happy, but she wanted him there. She was aware that to many people that still might sound selfish and inconsiderate, but Trevor would be touched. She could tell he wanted to see her badly by the urgency in his voice.

"Leila, can I come over?"

"Right now?"

"Yes."

"Ummm... sure."

That was only five minutes ago, and from her apartment she could see him jogging up the stairs and pushing her intercom button now. She let him up. Leila was taken aback by how good he looked. She hadn't seen him in weeks, maybe a month or two—she couldn't remember how much time had passed. She studied his face before stepping aside to let him in.

"Can I get you something to drink?" she offered, sensing that he was a bit uncomfortable being alone with her after so long.

"Yeah, water would be nice." He sat on the couch as she went into the kitchen. "The place looks nice, more spacious. No more cookware lying around everywhere."

"Thank you," she yelled. "Ice?"

"Who?" He asked nervously .

"Ice. In your water?"

"Oh … no thanks."

Leila returned with two glasses of water and sat. She hated the tension that was between them. Trevor seemed to be getting more uncomfortable by the minute, and Leila feared she wouldn't get to say her piece before he bolted out of there.

"Look, Trevor, I'm glad you called. I've been meaning to talk to you about a few things." She said. "I wanted to tell you that … that … I'm sorry for the way I treated you. I know how much you love me, and I wasn't exactly being fair when I didn't take your marriage proposals as seriously as I should've."

"Did I just hear you apologize? Hell must be freezing over right now," Trevor joked. "That's a first."

Leila didn't find the humor in it, but she smiled just to show she could be a good sport. "I'm serious right now. I thought you would be happy."

"Happy about what? Are you saying that you want to marry me now?"

Leila took a deep breath. Trevor wanted more than an apology, but that was all she was prepared to offer. That was all she planned for. A million ways of saying no to his question surfaced to her brain, but she found a way to push them aside. This was her opportunity to try something new, to think about someone other than herself and maybe still feel like her entire life wasn't being run by someone else. For once in her life, she was ready to let go.

"I'm saying that I want to talk about it more. Considering marriage is no longer off the table, because I still love you, Trevor. These past few months have been difficult, and I don't want it to be that way."

"What about all that stuff about me controlling you and not wanting to feel weak? Is that not how you feel anymore?"

She said nothing. This wasn't the response she was expecting. He was supposed to be elated that she was even saying the word "marriage." But instead he was challenging her. How dare he do that? She was mad at him for asking her those questions, but she was more upset at herself for not having an answer.

"You miss me, Leila, and I miss you, but things haven't changed. I'm still the man who loves you wholeheartedly, and you're still the woman who won't allow herself to love me back."

"I do love you, Trevor. Haven't you been listening to anything I've said?" Her eyebrow shot up, her frustration showing itself in her voice. "We can talk about marriage and babies, whatever you want, okay?"

"You're just saying this because you want things to go back to the way they were before. I know you, Leila. I know that's what you're doing."

"I'm not, Trevor," she said, shaking her head. "I'm really serious about this. I love you, and if marriage is something that you want, then I'm willing to consider it."

"You're not just saying that because you want things to go back to the way they were before?"

Leila felt vulnerable, but she didn't mind it that much because it was only the two of them to witness it. She had to do whatever it took to get Trevor back. "No. I love you." She kissed his hand. "I love you." And then his wrist. "I love you. I'll say it as many times as you need to hear it, because it's the truth."

Trevor pulled her into his lap. "I want you to be my wife and have my children, Leila. You mean the world to me. I will never stop loving you or being there for you … always."

She didn't say anything, just looked at him for a few moments and let his words simmer. It was hard. Leila couldn't explain it, but she wanted to allow herself this pleasure of appreciating the moment for what it was and not for the potentially bad scenarios that could come from it.

Feeling liberated, she lowered her head and kissed Trevor, slowly reacquainting him with her mouth. The feeling of having him close to her again made her want to connect more than their mouths. She started to unlatch his belt and take his shirt off at the same time. He maneuvered her back to the couch and positioned his body on top of hers. Leila felt her lower body begin throbbing for the intimacy it'd gone so long without before the ringing of her apartment bell interrupted the flow.

"Keep going. Whoever it is can come back later."

"Baby, no, we need to talk." Trevor tried pulling away from her. "There's something I need to tell you."

"Trevor, the last thing I want to do right now is talk," she said, annoyed at the lack of progression they were making toward the bedroom.

The bell rang again. This time, Leila reluctantly got up and moved to the intercom. "This better be one of my sisters or else somebody is about to get cursed out." She spoke into the mic. "Hello?"

"Hi. Is Trevor there?"

Leila glanced over at Trevor, who was quickly making his way over while trying to fix his clothes. "Who is this?"

The voice came again. "Is he there?"

Now Trevor was beside a disturbed Leila.

"I can explain; it's not what you think," he said to her before taking over the intercom. "Brandice, I thought I told you that I would call you when I was ready."

"You were taking too long."

Leila didn't know what was going on, but she knew it wasn't something she was going to tolerate, and she was perplexed as to why Trevor would think otherwise.

"Trevor, who the hell is this woman and why is she at my house asking for you?"

"Just hold on a minute. Let me handle this."

Against everything she felt, she took a few steps back, allowing him to go handle the crazy woman downstairs. Leila watched as he stoically stood, apparently unaware of exactly what he was going to do. Leila knew that whoever this woman was, Trevor didn't really want to speak to her. But why? Who was she, and what did she want? It was too much of him to ask of her to just stand aside. They might've been apart for a while, but he had to know better than that.

"Trevor, you're just standing there," she said with frustration. "I'm about to call the police." She picked up the cordless that was sitting in its cradle next to her couch. "I've already been shot by one crazy person. I'm not about to let another one in my house."

Trevor grabbed the phone from her hand. "No. Just stop talking so I can think for a second." He started mumbling things to himself. Things that didn't make sense to Leila.

"Think about what?" she said, taking offense. "What the hell is going on?"

The intercom rang again.

"Leila, let me up?"

Leila walked briskly back to the intercom. "Raven, is that you?" she asked with confusion.

"Who the hell else would it be? Let me up." Leila gave Trevor a questioning look, but he said nothing, just stared back at her. Something was definitely wrong; it was all in the air. Slowly, Leila shook her head as she pushed the button that would let Raven up.

"Whatever happens, just remember how much we love each other, Leila. Remember that we can get through anything together," Trevor said nervously.

What the hell? Leila thought. *Why is Trevor talking to me like somebody died?*

"Oh my God!" Her hands rushed to her face. All the feeling in her body dissipated, the lightness in her head increasing. Leila's knees buckled, and she fell to the floor crying hysterically. "Who died? Is it Brook? Oh, Lord, please say it isn't Brook," she cried out.

Trevor rushed to her. "Nobody died, Leila. I promise, no one is dead." He tried to comfort her, but by the tone in her screams it was easy to see that she wasn't listening. "Calm down, you have to breathe." He rubbed her back.

Leila tried to breathe, tried to believe that her sister was still alive, but her conscience wouldn't allow her to. It was like déjà vu, the way her mind went back to the day her mother was found dead. Everyone kept saying that it couldn't be true, that they would revive her. Leila had believed those people. She had faith that she would see her mother alive again. In the end it had all been lies, lies people told to calm her down.

Still crying, Leila allowed Trevor to pick her up and move her to the couch.

"I guess you beat me to it," Raven said, slamming the door behind her and locking it. She looked through the peephole. "I can't believe this shit is actually happening."

Leila ran to Raven's open arms. "See, I knew something was wrong. What happened?"

"I didn't get a chance to tell her, Raven. She's crying for no reason," Trevor said. "Did you see Brandice downstairs?"

Raven gave Trevor the evil eye, confirming that she had. Like she'd done so many times before, Raven calmed her little sister down with soothing words of reassurance and a cup of hot tea. When she thought it appropriate, along with the help of Trevor, Raven explained who Brandice was and why she was downstairs waiting to meet them.

"You got to be fuckin' kidding me," Leila screamed out. She couldn't remember the last time she had felt this enraged. If her father weren't already dead, she would have no regret in killing him herself. How dare he have a wife and child after he left us to fend for ourselves. He was supposed to be an evil bastard with no heart. Instead, he was just a selfish man who didn't like what he had first and decided to erase the slate and try again. Leila pensively focused her eyes on the cup of water sitting on the table. It was all she could do to keep from giving into her urge to break something, to throw a table across the room followed by plates and vases. Looking at the glass reminded her that for every action there was a reaction.

As much energy as she dedicated to staying calm, she couldn't stop the image of her father from camping out in her brain. The thought that he might have moved on and found a new family had entered her mind as a child, but just the thought was painful enough for her to deem it impossible. Now, his pride and joy was just feet away, and Leila wanted to throw up.

"Why did you bring her here, Trevor? You had to know that I wouldn't want anything to do with that bitch."

"Watch your mouth," Raven said. "You might not like what she represents, but you can't go around calling her outside her name—which is Brandice, by the way."

"Oh … so you're okay with this? You don't see how fucked up this is?" Leila knew her sister was right, but now was not the time for reason. Now was the time to get mad as hell and express it.

"Please. You know how much I hate that man, and seeing her brought it on stronger, but I'm too tired to fight right now. All we can do is open up that door, let her in, and hear her out."

Leila saw the sadness in her sister's eyes. She didn't want to upset her any more, so she turned her attention to Trevor. "Why would you do this to me?" Leila went back to her original unanswered question. "Why wouldn't you stop this from happening?"

She didn't know why, but for the first time in her life, Leila expected a man, Trevor, to save her. He wasn't supposed to work at the restaurant that her father and his daughter dined at every week. Or be the person who consoled Brandice by making her favorite meal. Just knowing that he had done all that, that Trevor was somehow a part of the series of events that led to this moment, meant that he was partly to blame for the knot in her stomach.

"Because it was out of my control. It's like fate the way she came into my restaurant. One thing lead to another, and here we are right now. I can't change what happened in the past, but I can be here for you now."

Leila heard him, but she wasn't sure if that was good enough. He'd withheld important information from her. What kind of love was that? Was that the kind of love Trevor expected from her, the kind that accepts his wrongdoings just because she loved him? She wanted to mentally work through the mess in her head, compartmentalize her thoughts and emotions to better handle this situation, but her sister had plans of her own.

"Trevor," Raven said, "let her in."

Chapter Twenty-Five

Brandice didn't know what to say. It was like a police interrogation room the way the three of them sat side by side across from her, piercing their eyes into her like she'd committed a crime by even showing her face. It was nothing like she had thought it would be. She was looking in the eyes of two of her sisters, and even though the deep frowns on their faces gave her the impression that they weren't happy to see her, she could finally deliver her father's message. Surely once that happened, once her sisters heard her out and realized that their father loved them very much and wished their mother hadn't kept them apart, they would feel better about her presence and maybe even embrace her as their sister. They just needed to know how great of a man Daniel Cartel really was, and Brandice would do that. With her memories and anecdotal stories, she would bring them together as a family the way her father would have wanted.

"Did you come all the way over here to look at us? Because we could give you a picture and you can go on about your way." Brandice tried to ignore Leila. Trevor had warned her that she was feisty and at times could come off as downright mean. She was beginning to think that the latter was all she would experience tonight.

"I'm sorry, it's just that I'm a little nervous. I don't quite know what to say or where to start."

"Really? Because you're the one who came looking for us. It seems to me that someone would have their stuff together before making a move like that… don't you think?"

"Leila, stop," Raven said. "Let the woman speak." She motioned for Brandice to continue. "You do have something to say, don't you?"

"Yes." Brandice felt her cheeks turning red. Never in her wildest dreams did she imagine her sisters to be so rude. It was like they had no sense of tact or hospitality. Leila had completely ignored her request for a beverage and didn't offer to take her coat. Didn't they know how childish and unruly they appeared? How embarrassing to be grown women who could easily be mistaken for teenagers by their actions. Apparently, none of that mattered to them. "As you probably already know, Daddy died of a stroke last winter."

"Who?" Raven asked.

"Our father."

"Your father," she corrected. "To us he's just Daniel."

"Well, okay," she said, annoyed by the interruption. "Before he died, he wrote a letter to me asking that I find his long-lost daughters. He wanted you guys to know how much he loved you and desired to be a part of your lives and how even after all the years you had to spend apart, he loved you and thought about you daily."

"What the hell are you talking about, *he desired to be a part of our lives.*" She mocked Brandice's tone. "That man walked out on my mother, leaving her to raise us alone, and he never looked back. He didn't give a damn about us," Raven said, now pacing the floor mumbling words under her breath.

"That's not true. Daddy tried to see you guys. He wanted to be in your lives, but it was your mother who kept him from seeing you. It was her, not him."

Brandice jumped back to avoid Leila's body as she lunged toward her. "Don't you ever fix your mouth to say anything about my mother. You hear me?" Leila said, trying to break free from the arms of Trevor, but he held her wrists tightly. "You don't know shit about my mother, and I swear to God, if you say one more lie about her, I will hurt you."

The look in Leila's eyes scared Brandice. She could tell her threats were not idle. But why was she so angry about hearing the truth? At least now they knew that their father wanted them. Brandice thought that, at least, was something to be happy about.

"I didn't mean to upset you. I'm just telling you the truth, Leila. I'm sorry it's so hard to hear, but I won't allow you to harbor inaccurate tales about Daddy. He was a good man."

Raven stopped her pacing. "Are we talking about the same Daniel Cartel? Because the man I know would never be classified as a good man." She sat on the table in front of Brandice, giving them the same eye level. "Daniel Cartel, born March 18, 1958?"

"Correct," Brandice said. "That's the one."

"Good. Since you like hearing the truth so much, let me enlighten you on the facts about good ol' daddy. He was a liar, a drunk, and a wife beater. The man had no boundaries on what he would do to my mother. Whether it was punching her face in or slapping her until her jaw cracked open, he didn't care. Your daddy broke my mother. He took a strong woman who deserved nothing less than perfection and walked all over her until she had almost nothing left. And when that wasn't enough, he would do it some more, making sure she could never recover from his beatings. Your daddy is nothing less than the devil, and I'm glad he's dead. My only regret is that I wasn't there to see his heart stop beating myself."

"Shut up," Brandice said loudly. "Shut up. I don't care if you don't want to believe the truth, but saying awful things about him out of spite is just wrong. If he could hear you now he would be so disappointed in you."

"Ha! Look who can't handle the truth now," Leila chimed in. "Fuck you and your stupid-ass father. He didn't do right by us, and he lied to you about the type of man he was. You can believe whatever you want. That's your business. But why would we lie to you? Why do you think we can't even stand to look at you right now? Huh? Trevor told you we didn't want to see you, and still it never clicked to you that maybe your father wasn't the man he pretended to be your whole life. He knew where we were. He knew how to find us if he really wanted to. But he didn't because he was a coward in life and apparently one in death."

"You two are evil," Brandice said with conviction and anger. "The man is dead. His last wish was to make things right with his daughters, and this is your response. Pure evil."

"So what if he's dead?" Leila responded. "So is my mother. And as far as I'm concerned, he's the one who killed her. He killed her long before she stopped breathing. We're not the evil ones."

Never in her life had words stung so much. It wasn't so much the words as the power behind them. Raven and Leila spoke with emotion that resembled hatred. It was hard to hear them talk, their voices marked with venom. On their faces and in their eyes was grief, but different from hers. Brandice couldn't stand to sit any longer.

Mentally, she read over the letter left by her father and then recalled the questions Leila had just asked her. Could any of their accusations be true? Could her father really have committed even a fraction of the inhumane acts they accused him of? Brandice couldn't believe that he would. He was Superman, for goodness' sake. Her best friend. She had to make them believe the truth or else her father would never be able to rest in peace. Brandice looked up at Raven and then Leila, and she knew that no matter what she said they would never want to know anything but what they already believed. From where she stood it seemed they were comfortable believing that their father was an evil man. It was what they wanted. So she sat there feeling defeated and incapable of doing the one thing her father asked of her.

"Brandice, don't cry. It's going to be okay." She had no idea that tears were rolling down her face until she felt the strong embrace of Trevor around her. "Please don't cry."

But she couldn't help it; the tears kept coming. It was all she could do after enduring the night. "My …my dad …he was a …good man," she managed through loud sobs. "He … really was. You met him, Trevor. Tell them."

"I know, I know," Trevor said, rubbing her back in soothing circles. "I know."

"Excuse me?" Leila said, clearly unhappy with his word choice. She stuck her neck out. "What do you know?"

Trevor and Leila exchanged challenging stares.

It was time for her to leave. Brandice knew she was causing more trouble than comfort. "I apologize for ruining your night." She wiped her face with her hand and stood. "Clearly, you're not ready to hear what I have to say, so I'll just leave."

"Hold up," Leila said. "We would like it if you didn't try to contact our little sister, Brooklyn. She doesn't need to hear any of this."

Just when I thought this night couldn't get any worse, Brandice thought. She looked at Trevor, hoping he'd rescue her from having to explain, but he said nothing.

"Your sister Brooklyn is dating my best friend, Jason. Chances are she already knows."

"Wait a minute. Was this a setup? Did Jason try to get with Brook so that you could get the 411 on us?" Raven accused more than asked.

"No, I promise he had nothing to do with this. It's just a small world, I guess."

Brandice was tired; she didn't want to answer any more of their questions, especially after the rude display they'd put on. "Trevor, do you think you can drive me home?"

"You don't know how to take a cab?" Leila said.

"Come on, Leila," Trevor coaxed. "I drove her here. It's late, and she's upset. I can't let her take a cab; it wouldn't be right. It'll be twenty minutes, and I'll be right back."

"Whatever, Trevor. I'm tired anyway. I'm going to sleep."

Trevor pulled Leila aside. "Don't be like that. I'm just trying to do the right thing here. As a man I can't let her take a cab when I have a perfectly functioning car right outside."

"Okay," she said with a hint of sarcasm. "Go ahead. I can take care of myself." Before he could say anything else, she continued, "Raye and I need to go over to Brook's anyway. I'll try to call you tomorrow."

"Don't do this, Leila. Don't use this as an excuse to walk away from us."

"I'm not. I just want her out of my house. It's late, and we both have work in the morning."

Trevor looked as if he didn't believe her, but with the tension in the room he didn't have a choice. He kissed an agitated Leila and escorted Brandice outside.

The car ride to her house was quiet, neither one knowing what to say. They passed the post office she frequented and the restaurant where Trevor worked, and to Brandice they both looked different. It was like in one short hour everything she knew and felt had been tainted. She couldn't help but feel different, changed by tonight.

Those women are delusional, Brandice thought. No wonder her entire family didn't want her to find them. They must've known how horrible they would be toward her and the lies they would say about her father. Raven was bad, but Leila was the worst with all her eye rolling and fist balling. *That kind of behavior would have driven Daddy crazy,* she thought.

Brandice knew she should apologize to Trevor for the way things turned out, for dragging him into the middle of the situation, but she didn't have it in her to feel as if she'd done something wrong by trying to do something good.

"Try to get some sleep," Trevor said upon reaching her house and walking Brandice to her door. "I know things didn't turn out the way you would have wanted, but you have to be patient. If there's one thing I've learned about Cartel women, it's that they're stubborn."

"That might be true, but Leila and Raven are not Cartels."

Chapter Twenty-Six

Don't complain about what you can't change.
Just play the cards you were dealt. —Wanda

"THAT'S IT. THAT'S THE WHOLE story, beginning to end." Jason brought his hands down from over his face. He'd just spent the last half hour telling Brooklyn everything he knew about Brandice being her sister.

Brooklyn sat on her bed Indian style. Tonight was the first time she'd asked Jason to come upstairs. She wasn't ready to do anything yet, but she wanted him to know that she wasn't hiding anything from him. Just lying together in her personal space where all her precious belongings were stored was intimate for her. It was supposed to be nice, quiet, and relaxing, with soft music and whispering.

Tonight was not supposed to be the night she found out that her boyfriend was the best friend to her sister, whom she had never met. It was shocking beyond an explanation, hearing him reveal the connection. It was like God himself had worked out this odd encounter between the two of them.

"What was he like?" she asked, holding a pillow over her chest. "I know he wasn't the most likable person, but what did you think of him?"

"That's just it." Jason turned to face her. "He was the best. Next to my father, I admired Mr. Cartel the most as a man. He was nice, smart, and always there for Brandice. He was even there for me when I needed advice and felt like I couldn't go to my own father. I think you would've liked him."

Brooklyn let out a loud sigh. She couldn't believe her ears. Just a few months ago she'd found out awful things about her father, and today Jason was telling her the complete opposite. She was confused about what was right, who was right. Her entire life, she had wanted to meet her father, experience him for herself, and now all she had were other people's stories, which weren't adding up. The empty hole she'd had in her heart for many years just got bigger.

Jason grabbed her hands. "You're mad at me. I knew you would be. It's just, I had to tell you."

"Mad at you for what? Telling me that you knew my father?"

"Yeah, I probably shouldn't have done that."

Brooklyn smiled. "I'm happy you told me. You could've kept it to yourself, but you didn't, even though you knew there was a chance it would upset me. You care about me, and I love you for that." She kissed his lips. "Don't ever think you can't talk to me about something, okay?"

"Man, I really didn't think you would take it this way. I was, like, freaking out about this, babe."

Brooklyn watched the relief finally come across his face. It almost made her want to cry. Jason was the best thing that had ever happened to her. Every day he amazed her more and more, the way he paid close attention to the things she liked and disliked or the way he wouldn't stop trying to make her laugh when she was having a bad day. Never in her life had anyone devoted that much of himself to her. It was like a fairy tale, and she wasn't ready to wake up. Brooklyn was getting used to having him around, loving her the way she wanted him to. How could he ever think she'd let something like him knowing her father interfere with what they had? Because that wasn't about to happen. As long as he kept treating her like his queen, she wouldn't leave.

"I know I never talk about why my mother and father split up. Until recently, I really never knew. But what you're saying about him just doesn't add up to what my sisters told me. It's like you're talking about a different person."

He moved closer, pulling her back into his chest. "What if they have it wrong? Maybe it isn't as bad as they remember."

Brooklyn thought about his words, but she couldn't give them any life. Her sisters would never choose to harbor thoughts about their mother lying beaten on the floor. Those images came from a real place. "No. I don't think that's even an option. I never met the man, but even as a child I knew he'd hurt my mother. It was all in the way she spoke, walked, like a woman who'd lived too much, experienced too much pain. He did that to her. Maybe he changed and turned into a different man, but that doesn't erase what he did to my mother or my sisters." She tilted her head. "Do you understand?"

"Yeah, I think you might be right," he said. "But how does all of this make you feel?"

This time Brooklyn sighed a little more lightly and smiled. "I'm good."

She was glad they'd talked, but she didn't want to dwell on this subject any longer. It was ruining the mood she'd originally set. "I'm going to get the paper. You go downstairs and get the cards. I'm feeling like some gin rummy." She hopped off the bed and began searching through her bag for a notebook while Jason went downstairs.

Brooklyn was pulling out her miniature card table from under her bed when she heard the doorbell ring. "Jason, can you get that for me?" she yelled.

"Uh huh."

Brooklyn smiled again. She found herself doing that a lot lately. *This must be the way Raven feels*, she thought, *always having someone there, working with you do get things done.* Now she knew how it felt to have more than a television keeping her company.

"Brook," Jason yelled, "Can you come down here?"

"Hold on." She wasn't quite finished setting up the board. "Give me a second."

"Brooklyn Cartel, get your butt down here, right this second."

It was Leila's rude self. Her sassy voice could be detected a mile away. Brook laid the blue felt board on her bed, slipped her feet in her green Celtics slippers, and walked down the stairs.

"What are you two doing here?" she asked upon seeing both her sisters standing in her foyer.

Saying nothing, Raven shook her head as she walked through the living room.

"Girl, you won't believe the kind of night we just had." Leila began offering an explanation until she realized that Jason was standing there. She looked at him with suspicion, walking in his direction. "Your friend Brandice really has some nerve, but I'm sure you already knew that."

"She came to see you tonight?" Jason said, his face on Leila but his eyes on Brook. "I tried to stop her, but she wouldn't listen to me. I told Brook everything, so you don't have to worry about her being the last to know."

Brooklyn watched Leila's face when Jason spoke to her. She knew Leila would've wanted to tell her about their father. It was probably the reason she was standing in her living room right now. Leila was the one who always protected her when she thought Brooklyn needed it. Having Jason say that he'd done that already would make Leila feel uncomfortable about their relationship. The way her eyebrows narrowed and her lips thinned proved just that.

"I know you guys must be really upset." Brook gave Raven a hug and then Leila. "This whole thing is really messed up."

"Damn right it is." Leila flopped down on the couch, setting her feet on the coffee table. "That bitch had the nerve to talk about Ma like she knew her. I swear, Brook, I was about to kick her ass."

"I told you about calling her out of her name." Raven rolled her eyes.

Leila theatrically scanned the room. "Her ass ain't here. So I'm going to call her whatever the hell I want to."

"I can't even talk to this woman right now," Raven told Brook. "You try."

"I don't know what to say." Brooklyn sat. "I just found out, and I've never met our father or Brandice."

"She really isn't a bad person," Jason blindly interrupted. "Once you get to know her, you'll see she means no harm."

Brooklyn loved Jason, and she knew he meant well, but she wished he'd never opened his mouth. When it was just the two of them he could say whatever he wanted, but when her sisters were involved it became family business.

"Why are you even talking right now?" Leila shot back. "Of course she probably has you believing all those lies about our father being a damn saint and how awful our Ma was by keeping him from seeing us, but you better not be filling my sister's head with that bullshit."

"What do you mean, Ma was awful? Did she say that?" Brooklyn asked Raven in shock. Even though Leila was the one who had said it, Brook knew she was liable to say anything when she was angry. Even as a child Leila would make things sound worse just to make her point. Plenty of times people urged her to become a lawyer instead of a psychologist because of her skills of manipulation.

"That's what she said. She came in all foul, talking out the side of her neck."

Brooklyn felt herself getting angry. She didn't know Brandice, and Brandice didn't know them. They might share the same blood, but that didn't give her the right to talk about their dead mother. She was way out of line. All of this was giving her a headache. "Can we talk about this tomorrow? I need time to think and digest all of this information."

Her sisters looked at her with concern.

"Sure, babe." Jason kissed her cheek. "I'll come by in the morning."

Brooklyn grabbed his hand, linking their fingers together. "No, I need you to stay."

She looked in the direction of her sisters.

"Oh, hell. You want us to leave?" Leila shouted in disbelief. "This is messed up, Brook. You don't even know what's going on with Raven and Sean, but you ready to put us out."

Raven slid off the couch. "Don't worry about it. We can discuss everything later. Just give me a call when you get a chance, little sis."

"What's going on with you and Sean?" Brooklyn asked.

"Nothing big. I'll tell you later." Raven embraced her sister and whispered in her ear, "I hope he's worth it." She eyed Jason.

Brooklyn felt her heart splitting. Part of her wanted to spend hours with her sisters, sorting this whole mess out the way they used to do as children. She wanted to be there for them the way they were always there for her. But then there was the bigger part of her that wanted to just be with Jason and forget about how messed up this situation was. She wanted to be happy, play cards, and laugh until they fell asleep. The father she never knew and the sister she didn't want to know were going to mess things up for her. It was a difficult decision, but tonight she was choosing Jason.

Brooklyn nodded her head in response to Raven and walked her sisters to the door.

"You okay?" Jason asked once they were alone again.

"Yup," she said, shrugging her shoulders. "Got the cards?"

He held them up. "You want to talk about this? Because it's a big deal."

Taking the cards from him, she said, "No. I don't want to talk about Daniel, Brandice, or my sisters. Let's just play cards. I got the board set up upstairs. Can you get some drinks out the fridge?" she asked, running up the stairs.

Brooklyn watched Jason go back into the kitchen from her balcony. Once inside her room, she allowed herself to let out a few silent cries of frustration, only enough to release some of the stress weighing her down. It was like God was determined to make her life difficult. With every leap of progress she made, Brooklyn felt like she was being pushed backward by a force she couldn't compete with. And she was pissed that Jason had to be involved. Already he'd witnessed what she thought was too many of her flaws, both personal and family related. Jason came from a good family with limited drama, and Brooklyn didn't want to scare him off with all of hers. Their sex life was nonexistent, he knew her darkest secret, and now he had the burden of knowing the ins and outs of her twisted family.

Brooklyn stopped her cries. Afterward she ran into the bathroom and ran a wet cloth over her eyes, taking a few deep breaths, making sure there were no signs of pain on her face.

When she came out, Jason was on the bed dealing cards. "You ready to play the cards you've been dealt, Ms. Brooklyn?"

Joining him, she responded, "That's the only way I know how to play."

Chapter Twenty-Seven

If you hear me speaking to you than acknowledge me. —Wanda

"I NEED TO SEE THE boys." Raven spoke into her cell phone while driving down the pike. She'd spent the last five nights sleeping on Leila's couch, trying to avoid the free therapy sessions being forced upon her. It was painful being minutes away from her family but feeling like she couldn't go home all because she'd finally told the truth about the way she felt. Sure, she'd hurt Sean, and that wasn't something she took lightly. It wasn't something she wanted, but in the moment, she couldn't take it anymore. All of the pent-up feelings that she tried to mask were dying to be released, and the words just came pouring out. She was a horrible person, which she knew. Any woman who could leave her husband for no explainable reason beyond "I don't feel like being here" deserved to be exiled from her children. That's why she didn't push the first four times she called and asked Sean if it would be okay to come by. She didn't push when he told her no and proceeded to make her feel like shit for the next ten minutes. But today, she wasn't having any of that. Today she needed to see her sons. The only thing that had gotten her through all the drama with her family over the past few days had been picturing the smiles and hugs of her children. She needed to see them, hold them, kiss them, and let them know that she was still their mother and she loved them.

"We don't have time for a visit today. I already made plans."

"I don't care, Sean. I need to see them today. I'm the one who birthed those babies. You can't deny me access to my own kids."

"You did this to yourself. You're the one who walked out on us."

"You, Sean. I said I wasn't happy with you and me, not the boys. And for the record you told me to leave."

"I can't believe you're going to blame me for you not being here, Raven. I'm not the one who quit. I'm not the one who only thinks about her damn self."

Raven pulled the phone from her ear. Sean didn't understand what she was going through, and she was tired of explaining it to him. He was hardheaded and unsympathetic.

She returned the phone. "Sean, I know you don't owe me anything and right now I'm not your favorite person, but I swear I don't know what I will do if I don't see my babies today. I'm their mother. I need them and they need me. So, please."

Raven waited for him to respond. The sound of the television playing in the background was her only sign that he hadn't hung up. "Fine" was all she said before hanging up and putting the first smile on her face in days.

Ten minutes later she was home. Back in her house, playing with her sons upstairs. They were so happy to see her when she walked through the door. Even Sean had to smile at the sight of their sons hanging on their mother's body so tight as to not let her loose from their grip. Tristan immediately pulled Raven upstairs to show her all the new toys he'd gotten that week. Raven figured Sean had taken them toy shopping to avoid telling them why Mommy wasn't home.

The thought of them asking for her, calling her name, and not knowing why she didn't come made her feel sick to her stomach. But right now she wouldn't think about that. All Raven wanted to do was enjoy her children and not think about how messed up her life was right now.

For hours she played video games, watched Nickelodeon, and drew pictures with broken pieces of crayons until the boys had to be put down for a nap. Raven sat in their room, listening to them sleep, and wondered how badly her decision would destroy them. She looked at her sons and wondered if her father had done the same thing. Had he scanned the faces of his two little girls and weighted out the pros and cons of ruining their family? Or did he just leave and never look back?

Brandice had said that he wanted to be a part of their lives but that for some reason Raven's mother wouldn't allow it. She didn't want to believe that there was any truth in that, but Raven couldn't help but wonder if one day she would have to explain to her sons that she, too, had wanted to be there for them but that their father had made it virtually impossible.

With Raven, her sisters, and her mother, her father clearly wasn't happy. All the terrible things he did to them could have been his way of handling his situation. Maybe he didn't know any other way to be there and still be a good person. Maybe being with them made him a horrible man and leaving was the best thing for everyone. With his new family he was happy. He was nice, productive, and loyal. All the makings of the great TV fathers Raven used to pray for.

Daniel Cartel was Raven's father, and for the first time in her life she believed that she had inherited something from him. Like him, she was a quitter. She'd quit her husband and taken away the security her sons were accustomed to, all to feel like a better person, a person she could look at in the mirror and not pity.

It was the reason she couldn't stand to look at Brandice, because she represented everything that could be in Raven's future. She represented what starting over could mean for the people she was quitting on, the people who would forever be scarred by the decisions she made.

She lowered her head into her lap and began to rock back and forth. It was how she used to soothe herself as a child, when no one was there to do it for her. Back and forth Raven rocked, trying to figure out why after knowing firsthand the pain of losing a parent, she would do that to her own children. Why hadn't she learned from the mistakes of her father but instead repeated his behavior? She thought and rocked, rocked and thought, only to come to the conclusion that she needed to do this for herself in order to be happy. In order to be the best mother she could be.

Sean cleared his throat, making his presence known behind her. He stood, leaning on the doorframe.

"You okay?" he asked in a caring tone.

Raven sat up. "They look so peaceful. My little angels."

"They're growing up so fast. Next thing you know they'll be teenagers, defying everything we say."

"Let's hope not. I'd like them to stay this sweet forever." She stretched out her arms.

After a few moments of silence, Sean said, "I made some sandwiches downstairs. You want lunch?"

Raven hesitated.

"Come on, Raye," he cajoled. "We'll eat and talk. I promise, no yelling." She agreed.

At the kitchen table where they'd spent so many meals, Raven chewed on a turkey club, not knowing if this would be the last meal they shared.

"You want to talk about it?" Sean broke the silence.

"What?"

"Your father and his daughter."

"No," Raven said without thought. Sean had used that delicate situation as a means to hurt her. She didn't want to give him any information just in case he wanted to do it again.

"I'm sorry about the way I told you," he said as if he could read her mind. "You know I'm better than that, right?"

What Sean had done was pure evil, and even Raven had to admit she didn't think he had it in him, but she also knew he was hurting at the time.

Not feeling like she had the right to hold a grudge, she said, "He's dead. The man died knowing that we were out there, and he never once came looking for us. Instead, he wrote a letter to his bratty daughter telling her to find us for him. Even in his death the man is trifling."

Sean bit into his sandwich and then sipped his soda. "I know you're not going to like this, but I have to say it anyway. The man was human, Raye. That means he wasn't perfect. He made mistakes, and hopefully he learned from them. At least you know he never forgot about you. He cared enough to write the letter, to send his daughter on a mission to find you knowing that there was a chance it could end badly. Don't you think he deserves a little credit for that?"

"No." Raye played with the bottle cap of her soda. "His gesture was too little too late. I shouldn't have to give him credit for doing a half-decent thing. Half-decent, Sean, not even whole."

"So what are you going to do? Continue being mad at a dead man?"

Raven couldn't tell if Sean was being sarcastic or not, so she didn't question him. She just answered truthfully, "Maybe."

"Raven, at some point you're going to have to let go of all this anger you carry around. It's not healthy for you, and it's not healthy for the boys to see you like that. I know you had it rough, and I'm sorry he did that to your family, but at some point you have to let it go, for yourself."

She pondered on his words. He was right. She did need to release the anger in her life, but she also knew it was easier said than done. And right now she didn't have the energy to let it go.

"I'll try," she said.

Sean smiled, happy to have seemed to help. "What about his daughter, your sister?"

"Don't call her that," Raven warned. "That's taking it too far." She emptied her plate in the trash and laid it in the sink before returning to the table.

"She is your sister, Raven, our children's aunt. You might not want to hear it, but it's the truth. So, what are you going to do about it?"

Raven pretended to think it over though she already had an answer. "I don't think I'm going to do anything about it," she said. "We might have the same father, but I don't owe her anything."

"But—"

"Sean, I can't, okay?" This was no longer a conversation she wanted to have.

"Okay." Sean got up and brought his plate to the sink, turning around he leaned against it. "Are you happy?"

Now Raven wished she had never ended the last conversation. She would choose talking about her absent father and new sister over discussing why she wasn't sleeping in the same bed as her husband, any day.

"I'm trying to be," she said, wanting to tell the truth but not saying too much. "It's just hard, you know."

Sean scratched his head and then crossed his arms over his chest. "I wanted to make you happy, Raye. I thought I was."

"You did, Sean. For a long time you were the only thing that made me happy. Knowing that I had you and the boys was always my joy."

"Then what happened? When did we stop being good enough?"

Raven pulled her loose hair into the band she had on her wrist as if preparing for battle. Never did she think she'd be in the position of having to explain her shameful and guarded feelings to Sean. But here she was, and she owed him the best truth she could offer.

"It became too hard," she began. "Like I was always working toward this goal that was impossible to meet, and I just got tired. Tired of trying to be a good wife and a patient mother. Tired of feeling guilty about wanting to be alone sometimes and not be bothered by you or the boys. Tired of trying to reach perfection all the time.

"My entire life, all I wanted was to have a family, with two parents and happy children. I looked at "real" families and I told myself that one-day that was going to be me. One day I was going to have a real family. I became obsessed with it, like, really obsessed with trying to create this picture-perfect family because as a kid that's all I wanted." Raye slid out of her chair and walked over to Sean. "All I wanted was to have a father at home who loved his family, a mother who was always smiling with happy children running around the house. And then I got it. I met and fell in love with you. We got married and had babies, and my fantasy was complete," she told him. "Only I didn't feel the way I thought I would."

"What do you mean?" He slid his back further down the counter. "I don't understand."

"I mean, in all the dreaming I did I was always the child, the one being taken care of, not the mother doing everything for everyone else. I never thought it would be like this, so hard and tiring all day every day."

"So you don't want to be a mother?" He asked with urgency. "Because you were the one who wanted to get pregnant both times. I didn't force that on you."

"I love being a mother. It's tiring and hard, but it's the best job in the world, and I love those boys upstairs."

The frown on Sean's face deepened as the disappointment in his eyes widened. "So it's me you don't want. You don't want to be my wife?"

"I don't know, Sean. That's what I'm trying to figure out," she said with a hint of optimism in her voice. "There was a time when all I thought about was making sure that you were happy coming home to me. Constantly striving to be the wife that wouldn't make you think about leaving me. Giving you everything I had. And I did it because I thought I had to in order keep you here. Sean, I just don't know if I have it in me anymore. I don't know how much of myself I can continue to give."

"Everyday I'm here because I love my family and I don't want to be anywhere else. I give too, Raven. To you, to the boys, I give."

"I know you do, and I admire how easily it comes to you. It's, like, effortless the way you care and give. But for me, I have to think and try and reenact whatever it is that I think I'm supposed to be doing. It's not natural for me, Sean. This confusion—it haunts me, and it's tearing me up inside."

"Tearing *you* up inside?" Sean's voice began to rise. He spun around, grabbed a plate from the sink, and threw it across the room, making it shatter against the wall. "What about me? I never would have married a woman who I thought would leave me out in the blue. It's like you've been lying about who you are our entire relationship."

"You said you wouldn't yell," she reminded him, pointing her finger to the ceiling. "The boys don't need to hear us arguing."

"Arguing? That's the least of their worries. Don't you get that?"

"Yes. I get that," Raven yelled back. "But can't we talk about this without all the shattered glass?"

If it were just the two of them in the house, Raven would have never stopped Sean's rampage. She probably would've given him more things to throw. But she knew how it felt to be woken up by the shouting parents, and she never wanted that for her kids.

"I'm sorry." He grabbed Raven by the shoulders, pulling her into him with light force, urging for her undivided attention. "But you leaving means that I could lose everything. My wife walks away, and my life crumbles because she's a part of everything I am. Don't you see how this is tearing me up, Raye? The woman I married couldn't do this, not to me."

Only inches apart the two of them stood, taking in everything that was said, neither one wanting to interrupt the other's thoughts.

Raven moved even closer to her husband, wrapping her arms around his waist and lightly kissing his chin. She knew her truth was bringing him pain that he probably never imagined she would cause. For so long she'd hid her inner thoughts from her partner because of the damage they would bring. Her heart was torn between doing the right thing by her family and doing what was right for her. Either way Raven wanted Sean to understand that the fault was on her and not him.

"Maybe I'm making the biggest mistake of my life by leaving right now, but that's something I have to do in order to be sure. Because it's not fair to you if I stay, still confused. I love you, Sean, but I love myself more. I'm not sure if that makes me a bad wife. It probably does, but it's the truth."

Finally, she had gotten it off her chest and out in the open. Raven had told him things she didn't even know were true. For so long she'd denied herself the opportunity to even think the words she'd just said.

She felt the strong arms of her husband around her waist, something she wasn't expecting.

"I'll give you six months to figure this out, Raven. If you want to leave then we'll get divorced, no questions asked. But if at any time you want to come home and be my wife again, then that's that. No turning back or saying you need space. I won't have you walking in and out that door." He pointed toward the front of the house. "We deserve more than a rash decision."

"You don't have to do this, Sean."

"Yes I do. This is my family, and I can't let it fall apart without saying that I did everything in my power to make it work. Now it's on you."

Chapter Twenty-Eight

THEY LOOK HAPPY TOGETHER. THAT'S what Brandice thought when she saw Jason and Brooklyn leaving his apartment in the late afternoon. They were laughing at some joke she told, both holding their stomachs and tossing their heads back. It looked like unadulterated happiness, something that Brandice hadn't felt in weeks, maybe even months.

Seventeen days had passed since she'd met her sisters. Every day she woke up and regretted ever going over there or even looking for them. It was like a bad dream that she couldn't escape. It haunted her to the point that she lay in bed at night crying, praying that someone would rescue her from this nightmare. That used to be her father's job. He was the one she would go to if she was in a funk and couldn't seem to find a way out. He would hold her, tell her all the ways she was a wonderful person, and then build her up again.

At night when she lay there, lonely and lost, she imagined he was there next to her. She felt his arms around her, but she couldn't hear his voice. It was faint and not clear enough for her to make out his words. She would try, really hard. She would try to press her fingers against her ears to block out all the noise in her house, hoping to zone in on his voice. But each night she failed. Each night she cried herself to sleep.

It was no surprise that her mother had showed up at her house a few days ago, forcing Brandice to get out of bed and put food in her stomach.

"You can't keep doing this to yourself, Brandice. This isn't worth it," her mother said as they sat in the kitchen, Brandice at the table and her mother over the stove heating up beef stew. "They aren't worth it."

"What does that mean ... they?"

"They ... those nasty girls who made you feel this way. If they don't want to know you then we have to let it go and move on with our lives."

"Our lives, Mom?" Brandice said. "Me. I'm the one that they hate. I'm the one Dad asked to do this, and I'm the one who can't seem to get it right."

"Your father wouldn't want you to go through all of this." Her mother stirred the stew before ladling it into two bowls. She placed one in front of her daughter. "Just wash your hands of the situation. You're better off without them anyway."

"Mom, why would you say that?" She pushed the bowl away from her. "I told you what Raven and Leila said about Daddy, and you said it wasn't true, right?" She gave her mother a long questioning look.

"Right." She placed a spoon in the bowl. "I have no idea where those stories came from, but if I had a guess, I would say their mother gave them that negative impression of Daniel."

"What do you know about their mother? Or her marriage to Daddy?"

"I told you before. I never knew the woman. All I know is that your father said she was a troubled woman with very little self-esteem. Not a strong woman at all. That's why he pitied her."

"What do you mean pitied?" Brandice didn't like that word, and if Leila and Raven were any reflection of their mother, she was having a hard time believing the low self-esteem part as well.

"Brandice, please. Eat your food and stop asking so many questions." Her mother pushed the bowl back to its original place on the table.

"Mom, what do you mean by pitied?" she asked again, not willing to leave the question unanswered.

"He told me he stayed with her for so long because he thought it would break her if he left. She depended on him, like she was a child. He only left when he couldn't take being with her any longer."

"That doesn't seem like Daddy. He would never leave us, no matter what the circumstances."

"Well, we never did anything to make you father want to leave, now did we?"

"That, Mom. The way you're talking right now. It's like you're speaking in code, trying to tell me something. What is it?"

"I'm not trying to tell you anything except to let it go, Brandice. If you have any respect for your father then you will let this go. Too many people have already heard about this. Jason's mother called me yesterday wondering if there was any truth to these rumors. God knows who else has heard those lies those girls are spreading about my husband. They are ruining our family name, and of you had any respect for this family then you would let it go."

"But Daddy—"

"Forget what your father said. He had no right to ask you to do that. I'm your mother, and I'm asking you to let it go."

Brandice sat looking at her stew and then began eating it. With every bite she took, she watched the smile on her mother's face widen. So she kept eating. But she knew something wasn't right. Even with her mother's words, Brandice couldn't get the look in Leila's eyes out of her head.

She wouldn't let it go.

And that's why she was across the street hiding in her car with a hat and big sunglasses on. She didn't want Junior to recognize her, and so far he hadn't. Not last night when she had followed him home and not this morning when he'd stepped outside to get the paper.

It was her only chance to get a glimpse of Brooklyn, who, to Brandice's surprise, looked more like her than she'd imagined.

Brandice thought back to three days ago when she had called Junior and asked him to come over to spend quality time with her. She was feeling down, and she needed her best friend by her side. She asked him to stop by, and he told her that he couldn't.

"Why not?" she asked, surprised that he didn't seem apologetic.

"I have plans today."

"What plans, Junior?"

"Plans with Brooklyn, Ice."

"I can't believe you would do this to me. After everything we've been through, you're going to choose her over me?"

"You know what? If you didn't go and mess everything up, I wouldn't have to choose. You did this without thinking about anyone else but your damn self."

"I did this for my father, Junior, and you know that."

"Did you ever stop to think that maybe your father wasn't always a saint? That maybe he had us all fooled?"

"Go to hell, Jason!"

After that conversation, Brandice decided that she needed to see the woman who was stealing Junior from her. So she drove to his house and camped out in her car, waiting for Brooklyn. And now she saw it. Brooklyn made him happy, and the truth was, they looked good together, laughing, having a good time, not at all worried about her.

Before Brooklyn, Junior never would have ditched Brandice, yet alone blamed her for doing the right thing. Brandice decided that Brooklyn was just like her sisters. She looked like a decent person, with that light smile, but she was evil too. Evil enough to keep Junior away from Brandice.

Junior was all she'd had left, and now he was gone too, just like her father, Brandice felt that all the men in her life were leaving her. There was nothing she could do about her father, but Junior was still here, still alive.

I'm just going to say hello, Brandice told herself. *There's no harm in stopping by when I'm already in the neighborhood.* She slipped her hat off and then her glasses before opening the car door.

Brandice knew if she gave it more thought she might chicken out, so she didn't think. She just moved. Across the street and into the view of Junior, who was now wrapping his arms around Brooklyn as they began walking along the street.

"Junior," she yelled out, waving to get his attention over the loud cars passing by.

With a disapproving look on his face, he waved back. "What are you doing here, Ice?"

"I was in the neighborhood so I thought I'd stop by." She moved her gaze from him to Brooklyn. "You must be Brooklyn." She extended her hand. "It's very nice to finally meet you. I'm Brandice Cartel."

Brooklyn took her hand. "It's nice to meet you, too." Then she looked at Jason. "I'm going inside to get something to eat." She started up the brick stairs.

"Maybe we could all go get something to eat," Brandice offered. "On me."

"Ice, just stop, okay," Jason said, signaling to Brook that he would handle it.

"Stop what, Junior? I'm just trying to get to know my sister. She might be your girlfriend, but she is my sister, Junior. Mine."

"Ice, she doesn't want to get involved in all of this. Everything that happened between you and her sisters is too much for her right now. And I'm not going to force her into anything just because you want me to. You need to leave." He pointed in the direction she had come from.

"She's my sister, Junior," Brandice said, feeling like she was talking to a brick wall.

Jason shook his head. "She doesn't even know you, and you don't know her. Brook, Leila, and Raven are sisters. You're just a stranger to them."

Chapter Twenty-Nine

Little girl, you worry me with the way you worry. —Wanda

LEILA LOOKED AROUND HER LIVING room trying to locate her cell phone charger. It had to be there; that was the last place she remembered having it. She remembered swinging it around her arm right before the movers invaded her house with what seemed like a million brown boxes all marked *Trevor's Stuff*. They were everywhere: in her living room, kitchen, bedroom, and even lined up against her hallways.

Leila had tried to ignore them when she woke up that morning and nearly broke her neck after tripping over a box on her way to the bathroom, but now she needed her phone charger and the damn boxes were in the way and no one seemed to think that they needed to be moved except her. She was mad that she wasn't going to have all her open space to juggle with and the peace and quiet she'd become accustomed to at night. She could get past all of that, but she needed her charger and she needed it now.

"Fuck!" she screamed out.

Trevor ran into the room carrying a knife in one hand and a carrot in the other. "What happened?"

Leila was grabbing her left pinky toe and hopping around on the other foot. "I banged my foot again on that damn box."

"Oh." Trevor shrugged and returned to the kitchen.

Leila followed. "Oh?" She grabbed an ice pack out of the freezer and placed it on her foot after she sat on the counter. "Oh, nothing. Don't you think you should unpack the rest of your stuff and not just your kitchen supplies?"

"I will." He added the chopped carrots to the boiling pot on the stove. "But I'm making you dinner right now."

"I'd rather not have another injury. If that means not having dinner, then so be it." She had an attitude.

"Leila, calm down. Just relax."

"I can't calm down. I can't even think with all this clutter in my house."

"Our house."

"What?"

Trevor stopped chopping and turned to face her. "Our house. You said 'my house' but you meant 'our house.'"

"Whatever. Just please, can you put your things away? It's been, like, three days."

"How about you start unpacking while I cook? By the time I'm finished, you would have made a major dent in the work."

Leila sucked her teeth. "Uh, no. My stuff isn't in those boxes. Your stuff, your job." She looked down at her injured toe, not liking what she saw.

"What's with all this possession? First it's 'my house' and now it's 'your stuff.' I don't hear any 'we' talk."

"When the situation calls for 'we' talk, then I will use it. But 'we' aren't about to clean up your stuff," she told him.

"Fine." Trevor wiped his hands on his chef's jacket and pulled the strings from his waist. "You cook your own dinner."

Leila stared him down. "You know I don't cook. But I can damn sure order some food."

"I can't believe you're doing this right now," he mumbled in anger. "I mean, I knew there was a chance you'd pull this crap, but I convinced myself that things were going to be different this time."

"What are you talking about, Trevor?"

"You, Leila. I'm talking about you. But I'm through talking. My boxes can stay right where they are because I'll be out of here tomorrow morning. I'm not doing this with you again." He stormed out of the kitchen.

"Doing what?" Leila hopped off the counter and followed him into the hallway. "What did I do now?"

Trevor didn't answer her, just grabbed his coat and threw it over his back.

"Where are you going?"

"I'm leaving. I don't have to deal with this hot and cold mess. You think I'm going to walk all over you if we get married, but look what you're doing right now. Treating me like a damn pet."

"So you're just going to leave me? Is that right?" she yelled. "What happened to, I'm going to always be here?"

Trevor turned around. "You don't want me here. That's why you've been bitching about every little thing since I moved back in. And I'm tired of it, so I'm out."

"Fuck the damn boxes, okay. They can stay. Just stop walking out on me, Trevor. Stop leaving every time we argue because that really pisses me off," she said, exhausted from all the yelling.

He shoved his hands into his pockets and blew into his closed mouth before releasing the air. "I can't keep coming back when you want me. That's how you pull me in every time, Leila." He held the back of his neck with both hands. "It takes more than love. It takes commitment, and you're not ready for that."

"I told you, I *am* ready."

"Then when are you going to tell your sisters that we're getting married? When are you going to start wearing the ring I bought you?"

Leila looked at him and then past him at the stained-glass door as if it would have an answer. "When the time is right. Right now, with all this stuff with my father, I don't want to bother them."

Trevor let out a sarcastic laugh and then gave her a pitying look. "This is what I mean. You are not ready." He turned to the door and opened it. "I'll get my things in the morning."

Leila wanted to scream. Why couldn't she get it right? Why did she have to go and mess things up just when they were getting back on track? It was like she couldn't help but destroy her relationships.

"I'm scared, Trevor. Okay? I'm scared," she said, crossing her arms over her chest.

He stopped, still not facing her. "I know you are. New things scare you, Leila, but that's not an excuse to stand still."

"No, Trevor, you don't get it," she said, sitting on a box. "You think I don't love you enough to marry you, that you don't have my whole heart … but you do, Trevor. I have never loved anyone the way I love you or even thought about being with a man they way I am with you.

"You got it, Trevor, everything. Of course I didn't mean for it to happen. I didn't think it would, because I was so good at keeping a safe distance from deep relationships, but somehow you got in, and you have it all. And that scares me because now you have the right to do anything you want with it. You might not hurt me. Maybe you will, but that's not the point. The point is that you have the power and the option, and I've been trying to get that back from you for a while, but for some reason you still have it. The more we're around each other the more you take, so sometimes I push you away. But it's a reflex. I don't even know I'm doing it until you walk away, and then you take it with you and my chest starts to feel like it's on fire so, please, stop."

Trevor shut the door, turned around, and slowly walked toward her. He reached out his hands, but she gently pushed them down out of frustration.

"Baby, you're crying. You never cry."

She ignored the tears rolling down her face as well as his attempt to embrace her. With glossy eyes and a runny nose, she said, "I don't know what else you want from me, Trevor, 'cause you have it all. Everything I have to offer is already yours."

Trevor sat. "I don't need anything else. Just you, Leila. That's all I've ever wanted is to be with you. To be the husband that you deserve, to have kids with you, to grow old with you. That's all." Exhaustion forced its way through his tone, body, and words. The same words he'd been speaking since the beginning.

Leila knew Trevor was being one hundred percent honest, and his words were what she needed to hear. She prayed she would be able to give Trevor all that he desired in their relationship, but she wasn't naive enough to believe that it would be that easy. And that's what hurt her so badly. She knew loving her wasn't easy for Trevor. He knew exactly what he wanted, and it was her. Knowing this gave her a sense of security that she had never felt with any man. Why could she not provide him with the same refuge? Her past was so much a part of the woman she was. As much as she wanted to grow, evolve, it would be a battle she fought every day. She felt overwhelmed not knowing how much of the battle Trevor was willing to fight with her. No amount of research or statistical analysis would give her that answer. Only time.

"Don't leave."

"I won't," Trevor said.

"Ever."

"No."

"Not even if ...when I piss you off or push your buttons or tell you to leave. You still have to stay."

"I will."

This was it. She knew she'd taken a huge step in the right direction, and it didn't feel nearly as soul killing as she'd expected. Feeling lighter, Leila stretched her arms out to rest on Trevor's shoulders. "I love you so much, babe."

"Girl, I'm going to spend the rest of my life trying to make you happy. Anything you want, anything you need, I got you. You know that, right?"

"Thank you, but how about we start with finding my phone charger? I really need and want that." Leila watched as Trevor began moving boxes around with ease, quickly returning with her charger in hand. "What else?"

Chapter Thirty

You can get burned in more places than the kitchen. —*Wanda*

No matter how hard Brooklyn tried to make out the name running across Jason's phone, she couldn't. Whoever it was had been blowing him up for the last hour, and she was beginning to wonder who the mystery person could be. He'd stepped out of her apartment twice this evening to answer his phone and stayed gone for about ten minutes each time. Not that she was suspicious or anything, but the look on his face every time a text came though was enough to catch her attention.

But he wasn't offering up any information on his own, so Brooklyn decided to keep her inquisitions to herself and continued to write at her computer. The thing was, the phone kept going off, and her concentration was shot.

She took her earphones out and laid them on the table where she sat. "Jason, is everything okay?"

He looked up at her for a second and then returned to banging his Blackberry's keys. "Uh… yeah," was all the assurance he offered.

Not convinced, she closed her laptop and walked to the couch where he lay sprawled out. "I need a break from work right now. You wanna watch a movie with me?"

Jason didn't answer. He was too concentrated on whomever he was texting.

"Jason?"

"Yeah." He looked up at her in confusion as if she were talking him out of a deep sleep. "What did you say?"

"Movie?" She pressed several buttons on the remote until she found something she wanted to watch. "Do you want to watch with me?"

"Yeah, sure."

She started the movie. Less than five minutes into it, Jason's phone rang... again.

"Hello," he said, answering it and walking out the front door once again.

Now Brooklyn was annoyed. Whoever it was, he obviously didn't want her to hear their conversation. And it must have been urgent given how his fingers had been glued to his phone all night and he had bolted out the door after one ring. *Maybe it's one of his parents or his job*, Brooklyn rationalized while she patiently waited for him to return. Which happened about ten minutes later.

"Aw, babe, you didn't have to wait for me." He pointed to the frozen screen.

"That's fine. I wanted to wait for you," she said, smiling as she waited for him to sit back down so she could once again rest her head on his chest. But her head never made it there because Jason's phone was ringing *again!*

"What the hell, Jason. Who is that?" Brooklyn knew her tone was out of line, but she could no longer hide her irritation.

"Whoa, calm down. I didn't know you had a problem with ringing phones," he said sarcastically, avoiding the question.

"Don't play me, Jason. You know I don't have an issue with that. But this isn't just a ringing phone. Whoever it is obviously wants your undivided attention, so I'm asking who is it?"

"It's not that serious, Brook. Look, I'm just going to turn my phone on silent." He did and then placed it on the coffee table for dramatic effect, but that didn't faze Brooklyn. She wasn't trying to argue tonight, and he wasn't trying to answer her question. She just pressed the play button, knowing that his phone would go off again and that this time she was close enough to read the screen.

And when it did silently ring, Brooklyn didn't waste any time widening her eyes and leaning forward until she made out the name "Ice" on the screen. She picked up his phone and handed it to him. "Is she who you've been running outside to speak to?"

Jason took the phone and ignored the silent flashing light. "She wants me to come over and hang out tonight," he said, "but I told her I was chillin' with you."

"It's fine if you want to go. I don't see why you didn't just tell me that from the start or why you had to sneak out to have a conversation with her."

The look on Jason faced showed Brooklyn that he was surprised by her response, and that bothered her a little. Ever since all this mess started, she'd never given Jason a reason to feel like he had to hide something from her.

"I didn't want to bother you while you were writing, so I stepped out. But are you sure you're cool with me leaving?"

"Yeah, I'm not a child." She tried masking her condescending tone with a smile. "I can survive on my own."

"All right." He leaned over and kissed her. "I'm going to run to the bathroom real quick before I leave."

Brooklyn sat in her living room as Jason made his way to the bathroom. The fact that he'd seemed preoccupied during their conversation didn't go over her head, and neither did his eagerness to leave. Even though she would never say it aloud, Brooklyn sort of felt sorry for Brandice. She could only imagine how it felt to have her best friend dating her estranged sister and being left out of that part of Jason's life. It wasn't her fault that Daniel had done terrible things, and it was unfortunate that things were this way. But there wasn't much Brooklyn thought she could do about it. Her loyalty was with Raven and Leila, and that's where it was going to stay.

His phone flashed again.

Brooklyn reached for it. *Damn, this girl doesn't quit,* she thought as she pressed Read on the screen.

I can't believe you're throwing sixteen years of friendship down the drain for some little brat who stresses you out with all her issues. She's trash and so are her sisters. My dad's only mistake was knocking up their train wreck of a mother!

Brooklyn read the message three times before she screamed out loud, "Bitch!"

Jason came running from the bathroom. Throwing his hands up in the air, he asked, "What's wrong?"

"I swear to God I will kill that bitch! Let me catch her ass in the streets and I will tear her head off."

"Who?"

"What did you tell her, Jason? About you and me?"

"Who?" He repeated loudly.

"Brandice. She said I stress you out with all my issues."

He looked at her with sorrow, but she ignored it. "Brook, calm down, please."

"No!" She tossed his phone to him. "I've never said a foul word about that trick, but now I'm about to kill her dumb ass." She was beyond pissed, and the only thoughts in her head were of the many ways she could bring physical pain to the daughter of her deadbeat father. There were baseball bats, knives, and hot baby oil involved in every scenario.

"Did you answer my phone, Brook?"

She ignored his stupid question but motioned for him to look at his phone. "She can say whatever she wants about me, even my sisters, but the moment she insulted my mother, she really fucked up."

He read the text aloud before looking back at her and apologizing. "I can't believe she said that. You have to understand, Brook, Ice is just hurting right now, and she's in a really bad place."

This was almost too much for her to take in, and her patience had left the room long ago. "Are you defending that bitch in my house, Jason?"

"She's not a bitch," he yelled back at her. "She's your sister!"

And that was the straw the broke the camel's back for Brooklyn. She went ballistic. "Fuck you! Fuck Brandice! Fuck Daniel Cartel!" she cried in anger, the tears burning her eyes. There was not much she could do to stop her body from shaking. Jason, just like his BFF, had crossed the line.

And, like clockwork, his phone rang.

"Ice," Jason shouted upon answering the phone. "What the hell is your problem?"

Brooklyn tapped her foot against the floor loudly, not wanting to hear the voice of the women she was about to murder.

"Don't be dramatic, Ice. That's not funny... I'm serious... Ice! Ice!" Then he turned to Brandice and said, "She hung up on me."

She shrugged her shoulders and rolled her eyes to the ceiling.

Jason looked around the room before spotting and grabbing his jacket. "I have to go, Brook."

"What? Why?"

"Ice. She's talking crazy, and I think she really needs me right now."

"Jason, I need you right now, and I want you to stay with me."

"I can't."

"You can't or you won't?"

"Brook, I don't have time for this banter with you right now. Ice needs me. Something isn't right with her."

"I know she's crazy! That's what I've been saying."

"I'll be back."

"No. Jason, I'm asking you not to leave. To stay here with your girlfriend, whom you and your friend just hurt."

"Don't do this, Brooklyn. Don't make me choose between you and her."

She sent him a hardened glare, speaking with her eyes until her mouth decided to chime in. "I'm asking you to choose."

Jason shook his head and turned toward the door. She sucked in a huge breath, exhaling only when he turned back around. "I love you, Brooklyn."

She didn't let his declaration work its way into her emotions. There was a cement wall there now, the same one she had used for years to block pain of the type she was experiencing now. "Are you leaving?"

"Yes."

"Then your love doesn't mean anything to me." Now it was her turn to walk away.

She'd placed a bet, rolled the dice, and lost.

Chapter Thirty-One

"WHAT DO YOU WANT?"

"Is that any way to speak to your mother?"

Brandice shook her head and gently pulled her mother into her apartment. Once inside, she embraced her mother as she had as a child, tight and long. "I'm sorry, Mother. It's just been a long day," she whispered in her ear before letting her mother go.

Brandice watched as her mother's eyes darted across her body. She knew her mother had noticed the weight she'd lost recently. It hadn't been much, maybe seven or eight pounds, but her clothes were starting to hang off her body in an unflattering way.

"Brandice Cartel, what are you doing to yourself?"

"Mom, I haven't had an appetite, that's all."

"No it isn't and you know it. This is all about those horrible girls, and I'm going to put an end to all of this foolishness. I let this go on long enough because it seemed important to you, but this has got to stop."

I'm done with them, Mom, and this time I promise you I will completely let this go. I don't know what I was thinking, but those women are incorrigible and don't deserve to carry the Cartel name."

"That's what I've been trying to tell you all along, Brandice. Some people don't have the sense God gave them. I hate to speak foul of your father, but he must've been intoxicated to be with someone so beneath him."

Brandice couldn't agree with her mother more. "That's what I tried to tell Junior, but he won't listen." Brandice replayed the phone conversation she'd just had with her *used-to-be* best friend. Their exchange had been harsh. She'd said things about Brooklyn that were out of line, but she wasn't about to apologize for any of them. However cruel her words were, that didn't take away from the fact that she believed every syllable. Junior could live in la-la land if he wanted, but not without her telling him where he could stick it. When she was sure that Junior was around dear little Brooklyn, Brandice had made sure to call his phone countless times after he'd told her he no longer wanted to speak with her. She would no longer be denied what was rightfully hers, and Junior was hers. The evil sisters could live bitter lives with each other. That was fine, but they would not ruin the relationship between Brandice and Junior without a fight. She hoped that her words would rattle the blissfulness for Junior and Brooklyn. At least this way someone else would feel an ounce of the pain and anger she'd been feeling for weeks now. The rejection from all three of her sisters, Junior, and Trevor (who had decided that it would be best if they didn't talk until things calmed down) was like a nightmare. No one seemed to care about her feelings or the toll this was taking on her life. It was all about those bratty women who somehow lived with themselves despite their immorality.

"Brandice." Her mother's voice brought her back to their current conversation. "Stop scrunching up your forehead like that. You're going to create lines."

"I'm sorry, but I was thinking about Junior and Brooklyn. I just wish they had never gotten together." The disgust on her face was evident. "Just looking at them together drives me crazy."

"Brandice, what do you mean Jason is *together* with Brooklyn?" her mother asked as she pulled clothes off the living room furniture and folded them neatly on the couch.

"I know, right? It's nauseating. I don't know what he sees in her, but they act like they're in love and whatnot. I can't stand it."

"This is not a matter to be taken lightly." Her mother spoke with urgency, putting her daughter on notice. "Now, that boy cannot be together in a relationship with a Cartel woman."

"Mom, believe me." Brandice let out a soft chuckle. "You don't have to worry about this one. She has no intentions of claiming the Cartel name or any of our family. Of the three of them, Brooklyn is the least of our worries." Off into her thoughts about her sisters again, Brandice almost she didn't notice the look of terror on her mother's face. It wasn't until she saw the beads of sweat dripping down her mother's now bright-red neck that she asked, "Mother, what's wrong?"

"You!" she yelled. "I told you to leave this alone, but you wouldn't listen. You just had to go putting your nose where it didn't belong, and now look what you've done! You've ruined everything!"

"Mom!"

"No, Brandice!" her mother shouted even louder. "I begged you not to do it, but you just wouldn't listen to me, and now your father's good name will be ruined forever."

"What are you talking about?"

"I'm talking about you opening a can of worms that would have been better off closed. "I knew this would happen, and I warned Daniel, but he wouldn't listen to me. He just hated the thought of keeping these secrets from his precious little angel."

"Listen to you about what, Mom? I'm lost right now."

"Now, I loved your father to death. He was a good man who'd made mistakes in life, but I was able to look past all of that. When he told me about his three daughters, I stood by him. I even chose him over a relationship with my mother. But there is only so much a woman can take, and I had to draw a line somewhere. I mean, I was a respectable girl from a good family, and I couldn't bring more shame to my mother than I already had."

"What are you saying?"

"I'm saying that your father had one more child, but not by the same woman. After he left his first wife, he met a woman he claimed didn't seem like the type to use drugs. Once he found out about her addiction, he left her, and that's when we met. Soon after our engagement, your father got a phone call from the Department of Social Services saying that the woman had died from a heroin overdose and had listed him as the father of her newborn son. He wanted to keep him, but I just couldn't do it to my family. It was too much, four children and we weren't even married yet. I told Daniel that I couldn't marry him. He just had too much going on in his life, and it wasn't fair to me to have to deal with so much at a young age.

Daniel decided that we belonged together and that he would find a home for his son. One of his friend's wives was having trouble getting pregnant, and they were looking to adopt. Your father arranged for them to adopt his son under the condition that he be in the boy's life. We got married months later and had you."

"Mom, what are you telling me?"

"Open your eyes, Brandice." She narrowed her eyes in annoyance. "Jason is not your friend. He is your half brother."

And those were the words that echoed in her head, as she stood in her bedroom alone. Brandice had asked her mother to leave her alone to grasp the information she'd just received, though grasping was the last thing on her mind. She'd heard enough to make her throw up several times in the last hour, and every time she thought about her mother's words she could feel her stomach start to turn again. It sickened her to think that her parents would do something so selfish as to give away a baby just because it didn't fit into their perfect little world.

He's your half brother

Her head began to spin. As much as she didn't want to think about her mother's words, they wouldn't leave her. It was obvious that her parents had planned to take their secret to the grave with them. Hell, her father had done just that!

She felt the contents in her stomach start to shift as images of her father bombarded her memories. Never in a million years would she put this type of act on the man she loved, respected, and praised so much as the honest, genuine father he was to her. He'd been nothing short of everything to her life. If the man had told her that grass was red, Brandice would never have doubted him. Instead she would have spent her days trying to convince the rest of the world that it was wrong and her father, Daniel Cartel, was right.

The contents of her stomach began to travel upward as new images of Raven, Leila, and Brooklyn appeared behind her eyes. Her father had told her to find his daughters and to tell them that he loved them very much and was saddened that he couldn't be a part of their lives, but it was all a lie. He chose not to be there for them just like he chose to give Jason to another family. Her father had abandoned his children and had sent the only child he actually took care of to do his dirty work for him. Leila had said that he was a coward. She also said that her father had used his hands to physically bring pain to their mother. They were right, and she was wrong. Wrong for believing in a liar and for doubting everyone around her. How could she have been so blind? How was she the only one who didn't see her father for the man he truly was?

Now the contents were leaving her mouth and landing on the floor as she bent over her bed, too weak to make it to the bathroom. Brandice didn't bother wiping the excess off her face or changing her stained shirt. She deserved to look and smell like shit. She was the product of two ruthless human beings and deserved all the disgust she was feeling. She would never be the same person again. Her entire life as she knew it was a lie, and she had nobody to run to. That thought made the spinning of her head move faster. There was nothing she wanted more than to talk to her father, beg him to tell her that this was all a huge mistake and to restore her faith in him and in herself. But that was an impossibility she couldn't afford to entertain. So she thought about calling Jason, apologizing for what she had said, and falling into his huge embrace. She could feel his arms around her and his whispers in her ear telling her that no matter what he would always be there for her and with her. But that, too, was a distant memory. Brandice was through lying to herself. She knew there was no chance of Jason forgiving her or even comforting her once he found out what her father had done to him. His relationship with Brooklyn would be ruined, and Brandice knew that somehow this would all be her fault. So, no, Junior was off the list as well.

For a minute she thought about Raven, Leila, and Brooklyn. She needed to tell them she was sorry about everything, especially showing up and turning their lives upside down. She wanted to tell them that they were right about everything and, yes, her father had abandoned them just like he did Jason. But she didn't even bother picking up the phone. Those women would never accept a word she said. They would never open their arms to her, hold her, reassure her, and make her feel wanted, good, worthy, secure, or loved, and those were the things she needed most right now. If only she could think of one person who wouldn't judge her, who could see past the bad and find the heart she had once allowed to beam brightly. She just needed someone, anyone... but there was no one.

I will always love you, Angel.

The voice was clear and soft, yet strong. It was her father. Brandice fell back onto her pillow, slowly letting her eyes settle on her ceiling. Her breathing began to steady; he'd come back for her just as unexpectedly as he'd left.

I was always there for you.

He was right. There was never a time that her father didn't shower her with love and attention. He never abandoned her once. He made sure she was always taken care of. She was the center of his life and he of hers.

Don't give up on me.

"I won't, Daddy," Brandice replied softly as she felt her body coming back to her. Her father, even in his death, still came to her rescue when no one else would. So what if he'd abandoned her other daughters? They still had each other. And Jason had turned out just fine as far as Brandice was concerned. They could all find fault in her father's decisions, but she wouldn't be naive and take on their life experiences. Daniel Cartel was her father, and in that moment, she decided that was all that mattered.

It was that realization that led Brandice to the awareness that she didn't belong here, not without her father. He was the only one who understood her and loved her unconditionally. She needed to be with him. So, in one quick motion, she slid off her bed and glided to her bathroom, where she stored all her over-the-counter medications. Over her sink she glared at herself in the mirror and smiled at the image she saw. The vomit-stained shirt didn't bother her, nor did the dried vomit on her face, for this image was a part of the life she was about to leave behind. Brandice opened her medicine cabinet, grabbing the first three bottles she found. Satisfied with the choices, she made her way back to her bedroom and sat on her bed Indian style. She carefully read the appropriate doses on each bottle and poured twice as many of each onto her bed.

There were four red pills, four blue pills, and four white ones, each in a separate pile. She ran her fingers through the capsules, mixing them before she grabbed them with one scoop, created a wad of saliva in her mouth, and tossed them back by threes.

Brandice gently lay back on her bed with that same reassuring smile on her face before closing her eyes and saying, "I love you too, Daddy."

Chapter Thirty-Two

I didn't have three girls so y'all could comfort yourself.
Be there for your sister. —Wanda

MOTHERLESS. FATHERLESS. IT WAS A hard reality to live every day knowing that the people who brought you into this world either were forced out of it or chose not to share it with you. The love you miss out on, the smiles that you will never see, and the comfort of stability that never knew your name will undoubtedly shape the person you end up being. Raven, Leila, and Brooklyn knew that. But that didn't make it any easier to live it out. There were times when knowing wasn't enough. On days like this, they suffered more.

"He just left, walked right out on me." Brook wasted no time calling her sisters over to her place after Jason left. She had no tears to shed, only anger to release, and she knew Leila would assist her with that.

"He said he loved you, little sis," Raven said. "You guys can work through this."

"Forget that. He walked out on the best thing that ever happened to him, and he deserves to suffer for that mistake," Leila said. "Plus, that nutcase totally disrespected you, and Junior didn't stand up for you. What kind of a man does that?"

She was right, and before now Brooklyn hadn't even thought about that fact. Jason had never once scolded Brandice when he had the audacity to answer her call in the middle of her rampage. But he'd come back. Brook was sure of that. And when he did, she would tell him that she couldn't play second fiddle to Brandice. Not after tonight.

"Well, what do I know? I walked out on my husband and my kids." Raven poured herself another glass of wine.

Leila took the bottle of wine out her sister's hand. "Stop saying that, Raye. You just need time, but you're going to go back home to your beautiful children and your amazing husband."

"Yup, Sean is the best. He's always there for me, he's loyal, and he loves me to death," she said in a low, lethal tone.

"Wow, Raven, you do realize that you just described a dog, not a husband?" Brooklyn said, shifting her body to face her sister. "I don't know much about marriage, but that sounds awful."

"I don't know if I'm supposed to leave, but I do know that just because I want to isn't a good enough reason to walk away forever."

Leila asked, "Are you happy?"

"Happiness isn't everything."

"Who said?"

"What if I left for good and that made me happy? I would be just like him, and I can't stand knowing that I'm this close to being like the only person I've ever hated."

"You will never be him. The evil that man possessed can only be matched by the devil himself."

Raven positioned her back comfortably at the bottom of the couch, releasing her wine glass for the first time since she had first filled it an hour ago. "You say that because you love me, but to any outsider I'm no better than him."

It was true. Nobody wanted to say it, but they all knew that Raven was right. The sad truth was that Leila and Brooklyn would support her either way. She was their sister, and they didn't want to see her suffer for the rest of her life just because she was afraid of resembling Daniel. It was a double-edged sword that shaped their lives, causing deep analysis and contemplation with every decision each sister made. How would they ever discover the women they wanted to be when they were too busy making sure they never turned into their parents? The clarity that they did hold was trapped in between masses of confusion, and that confusion was cancerous.

"How did we become the bad people? Huh?" Brooklyn asked her sisters. "It's like no matter how hard we try, we can never be normal, happy people."

"Lord knows I'm trying," Leila said. "Trevor asked me to marry him again, and I'm trying my hardest to let myself go through with it. But it's so hard. Every morning I wake up and think of a million reasons why this is going to backfire on me."

"Oh my God! Congratulations!" A giddy Brooklyn hugged her sister.

"Thanks, but I feel weird, like an alcoholic that has to work every day to be sober. Love is supposed to be comforting and freeing at the same time. All I feel is anxiety, every minute of every day, and it drives me crazy."

"Me too," Raven said.

Brooklyn said, "Me three."

"You know, I have these high school students. They look at me and see everything they want in their futures, and it kills me, because I used to be them. I wanted everything I have, and sometimes I still do. But there is something in my soul, my spirit, that won't let me be content," Raven said with blank eyes. "I wake up some days and all I want to do is start over, figure out where I'm broken, fix myself, and finally get it right. But I've tried, and nothing changes. The next morning comes, and still I'm broken."

"You're not broken, Raye. You've just been through some stuff." Brooklyn tried to console her eldest sister though she had similar thoughts about herself.

"I don't know what I am. But I think after all these years of living and trying, I've finally come to the conclusion that happiness and normalcy grace the lives of those that God chooses, and that just isn't us."

The mood in the room shifted from solemn to depressing. Usually this was when Raven would give reassuring words describing each sister's brilliance and beauty, but it was clear she had no words along those lines today. These moods didn't come often, because the sisters had learned how to not let these feelings surface but some days, there no antidote could outmatch the truths they tried to keep hidden.

Days like this made tomorrow seem impossible but at the same time inescapable, and that feeling alone was enough to pull the sky down to eye level. Loneliness, crowdedness, clarity, and confusion bombarded the core of the sisters' beings. Days like this had a way of reminding them of their imperfections while simultaneously coveting their beauty.

Each sister fell into her own conscience, shuffling through her individual circumstances, trying to heal her bruised thoughts. Lord knew they were in no position to aid each other.

Leila's cell phone vibrated, interrupting their judgments.

"Hey Trevor, what's up? Why was she calling you? He said what? Oh, you have got to be kidding me! Are you out of your mind? I'm not going down there… No, Trevor. You can do what you want to do, but count me out… Don't yell at me. *My* sisters are here with me now, and they are the only sisters I care about."

"What was that about?" Brooklyn and Raven asked in unison.

Leila poured the rest of the wine into her glass and downed it in one gulp before doing the same to both her sisters' glasses.

"Leila?" they asked, wondering what had caused her uncharacteristic silence.

"Brandice is at Mass General Hospital. The trick tried to kill herself."

Chapter Thirty-Three

JASON DIDN'T KNOW WHETHER HIS ears were playing tricks on him or if he really had heard Mrs. Cartel. He was still in shock from finding Brandice lying sprawled across her bed, half dead in her apartment. After his failed attempt at waking her up, he had dialed 911 and then Mrs. Cartel. The ambulance had arrived within minutes, strapping Brandice to a gurney before taking her to the emergency room. Jason trailed the ambulance and waited outside the hospital to meet Mrs. Cartel.

His head was spinning, and no matter how hard he tried, Jason couldn't stop his heart from moving at rapid speed. He knew he wasn't physically responsible for what Brandice had done, but that didn't relieve any of his pain. Time after time, Jason had ignored signs that Brandice was hurting because he didn't want to upset Brooklyn or her sisters. Now doctors were trying to save a life Brandice had chosen to give up.

"Jason, I didn't want to be the one who had to tell you this." Mrs. Cartel spoke softly.

This was her third time repeating herself, but Jason still didn't comprehend. He tried to swallow, only to find no liquid left on his tongue. Then he tried to steady his shaky legs, but he couldn't find feeling beneath his thighs. Rage built inside him by the second, and every time he tried to blink away her words, her face, Jason opened his eyes to find Mrs. Cartel still standing in the secluded hospital corridor where she had insisted they have a "serious talk."

Jason looked down at the woman for whom, until this very moment, he'd had the utmost respect. Now, all he wanted to do was slap those words out of her mouth until she took that blank stare off her face. Never in his life had he had such an overwhelming desire to lay hands on a woman, but Mrs. Cartel was pushing his patience.

"Son, I wish I could offer you more," she broke the silence. "But my daughter needs me right now."

Jason shoved his hands in his jeans pockets as the urge to strangle this woman grew. How dare she drop a bomb on him like this and then walk away.

"I'm not your son!" he called out as Mrs. Cartel walked past him towards Brandice's room. She stopped, slowly turning on her toes to once again reveal her unmoved facial expression. "I know that. But Daniel was your father, which makes his daughters your sisters, including Brooklyn.

Jason could no longer keep his composure. One after the other, his fists emerged from his pockets, punching thin air. This had to be a dream, he thought, a nightmare that he couldn't wake up from.

There is no way that I'm related to the Cartel family. Just saying those words in his head made chills appear on his skin in between the hot flashes.

Depleted of all energy, Jason relaxed his back against the cinder-block wall and then slid his body to the floor. There was very little use of searching for lies in Mrs. Cartel's words. Jason had known her his entire life, and Mrs. Cartel wasn't the joking type, especially when it came to her family.

The details were still unclear to him, but Jason knew that at the end of the day he was the biological son of Daniel Cartel, the older brother of his best friend and dating his half sister.

The last two realities prompted tears to form in his eyes, but Jason wouldn't let them fall. He wiped his eyes with the sleeve of his shirt. Jason was too tired to cry, too tired to let his emotions win right now.

"Jason!"

He stood upon hearing his name being shouted down the hallway. Jason forced a smile but then realized they were in a hospital because Brandice had swallowed a bottle of pills. His lips straightened as he slowly waved Trevor and the man with him over.

"Is she okay?" Trevor asked once arriving within inches of the distraught Jason.

"The nurse says that they have pumped her stomach but she's still not out of the woods yet." He turned his attention to the gentleman standing next to Trevor, whose look of concern matched his.

"This is Sean," Trevor interjected. "Raven's husband. I was with him when I got the call."

Jason felt his head get lighter as he realized that he was technically meeting his brother-in-law for the first time. He extended his hand to Sean. "We just have to sit around and wait for another update."

"Has anyone told the sisters?" Jason asked, shifting his eyes between both men.

Jason watched Trevor's chin as it lowered. "I called Leila," he told them. "But I don't think they're coming."

"This needs to end now," Sean said. "Their sister tried to commit suicide, probably because of the shitty way they've been treating her, and those women still can't move beyond their own feelings." He sucked in a violent breath. "They are sisters, for Christ sake."

"I agree," Trevor chimed in. "I knew Leila was stubborn, but this goes beyond any of that. This is just heartless. And you know they are all probably convincing each other that they aren't doing anything wrong."

Jason didn't want to listen to any more of their assaults on the Cartel sisters. It was hard enough for him knowing that had they said all these things an hour earlier he would have been right along with them. Giving his judgments about the pure evilness that they were displaying, he would have thrown in a couple of "selfishes," "disrespectfuls" and "unGodlies."

Now, Jason couldn't say those things. He was going through his personal bout of emotions, and hatred was one of them. Trevor and Sean had no idea what it felt like to be passed up, deceived, and forgotten by your own father. Jason had only begun to question what was so different about him that Daniel didn't want him as a son but loved the hell out of Brandice. Daniel Cartel had done this to all of them. He was responsible for his daughter's attempt at suicide and the unsettling bitterness of his other daughters. Daniel brought five children into this world and only gave a damn about one. And that, Jason decided, was the root of all of their issues.

"I'm going to give Raven a call," Sean said, taking Jason from his thoughts. "She can talk some sense into her sisters."

"No." Jason put his hand up. He didn't want to have to see Brooklyn or her sisters right now. So far he was holding it together, but he knew that as soon as he saw her he would fall apart. "I've had enough drama for today. If they don't want to be here then they shouldn't come."

Chapter Thirty-Four

Forgiveness will free you from an unhealthy attachment.
Don't you want to be free? —Wanda

"WHAT DO YOU MEAN SHE tried to kill herself?"

"Raven, I mean exactly what I said," Leila responded as she rocked her body slowly in her sofa chair. She still had her cell clamped tightly in her hand. "Trevor said he was on his way to the hospital and that we should come too."

"What did you tell him?" Brooklyn asked.

Leila didn't respond with words, just a knowing look.

"Leila! I can't believe you!" Raven shouted as she sprang to her feet.

"I know, but what was I suppose to say?" Leila asked her sisters for an answer along with empathy for her response. "He caught me off guard."

"We have to go to that hospital," Raven said as she slid into her shoes and searched the room for her keys. She was at the front door when she realized she was the only one moving. "Why are you guys still sitting there? We have to go!" She looked at an unmoved Leila. "Brook, let's go."

Brook didn't move either. "If we go and she's dead, then everyone's going to blame us for it. If we go and she's alive, she's just going to blame us for driving her to do it. I don't want to deal with that."

"Why can't we just stay here and say a prayer for her?" Approving her own idea, Leila extended an arm to each of her sisters. "Dear God," she began.

"Oh, Hell no!" Raven slapped Leila's arms down. "You two are seriously crazier than I ever thought. How are you going to pray and not even mean it?"

"We do mean it. I hope she doesn't die."

"Me too," Brook added.

Raven had heard enough. "We are not going to sit here while our sister is fighting for her life." She tossed jackets at both her sisters.

Leila caught her jacket and laid it to the side. "She isn't our sister."

"Yes she is!" Raven didn't like the taste of those words coming out of her mouth, but now wasn't the time to explore that. "She has our blood running through her veins. We don't have to like it or her, but this is wrong, you guys."

She said in a softer tone, "What would Mummy say if she knew we were acting like this?"

"Don't do that to us, Raven. Just because she's gone doesn't mean we have to act like saints."

"Leila, we don't have time to argue about this. We're going to the hospital because it the right thing to do, not because we want to."

"That's just as bad as us staying here and praying," Brook said.

"She tried to kill herself, y'all." Raven sat on the arm of Leila's chair and let her words sink in. Raven knew that forgiveness wasn't high on any their priority list and that to them, Brandice and Daniel were one and the same. Raven glanced at her sisters as they sat, each looking in no particular direction. This was hard for them. Going to check on Brandice meant relinquishing anger that they weren't ready to give up. It meant that after everything was said and done they were still sisters. Maybe, Raven thought, if they could have come to this on their own, it would have felt better. And she knew that's what was keeping them in their chairs.

"All right, let's go." Brooklyn stood, walked over to Leila, and took her hand. "You ready?"

"No," Leila said positively. "But I'm going anyway."

Chapter Thirty-Five

Thirty minutes later, Raven, Leila, and Brooklyn slowly walked through the emergency room lobby, where Trevor met them. The car ride to the hospital had been silent and slow as Raven drove the speed limit and graciously allowed cars to pass them on every street.

"I'm glad you guys decided to come," Trevor said as he hugged Raven and Brooklyn. He pulled Leila into his arms and held her tightly before releasing her body and taking her by the hand. "Your sister is down the hall."

Trevor looked back at the women, expecting some resistance after referring to Brandice as their sister, but he received none. Each woman walked stoically, eyes forward, with no sign of emotion on her face.

"Is she going to make it?" Raven asked as they approached the room Brandice was assigned to.

Trevor nodded. "The doctors are confident that she will, but she's still under observation.

The sisters took in his words, all the while locking eyes with each other. A weight was lifted off of them knowing that she wasn't dead, but they still felt uneasy.

"Trevor," a woman called as she emerged from the room. "Who are these people?"

"Mrs. Cartel, this is my girlfriend, Leila, and her sisters. They came to check on Brandice too."

"Oh, that's nice," Mrs. Cartel said. She walked toward the women. "Maybe you shouldn't be here. This isn't the place for your drama."

Before either of them could respond, Jason gently pulled Mrs. Cartel's arm, making his presence known. "They have just as much right to be here as you and I."

"You don't have a right, Jason."

"I have every right, and you know it."

Brooklyn had never seen Jason so unhinged and disrespectful, and it embarrassed her. "Jason, stop acting like this. I know you're upset, but you're being rude."

Jason never took his eyes off Mrs. Cartel. "Brook, stay out of this, okay?"

"Wait a minute now," Leila jumped in. "Don't talk to my sister like that."

"Leila, don't," Brooklyn told her sister before taking both Jason's hands in hers. She looked into his eyes and saw nothing but pain. He was hurting badly, and that caused Brooklyn pain. She wanted to make his aching disappear the way he'd done for her. Brooklyn stretched her arms around his neck, pulling his face down to hers. Brooklyn felt the eyes of her family on them, but she didn't let that stop her from connecting with the man she loved right now. "It's going to be okay, baby. I promise."

With tear-filled eyes, Jason told her, "No, it won't. It will never be okay."

"Baby, yes it will. Brandice is going to be fine, and so are we. Everything is going to work itself out," Brooklyn tried convincing him. "Come here." She pulled his face to her, gently placing her lips on his. Jason pulled away from her as soon as their lips touched, causing everyone around him to jump back.

"Dammit, Brook, don't do that!" he shouted, wiping his thumb across his bottom lip in disgust.

Brooklyn was mortified. Never in her life had she publicly shown affection to any man, and Jason had just shown all the people closest to her that her affection wasn't the kind he wanted.

"I'm sorry, Brooklyn, but I have to get out of here." He turned to Mrs. Cartel. "Your family ruined my life, and I will never forgive you," Jason said as he stormed down the hall, disappearing around the corner.

"Jason! Jason!" Brooklyn yelled after him, but he didn't stop. "What the hell is going on?" She directed her question to Mrs. Cartel.

"I don't think you really want to know, dear."

"Please" was all she could say.

Mrs. Cartel gave her a warning look. "Due to their constant meddling, Brandice and Jason discovered that Daniel is Jason's biological father."

Brooklyn went numb as she assessed what she'd just heard. It didn't take her long to fully comprehend that she'd been dating her own brother. Her sisters and their men grew very quiet, and all of their eyes were focused on her. Brooklyn glanced at each of them; taking in the sorrow and pity they all offered her in their facial expressions.

Pitiful.

She smiled first and then let out a soft chuckle, allowing it to grow into a full and hearty laugh. It was the only reaction that made sense. Of course Jason was her brother. Life just wasn't supposed to go her way. Just when she thought that normalcy was coming within her reach, the universe had a funny way of saying, no, not today.

"Brook, sweetie, why are you laughing? This isn't funny."

"Yeah, you don't have to feel embarrassed. There is no way you could've known."

"I know. That's what's so funny." She laughed harder, ignoring the concerned looks from her family. "Tell Brandice that I hope she feels better." She kissed both her sisters on the cheek. "I have to go."

"Brook, wait," Leila said. "Let us come with you."

"No. Please. I just want to be alone so I can feel in peace, okay?" she said softly.

Raven tugged at her baby sister's arm, tears streaming down her neck. "Are you going to be okay?"

Brooklyn thought about her sister's question like it was worth a million dollars and gave her the best answer she could think of. "Maybe."

Epilogue

I DON'T THINK THAT I can remember a time when I felt completely comfortable or even halfway comfortable in my own skin. Even admitting that makes me feel further away from reaching this comfort.

I appreciate being here, having life, and being able to make choices every day. However, I feel that some choices made for me before I was even born are more influential on my life then my own.

Growing up, I had dreams and aspirations like most children. I wanted to run the world, be able to buy out the toy store, and become a princess. I also dreamed about feeling true happiness. I wanted to see my mom smile more, cry less, and marvel at her surroundings. I dreamed about how it felt like to be loved whole-heartedly by someone. I dreamed about loving myself, but I couldn't.

I saw too much anger, felt too much pain, and heard too many stories about myself, how I got here, who brought me here, and why all of this wasn't supposed to be.

My mother was the strongest woman I've ever known. I say this because each day I saw her fight. She fought to be happy, to love again, to find herself, and to give me a better life than she had. My mother taught me what it means to be strong, how to overcome obstacles, and how to live through tough times. My mother was a survivor.

However, when I sit back and analyze my life with her, I know my mother was never truly a happy person. She lived for her children. We were always aware of that, and it made me sad. I wished I could have made my mom smile more, given her life back, filled her heart with the love she craved. But I was just a child, and though I knew more about this world than I should have, I didn't know how to do that for her. My sisters and I tried, though. Becoming a princess, running the world, and buying out the toy store became less important. We wanted to make mummy happy, proud, content, relaxed, and comfortable in her own skin, in our lives, or maybe just in us, her daughters.

Leila was Mummy's go-to daughter. She would call Leila into her bedroom some nights and the two of them would talk for hours about life, love, God, and probably a bunch of other stuff. Mummy always said Leila was born with the gift of wisdom that could help people one day.

Even though she learned from those intimate talks, I think they hardened Leila also. She listened to my mom, felt the pain in her words, and somehow internalized them as her own.

It's not her fault that she sees the world in black in white. That's just life. Leila's trying, though, and I know this because she thinks about changing. Even though her thoughts don't always coincide with her actions, I know she's going to get there one day.

Now, Raven came out of the womb knowing exactly what she wanted out of life, and I don't think a day went by when she wasn't completely consumed with having it all. Raven hated growing up poor, so she wanted money. She hated not having a father and she was determined to have one for her children. She has all of that now, plus more, but she's not happy either.

Raven's not the type to ask for advice. But I think that's the reason she is so unhappy, because she never took the time to really get to know who she really was or what she really wants out of life. You see, Raven was and still is caught up in the struggle of our childhood, and she didn't fully develop as a person. Struggle will sometimes do that to you. It's going to take a while to reverse her mindset, but if Raven is one thing, it's resourceful. She'll figure it out.

Together the three of us are twisted, confused, focused, intense, and careful. But most importantly, we identify ourselves as Wanda's Girls. Everything we are, good and bad, is because of our mother. Before today, I would have told you that she was the most influential person in my life. Now I know that this isn't completely true. My father, whom I've never met, never spoken to, and barely know anything about, has shaped me more than anyone in the world. His absence is the biggest presence I've felt. I'm aware of how weird that sounds, but I think of him all the time. I wonder if he ever loved me, ever missed me, ever wanted to know how I was doing.

When I was molested in that bathroom, screaming out for my daddy to save me, and he never showed up, that's the first time I knew that I had the ability to hate someone. For reasons I can't explain, my father, not the man who assaulted me, gained every ounce of that hatred. I blamed him for not protecting me when I really needed him.

After that day, I counted how many milestones in my life he missed. My hatred grew simultaneously with his absence.

Notification of my mother's passing appeared in the local newspaper, and I remember thinking that he would show up for the funeral. My father used to love my mother, and now she was gone. He had to come. He would redeem himself for years of disappointment by wiping the tears from Leila's eyes and holding Raven's hand because he used to love this woman.

He never showed up.

I no longer hated my father after that day. There was no energy left for that because I lived in complete terror.

Although my parents couldn't be in a healthy relationship, my mother consistently told us that my father loved his little girls very much, and in a way that made me feel better about who I was and who brought me here. So when he didn't show up to her funeral, I began thinking, what type of love was that?

The biggest lesson my father taught me is that I can love myself far more efficiently than anyone else could. At least I know I'd show up to my funeral if no one else did.

I can admit that because of him I'm afraid to love intimately. The thought of sharing myself with a man doesn't sit well with me. I'm not one of those girls who looks for love in "all the wrong places" because my father never loved me, although sometimes I wish I was.

My strongest desire is to be able to look in the mirror and know for a fact *that the woman staring back at me is worthy of love. I want to reach a point where I love myself in the most normal way possible.*

Today, I know that in order to reach that point I have to work through some things and let other things go. Jason is one of those things I have to let go because it isn't normal to be in love with your brother. It's ironic that the first person I found myself loving and trusting turned out to be the one person I can't have. That alone used to be enough to make me want to give up on myself. But not today. Today, I'm determined to smile more, live more, feel happiness more, and eventually love others and myself more.

I realized that I couldn't help who made me, shaped me, or even hurt me. I can't change that. I shouldn't—scratch that, I won't let it dictate who I am.

For a while I've been trying to discover what I needed to write about, and now I know that this is a story I want to tell. My story. Thousands of women grow up fatherless, left with questions and no answer. Maybe I can help these women as I learn how to help myself cope.. Cope with being me.

CPSIA information can be obtained at www.ICGtesting.com
Printed in the USA
BVOW072029301012

304216BV00002B/8/P